Montana Fire

Montana Promises
Book 3

Vella Day

MONTANA FIRE

Print Edition
www.velladay.com
velladayauthor@gmail.com

Cover Art by Sloan Winters
Edited by L. Watanabe and Rebecca Cartee
Published in the United States of America
E-book ISBN: 978-0-9899759-6-4
Print Edition ISBN: 978-0-9899759-7-1

Acknowledgments

Special thanks to Dawn Drollinger, Montana Deputy State Fire Marshal, and to Gordy Hughes, Fire Marshal of Missoula, Montana for answering all of my questions. You guys rock. And to Marla Monroe for all her medical advice.

Chapter One

"I heard you took a bullet for the bride."

Even though the voice from behind sounded impressed, Jamie Henderson was determined to block out that nightmare. Forever. She softly let out a breath, willing herself to stay calm, and absently rubbed her arm where she'd been shot.

"That's true."

Why did Max Gruden, the man her best friend had paired her with to dance, have to bring up her past? Damn him. It was hard enough going through the motions, pretending to be happy, but it was Amber's wedding day. For her, Jamie would try.

She pressed her palms down the overly big bridesmaid dress then smoothed her long hair, but the blonde wisps refused to stay down. She inhaled and turned around. There might be nearly two hundred people in the middle of a decorated barn, but her world seemed to have shrunk to just the two of them.

She'd never been this close to Max Gruden before. She couldn't help but drag her gaze from his polished boots to the top of his head. His snug jeans and crisp white shirt with a bolo tie, spoke of a man who didn't indulge in excesses. He wasn't bad looking, either.

Who am I kidding?

His combed back brown hair that curled just at the collar, combined with the dark stubble and white smile made him very handsome. Then there were his eyes. She'd never seen anything like them before. The irises were a unique tint. Kind of caramel, like the color of those chewy candies that stuck to her teeth. Nicely spaced apart and set deep, his alluring eyes gave him a look of mystery—or were those etched lines shooting from the corners a result of worry? Upon further study, she'd have to say he looked close to forty.

He placed a hand on her shoulder. "Are you okay?"

She didn't know if he said that because she'd been focusing on his face too long or because she hadn't taken a breath in a few seconds. "Yes. I've been through a lot. I space out sometimes. Sorry."

She inhaled, and his clean, spicy scent with a hint of mint caused more chaos inside her. That wouldn't do. Max wasn't her type at all. He carried himself with control and power. Jamie was used to a more quiet man.

The wedding party music struck up, and Max gazed down at her. "I get it, believe me. I know you've been through a recent trauma, but could I persuade you to have this dance with me?"

Max had experienced his share of woes, too. Having his wife and young child burn to death at home because of revenge would break the strongest of men. "I'll dance, but I'm not ready to talk about what happened." Not that he'd asked her to.

"Deal."

He held out his hand. When their palms touched, his warmth spread up her arm, and her pulse raced. As they eased their way to the dance floor, Jamie fought his allure.

Amber Delacroix Carter, the new bride, had been in deep conversation with Max a half hour ago, no doubt filling his head about Jamie's issues regarding her former boyfriend, Benny Ford. Amber had suspected Benny of killing hospice patients at the hospital then murdering Amber's brother—which was why

Benny had shot at Jamie's best friend.

Just as he was about to pull the trigger, Jamie stepped in front of Amber to protect her. Even after six months, the emotional pain was only now beginning to diminish.

Jamie's rational thought returned and she pursed her lips. She needed to make sure Max understood that she was only dancing with him because it was her obligation. "Just because I agreed to a dance, doesn't mean I'm going to spill my guts," she repeated. She hadn't meant to sound so bitchy, but her stomach was swirling.

The lines around his eyes crinkled. Damn him. His whole face lit up when he smiled, creating a devilishly handsome appearance. "That's fine, but if those guts happen to spill, I'm your man."

"I'll remember that." She couldn't afford to be tempted, especially by someone like him.

This was a wedding, not some therapy session. Jamie was tired of talking about her botched romance. Even if she got over Benny's betrayal and violence, those poor victims would still be dead.

Max guided her next to him, walked side by side for three steps, and then rotated her backwards as he executed a step-together-step. The man was smooth, almost as if he didn't have to think about how to move his body.

"Relax. Enjoy the music." There went that smile again.

How could she relax with his hand on her back, the heat of his body pouring into her, and his masculine scent messing with her brain? Not to mention his sensitivity to her desire not to share.

Answer? She couldn't.

Throughout the song, Max guided her around the makeshift dance floor, keeping perfect beat to the music. Because of his strong lead, she didn't have to think where to put her feet. He also didn't ask her any questions, for which she was thankful.

The volume lowered and the wedding planner stepped up to the microphone. The dance was over, and Jamie wanted to step off the stage, but Max kept a strong grip around her waist.

"Okay, now," the woman said with more enthusiasm than should be allowed. "How about a hand for the newlyweds?"

For the first time since Jamie had stepped on stage, happiness filled her. Amber Delacroix had found two perfect men, and Jamie couldn't be more pleased.

As soon as the crowd noise dimmed, a slow song filled the cavernous barn. The woman leaned close to the mike again. "This song is for everyone. Come join Amber, Cade, and Stone to show your support."

Before Jamie could excuse herself, Max drew her near, his strong chest pressed against her body. She wanted to protest, but decided one more dance wouldn't hurt. She had to admit that being in his arms was nice. Comforting even. She'd been alone since Benny's arrest, and she hadn't liked it.

After a few minutes of dancing in silence, her curiosity got the best of her. "Can I ask you something?" Jamie had to crane her neck to look up at him. She was only five-foot-two, and Max was almost a foot taller.

"Sure."

"It's a bit personal."

"Ask away. I'm an open book."

"It's about your family."

He nodded. She didn't know how he could be willing to talk about something so painful. She wished she could. "How did you move on after the death of your family?" What was his secret?

Max looked over her head as they swayed to the music. "I didn't for a long time. In fact, I kind of went on a ten-year quest. I became so obsessed to bring the arsonist to justice that I lost a lot of my friends. That was a mistake. Being alone isn't healthy for the soul."

Ten years was too long to wait. She, too, had lost some friends. "You seem happy now." He must have done something different.

He glanced down at her. "I am. It helped that we finally caught the man responsible for the fire."

"My ex-boyfriend was caught, too, but it's still hard."

"I hear ya. If I had to give one bit of advice, it would be to surround yourself with good people. If I hadn't, I would have sunk into a deep depression. But it's not easy. I had to force myself to go out, have fun, and help others."

The advice sounded good. "I'll try that." Max was right. Moving on was hard.

In the beginning, her friends called all the time. Jamie even made it to their weekly happy hour, but when she changed jobs, she'd been too busy to meet with them. Or maybe, she'd just let her past rule her life. She hated what was happening to her, but she seemed unable to stop the decline.

Max twirled her around, keeping her close. It was as if he wanted to let her know he could be a friend if she would let him. The problem was that Jamie wasn't sure if she was ready to let anyone get close to her again.

The music ended, and Max glanced down at her. "Ready to eat?"

Many of the couples were leaving the crowded stage, and he could sense Jamie had had enough of being this close to him. He worried she'd come up with some excuse not to sit at their wedding party table, but he wasn't about to let her. He was serious when he said she needed to surround herself with friends.

She bit down on her bottom lip and he could almost see her mind spinning. "Sure."

Glad to get past that hurdle, he led her to her seat. Jamie

intrigued him. A tiny thing, she had shoulder length blonde hair that seemed determine to curl at will, big blue eyes the size of the sea, and porcelain skin that could use a bit more color.

After holding her in his arms, and feeling the tension in her body, this wedding seemed to have taken a toll on her. He understood why. Between the men he worked with at the police station and the firehouse, together with Jamie's best friend, Max had learned a lot about her. After years of struggling with his own demons, he'd finally gotten closure over the death of his family. Jamie seemed to be at the stage where he'd been before the arsonist's capture. Max not only believed he could help her—he wanted to help her.

When Jamie was speaking with Amber earlier, he'd caught the spark of life inside her, and a sudden urge to put a smile back on her pretty face shot through him. But Jamie was skittish. He had to be careful. He hoped he had the skill to make things better.

✧ ✧ ✧

Four blocks from the free clinic, Jamie gathered the food sacks and a cardboard coffee holder from the passenger side seat. As she slid out of her car, a cold wind blasted her face. *Brr.* March in Montana was usually warmer—as in ten to fifteen degrees warmer. *Stupid weather.*

Jonathan, a homeless man she saw often, was slumped on the steps that led up to the abandoned warehouse close to where she worked. Jamie couldn't imagine having to live outside. Even though both he and his occasional friend, Larry, had told her they weren't the indoor type, they couldn't be happy about winter sneaking back in.

As Jamie drew near, Jonathan sat up straighter. "Hello, Miss Jamie."

She scanned his face, not liking his color or the way he was rubbing his leg. During a rare moment, Jonathan had confided in her that he'd served in the war and had a piece of shrapnel in his calf. She'd offered to take him to the VA hospital to have it checked out, but he refused to go. Said doctors freaked him out.

She lifted one of the white bags. "Stopped by for an early lunch on my way to work." He'd told her it made him feel like a charity case if she went just for him, so she always showed him her bag, too. She handed him his meal, along with one of the hot drinks. "For you."

Jonathan grinned, and for a moment, he looked to be on the good side of sixty. His teeth might be even, but they were heavily stained as if he'd spent his life smoking and drinking coffee. Years ago, he might have been a handsome man, but exposure and poor nutrition had dulled his hair and made his beard scruffy. He once told Jamie that his daughter was her age, but that they hadn't spoken in years. She wondered if his daughter knew how lucky she was to even have a dad.

He guzzled the drink. "You're a true angel."

"Where's Larry?" Jamie always brought a meal for him, too.

"You know him. He comes and goes. I'm sure he'll stop by at some point today."

Jamie nodded. "Larry always said Montana's too damned cold, and he'd be right today. Maybe he's on his way to Florida."

Jonathan's lips tilted upward. "Talks about going all the time. That's his dream."

What's your dream, old man? She wouldn't ask. Privacy was respected in this part of town.

He glanced up and grinned. "Knock, knock."

She loved when he told her his corny jokes. When her dad had been alive, he used to do the same. "Who's there?"

He leaned forward. "Cows go."

"Cows go, who?"

"No, cows go moo!"

She laughed. It wasn't really funny, but the delight in his eyes made her feel warm inside. "Good one."

He never expected her to stay more than a minute or two, but they seemed to connect when she stopped by. Because she'd never mentioned how Benny had gone crazy and murdered some of her hospice patients, Jonathan was one of the few who didn't look at her with pity.

His brows rose. "I got more." His glance shot off to the side, and a quick splash of worry replaced his joy.

"I wish I could stay, but I don't want to be late to work." She bent over and set down the other coffee and bag that contained a ham and cheese croissant. "In case Larry comes."

A strong gust of wind from behind forced her to take a step forward. When Jonathan reached up to steady her, the strength in his fingers surprised her. She straightened and smoothed out her coat, a bit embarrassed at him helping her. "Thanks."

"Take care, missy, and thanks for this." He raised his cup then nodded to the extra food.

You, too, old man. With a bit more pep in her step, she walked the remaining three blocks to the free clinic where she worked as a nurse, and ducked into the warm interior. Her good friend and fellow nurse, Sasha Langley, breezed out of the hall door into the patient waiting area. "Cold, huh?"

Jamie's nose must be red. "What's up with this weather? It was almost sixty degrees yesterday."

"I know, right?"

Sasha called a Mr. Talbot to the back, and Jamie followed them through the doorway and down the hall. Sasha took her patient into Exam Room 3, while Jamie continued on to the break room, where she stored her gear and spread out her early lunch.

Once she finished eating, she went to work, checking charts and handling more patients. Person after person piled into the clinic and the day seemed to fly by. This was one reason she loved this job. It kept her mind off the betrayal, and how stupid she'd been not to see the signs of Benny spinning out of control.

Jamie's last patient was an adorable little girl with a mean sore throat. Katie had been in several times over recent months. Poor thing. Her immune system just couldn't keep up. A few times, Jamie caught her sucking on her toys, and suggested to Katie's mom that part of her daughter's problem might be her chewing on unclean items. Her mom explained that they always stopped at a particular fast food place before they came here so that Katie could collect the free movie toys. Jamie never mentioned it again.

Once she sent the family on her way, she headed to the front to put the file away.

Jamie's boss, Dr. Yolanda Withers, stepped next to her at the desk. "Thanks for locking up tonight."

Most of the time, Yolanda closed, but she'd asked Jamie to do it this evening because Yolanda had been fighting a migraine all day. "No problem. Put a heating pad on your face and rest."

Yolanda gave her a weak smile. "I plan to." Yolanda lifted the lanyard from around her neck, unhooked the key, and handed it to her. "I guess you'll be needing this. See you tomorrow."

"Take care."

The last of the stragglers left the clinic, and at nine on the dot, the rest of the staff departed. Before Jamie could leave, she shut down the office computers then made sure the Lab had picked up all the samples for testing. Fatigue had victoriously climbed all the way up her body, and she couldn't wait to collapse on her sofa with a glass of wine and watch some reruns before hitting the hay. Her best friend Amber's wedding this past weekend hadn't given Jamie a chance to rest.

Max Gruden's words of advice were still swirling in her head. The astute observations he'd made after dinner had unsettled her at the time, but the more she thought about them, the more she realized he was right. Only she could take back her life.

Jamie slipped on her coat and grabbed her purse. "Time to go."

She set the clinic's alarm, doused the overhead lights, and locked the door. Yolanda had asked the staff to park next to the vacant warehouse so the patients could have the good spaces in front of the clinic. If only the city would install a few more streetlights in this part of town, walking in the dark wouldn't be such an issue.

While the temperature was above freezing, it was still damned cold. Jamie drew her coat close, and hugged her purse to her side. Keeping her head down, she rushed toward her car.

She'd walked about fifty feet when slow moving headlights coming toward her drew her attention. Jamie might not have noticed had they not pulled to the side, stopped for maybe ten seconds then started toward her again. Were they looking for an open store at this hour? The street was all but deserted, and the shop windows were dark. This part of town wasn't the best place to be at night. Anxiety sped through her veins.

A couple hundred feet ahead of her, the van drove into the middle of the road, angled toward her, and stopped. With the lights blinding her, Jamie squinted and looked away. The driver and passenger side van doors squeaked opened and, seconds later, slammed shut. Footsteps hit the hard pavement with thuds. Or was that her heart pounding hard against her ribs?

Oh, shit. Her sixth sense told her something was about to go down, and she was caught in the middle. Jamie swiveled her head right, then left, but detected no one else nearby.

Act casual. Jamie spun around to retrace her steps, pretending she'd forgotten something inside the safety of the clinic.

"Hey you. Stop!" The man then shouted something else, but she couldn't make out the words.

Her pulse escalated. *Run!* Sprinting toward the clinic, she pumped her arms, her purse beating against her side. Oh, God. Footsteps sounded behind her.

Her legs weakened as she drew near the clinic door. If she thought screaming would help, she would have yelled her lungs out. When Jamie finally reached the front, she grabbed the door handle, and tugged to open it. Locked. Fuck. Heart racing, she unzipped her purse with shaking fingers, and fumbled for the elusive key. Damn it. She should have hooked it on her own keychain.

"Come on, come on."

She glanced down the street. Two men, wearing baseball caps tugged low over their eyes, closed in on her. Her stomach churned. One continued in her direction, while the other slid behind the building next to the clinic. What the hell was going on?

Hurry. Cold metal contacted her now warm skin. She grabbed the key and shoved it into the lock, but it snagged. "Shit."

Her eyes teared from the cold, making it next to impossible to see what she was doing. Jamie opened her mouth to gulp in air and pushed the key in harder. She wiggled the metal back and forth. On the third try, it finally went in. Her heart lurched. She turned the lock, yanked open the door, and rushed inside. She took one step when her addled brain clicked into gear.

Lock the damn door. Leave the silent alarm on.

If she didn't punch in the code within thirty seconds, the security company would send help. After Jamie flicked the deadbolt closed, she ran toward the hallway door, the glowing Exit sign providing the needed light. A tight band squeezed her chest, making it damned hard to breathe, let alone to think.

Jamie was halfway down the hall, when shouts sounded from the front, and the door rattled. *This can't be happening.* To hell with the security firm. From the side pocket of her purse she extracted her phone. A few quick swipes brought up the keypad, and she pressed 911.

Jamie had to find someplace to hide. She pushed open Exam

Room 4, locked the door, and plastered her back against the wall, her heart banging against her ribs. She didn't dare turn on the lights for fear they'd find her.

The phone seemed to take forever to ring. "911. What is the nature of your emergency?"

Finally. Jamie strained to hear the intruders, but she couldn't, not over the pounding in her ears. "I'm at the free clinic on First Street," she whispered. "Two men got out of a dark van, and are now trying to break into the clinic." Her tongue stuck to her dry mouth.

The woman told her to stay calm, that officers were on the way, and to remain on the line.

Stay calm? Really? "I'll try."

Jamie slumped back against the wall, her body shaking. Nothing made sense. Why were they chasing her if they planned to break into the clinic? Why not wait until she was gone before trying to steal something? Yolanda had told her that after a gang had robbed them of drugs last year, she'd called the city and insisted they put in an alarm. They had. A lot of good it was doing Jamie now. Hopefully, the cameras would catch these guys in action.

"Ma'am?" The voice on the other end broke through her thoughts.

Jamie swallowed to wet her mouth. "Yes?"

"Where are you?"

She needed a moment for the words to sink in. "In the clinic." Hadn't she said that?

"I have two officers at the front door. They need you to open up."

Relief poured through her, but her legs had turned to rubber. She straightened and groped for the knob in the dark. After twisting it open, Jamie moved as quickly down the hallway as her body would allow. She drew open the heavy wooden door that led to the waiting room, and hurried to the entrance.

Red, blue, and white flashing lights spun around the room, creating a kaleidoscope of color. Thank God, help was here.

Jamie unlocked the door and opened it. Standing in front of her was Thad Dalton, another of her friend's fiancés, and someone else she'd seen at this weekend's wedding.

"Jamie?" Thad ran his hands down her arms. "Are you okay?" The second man, who Thad introduced as Trent Lawson, turned on the overhead lights.

"Yes."

Thad led her over to the chairs and had her sit down. "Tell me everything."

In starts and stops, she explained about locking up then spotting the van that had stopped in the middle of the street. Questions about why this was happening kept bombarding her. Hadn't she been through enough?

"Did you get a look at their faces to see if you knew them?" Trent asked.

"No. I'm sorry. They wore baseball caps and kept their heads down."

Thad leaned forward. "Can you remember if they were close enough to see you lock up?"

She racked her brain, but no memory surfaced. "I don't think so, but maybe."

"Is the place alarmed?" Trent asked. "We spotted the cameras. That should help us catch these men."

Oh, crap. "Yes." She jumped up and punched in the number for the alarm, then returned to her seat.

"I'll ask one of the men to call the security company." Trent asked her for the company's name. "I need to let them know everything's okay."

"It's AA Protection Services," she said, surprised she remembered.

Once he spoke into his shoulder radio and gave the other officers the information, Trent dragged a chair around to face her. He took out his iPad, probably for taking notes, and looked over at Thad. "If they were here to rob the place, they'd probably assume any clinic with drugs would be alarmed. Perhaps they wanted the key."

"Even with the key, they'd have to punch in the code," she said.

Trent raised his brow. "Maybe that's what they needed you for."

"You think?" Crap. Had karma decided she'd done something wrong in her past life and deserved this punishment?

Trent firmed his lips. "I have no proof of anything. It was just speculation. I'm sorry."

She understood why he'd said it.

"You're safe now, Jamie," Thad said.

It was as if he could read her mind. Or had he noticed how she'd woven her fingers together? She stopped tapping her foot, and tried to slow her rapid breathing.

"I know." She trusted Thad. Her friend and therapist, Zoey Donovan, was a lucky woman to have snagged him.

"Could these two men have been teens?" Thad asked.

Teens? He worked for the Street Crime Unit who dealt with gangs. "Not unless teenage boys have really deep voices." Jamie told him about the man shouting. She then closed her eyes for a moment to picture them. "They were large, but it was too dark to see much of their shape. I do remember that the one who ran around to the back had a slight limp."

Trent jotted that down. "Can you describe the van?"

Weren't all vans the same? "Black. Big. As I mentioned, as soon as I thought I might be in danger, I spun around and didn't think of anything other than getting to safety."

Trent relayed her information about the vehicle to someone on the other end of his radio mic.

"You did good," Thad said.

Jamie held out her hand. "Then why am I shaking?"

"Because you went through a trauma." Thad then glanced at Trent. "We should have someone patrol the place for the next couple of days."

"I'll let the captain know," Trent said.

After a multitude of questions that ranged from who normally locked up, to if she had been aware of the many thefts in the past, two patrolmen knocked on the front door. Trent let them in.

"We checked a four block radius, sir, but spotted no one," one of the cops said.

"Thanks," Trent replied. "Keep an eye out for anyone suspicious. We don't need them returning."

Thad tapped her knee. "I bet you want to get out of here."

He had no idea. "Yes, but I need to call my supervisor and tell her what happened."

Trent returned. He swiped his iPad. "Give me her number, and I'll take care of it."

"I appreciate it." Jamie was too torn up to go over the event one more time. She looked up Dr. Yolanda Withers' contact information on her cell and gave the information to Trent.

Thad stood. "I want you to stay with us tonight."

He was the sweetest man alive. Jamie rose and placed a hand on his arm. "I appreciate the offer, but I'll be fine. If you could drive me to my car, and maybe follow me home, I'll be good."

He shook his head. "Not going to happen."

Chapter Two

When Thad escorted Jamie into his house, it was close to ten thirty at night. Her body ached with both fatigue and frustration. Zoey should have been in bed, but there she was standing at the kitchen island with a cup of coffee in her hand, her brows pinched.

Zoey set the drink down and rushed over, opening her arms to hug Jamie hard. "Oh, Jamie. Are you okay?"

Her friend acted as if the thugs had actually harmed her. "I'm fine. They didn't get me."

Only after Thad and Trent arrived, had she realized things could have gone very wrong. She shivered, pushing aside the fact she'd been seconds away from possibly being attacked or killed.

"Thank goodness." Zoey leaned back and held Jamie at arm's length, running her gaze up and down her body. "You don't look any worse for wear."

"I'm just a bit shaken. That's all." Jamie slipped out of her coat and draped it over one of the center island stools.

"I made some decaf for you. Black. Just the way you like it." Zoey handed her a matching mug.

"I can really use this." Jamie brought the rich smelling brew to her lips and sipped. Divine. It was the perfect temperature—warm without being tongue-burning hot.

Thad waved the satchel he'd let her gather from home. "I'll

put this in the spare bedroom."

Jamie appreciated he was giving them some space. "Thanks."

While she might appear calm on the outside, her stomach was churning up a storm, and anger was close to the boiling point. The near violation was beginning to sink in.

Zoey picked up her mug. "Tell me what happened."

"You going to charge me for the session?" Jamie gave her former therapist a smile, trying to lighten the mood.

"No, missy. Now spill."

Jamie inhaled. "The one time Yolanda asks me to close up, some thugs decide to rob the place." The injustices of this last year came crashing down on her and she squeezed the cup tighter.

Gravity tugged on Zoey's lips. "Thad has a punching bag in the garage. Want to take a whack at it?" Zoey acted like that would help.

"I would if I knew I wouldn't break my hand."

"Come here." Zoey wrapped a comforting arm around her shoulder, and led Jamie over to the sofa in the family room and sat down next to her. "No one would argue that what happened to you was terrible, frightening, and undeserving, but this might be a good thing."

Jamie studied her friend, checking to make sure her eyes were clear. "You might be a shrink, but are you sure you haven't been smoking some wacky weed or something?" Even though every cell in Jamie's body vibrated with irritation, Zoey's words eased her concern.

Her friend set down her nearly empty coffee mug on the wooden table in front of them. "Anger can sometimes be a good motivator."

"Really? If that's the case, I should go on tour. With how pissed I am, I could motivate the hell out of people."

Zoey smiled. "I wasn't talking about motivational speaking."

Jamie sipped her coffee, some of the frustration dissipating.

"I'm not really following you."

"All I'm saying is that while you're riled up, it's a good time to take action."

"Action, as in trying to get the store owners to clean up the street, kind of action?" Then where would Jonathan, Larry, and those like them live? "Or action, as in bugging the city for more streetlights, and maybe even a few policemen to patrol the area?"

"I like those ideas, but I was thinking more along the lines of taking a class in self-defense from the police department."

Jamie had considered doing that after a female friend had been mugged a few years back, but time always got away from her. "Given my size, I think I'd be better off learning to shoot a gun."

Zoey winced. "I thought you hated weapons."

"I do, more than anything, but I'm tired of being a victim." When Max spoke to her at the wedding about how she seemed to think of herself as one, she'd stomped off. She could see he'd been right. "In truth, I wouldn't feel good handling a gun, and I certainly could never shoot anyone, but having one close by might make me feel more secure."

"I'm all for whatever makes you feel more comfortable."

While Jamie didn't really care for the gun option, if Zoey hadn't had a stun gun when one of her loose cannon clients attacked her, Zoey could have died. "Working the night shift twice a week at the clinic probably isn't a smart choice on my part. I guess I could ask for days only." Jamie shrugged, trying to think outside the box. "Or I could get a job in a better neighborhood. The problem with that is that I like working with those in need. Besides, I really like my coworkers."

"Keep thinking. Something will be a good fit." Zoey's smile brightened.

"I can't quite tell which solution you like the best, but your eyes lit up when I said I could quit my clinic work. Are you suggesting I go back to the hospital?" Jamie wasn't convinced it was any safer there.

Zoey shook her head. "It's not up to me to decide. You're the one in control. It's your life."

"Control. Right. My life has been out of control ever since Benny tried to take away my pain."

"Well, keep thinking. More options equate to more power."

Jamie leaned back against the sofa, her mind going in ten different directions. "It's strange."

"What is?"

"My rage is actually wearing off,"she said, inhaling.

"That's good, right?"

Hadn't Zoey just said that anger was an excellent motivator? Maybe it had already done its job by allowing her to consider her next course of action. "The problem is, now I'm kind of scared." It had been a long time since Jamie had admitted something like that.

Zoey slid Jamie's mug from her fingers. "Come here, you. I bet you could use a hug."

For the first time since she had spotted the men, Jamie really smiled. "You have no idea."

Max Gruden rolled over in bed thinking the loud noise came from one of his many bad dreams. When the vibrations in his head refused to stop, he cracked open an eye and spotted the glowing cell on his nightstand. "Damn." Picking up his phone, he glanced at the clock instead of looking at the name on the screen and answered. "Gruden. It's one in the fucking morning."

"Sorry. It's Rich."

Christ. Max had worked with the man for years. The guy had to know by now how precious sleep was to someone who suffered from insomnia. "What is it?" Max barely kept his voice civil.

"There's a fire raging at the old warehouse on First Street."

The word *fire* had Max sitting up, his feet hitting the cold floor. Arson investigators usually arrived after the coals were cold. "Tell me more."

"About half an hour ago, I was driving down First Street—don't ask—when I spotted the fire and called it in." The excitement in his voice urged Max to hurry.

He rummaged through his closet for something warm. "What can we do?" His brain was still fuzzy.

"Fuck, Max. I thought it would be easier to locate the source if we witnessed the fire first hand." Rich Egland had been an inspector way back when Max had first joined the Rock Hard Fire Department more than eight years ago. Now, he worked for Max.

Rich's logic finally sunk in Max's sleep-weary brain. "You're right. It'll be easier to determine if arson is involved. Appreciate the heads up. I'll get there as soon as I can." He disconnected the call before Rich could say more.

Once dressed, Max rushed to his car and headed to the outskirts of town. As he neared the warehouse, his heart pinched at the sight. The place was lit up like a Christmas tree. Bad memories assaulted him, but he pushed them back. He'd found closure, or so he wanted to believe.

The closest he could park was a block away. Max hightailed it to the blaze. Flashing his new fire marshal's badge, he spoke with a cop guarding the perimeter.

"Go ahead, sir."

Spotting Rich, Max picked his way over to him. "What do we know?"

"Fire's going fast, eating up the place from west to east. There are multiple source points, too."

That screamed arson. Sirens sounded and another truck pulled into place. Behind it was an ambulance, and he and Rich moved out of their way. The last few fires had been linked to gangs. "You have a chance to check for graffiti?"

Rich shone his light on the far right side of the building that had yet to burn. "It's too dark to tell the colors, but it looks liked the same gang related swirls."

"Fucking kids." As Max studied the intensity of the flames, the back of his head and legs began to chill. "You take a photo of their handiwork?"

"You bet."

"Guess it was good you got here in time."

Rich clicked off his light. "You're right about that."

About five minutes after Max arrived, a loud explosion jarred him out of his reverie. A ball of flames shot from a top floor window of the abandoned warehouse, sending exploding glass in their direction. The powerful blast tossed him a good five feet before dumping him on the ground like a rag doll. Holy fuck. He broke his fall with his forearms, but his knees took the brunt of the impact. Jesus, his achy body didn't need that.

Before attempting to get up, Max assessed the damage, but decided nothing of importance had been harmed. Fuck. After working as a fireman for six years, he should have been prepared for that. He hoped no one else was caught in the flying debris field.

Max glanced over at his assistant who was a decade older than he was. "You okay?" Even with the light from the fire, it was too dark to see much.

"Think so."

Max scrambled to his feet and helped up Rich, who grunted and wheezed a bit as if the impact had knocked the wind out of him. Max brushed off some burning embers that had landed on the sleeve of his good coat. Crap. The cracked leather had seen better days, but this jacket held a lot of sentimental value.

"Son of a bitch. I guess there's a reason why we wait until the fire's out before we do our job." His wife had given him the coat on his thirtieth birthday. Guess after thirteen years, it might be time to retire it.

"Yeah, but how often do we get to see a fire like this burn?"

Once is often enough. "You're right. It'll save us time, too. Won't have to interview the firemen."

As Rich flicked the glass off his jeans, Max stepped farther from the crackling building. After a few more minutes of studying the blaze, his curiosity about how the fire started got the best of him. Stepping around the hot debris, he edged toward the side of the building where the fire was only now making its way. Rich followed.

"I wanted to check and see if the gang left a taunt," Max said.

Each of the previous fires had a design as well as some kind of warning. Between the graffiti markings and the accelerant, he'd know which gang started the fire. The punks were quite repetitive in their destructive process.

Before Max had the chance to shine his light on the side to check for spray paint, the side door burst open and one of the firemen lumbered out, carrying someone on his back.

"Holy shit," Rich shouted. "There was someone inside."

"Jesus Christ." Max's heart lurched.

Two paramedics rushed to the fireman's side and helped the injured man onto the gurney. Forgetting about the source for the moment, he and Rich dashed toward the ambulance where the paramedics frantically began work. One look at his body had Max's stomach in near revolt. The man was covered in blood and ash. Max held his breath, trying not to gag from the putrid stench of burnt flesh.

Horrendous images of his own home being consumed by fire flashed in his mind. *Don't think about them. Not now.* He needed to focus on this case.

Hands clenched, Max wanted nothing more than to beat the shit out of whoever had started the blaze. The victim groaned and thrashed. Max didn't recognize the old man, but he doubted anyone would. Most of the salt and pepper beard on his left side had been singed off, and his shoulder appeared burned. Blood trickled down his forehead. The rest of his body was covered in soot. From the nature of his injuries, the poor guy might not last long.

Paramedic Drake Longworth placed an oxygen mask over the man's face then covered him in a sheet. The man opened his eyes for a few seconds and grunted. The guy's body then shook as if he was going into shock.

"Max, can you stand back? I need to get him into the ambulance." Drake motioned with his head for Max to move out of the way.

"Let's give him some space," Rich prodded.

This tragedy was horrifying, purposeless, sad. Max strode back toward the far side of the building again. The gang fires had stopped a few months ago, so why restart now? Both he and Thad Dalton thought they'd caught the arsonist.

The fire trucks were making good progress against the blaze. Smoke was billowing out of the building, forcing him to stand far enough away to avoid the toxic fumes from clogging his lungs with soot.

As much as he wanted to go inside and check for an accelerant pattern, it was too dark, too hot, and way too dangerous. They'd have to wait until tomorrow to investigate. A set of headlights pulled into the lot near the fire trucks, and Detective Trent Lawson exited his car.

"The circus is about to begin," Max announced.

It didn't matter that Trent was a capable guy—and Max's best friend. The more people who came to the fire, the higher the chance something important would be disturbed.

Rich nodded to Trent. "If you want, I can wait around and make sure RHPD doesn't muck up our evidence."

It was Max's job now to stay behind. Four days ago, he'd replaced the former fire marshal, who'd stepped down from the position due to health reasons. Now Max had double duty—he was both the arson investigator and the fire marshal for the small town. The fire chief said Max's police background, coupled with his fire science degree made him a better choice than Rich.

Since then, Max had worked pretty much non-stop, only taking time off for his friends' wedding. Last night, he'd spent hours creating a spreadsheet for the cyclic maintenance inspection of existing buildings around town. His predecessor hadn't kept the files electronically, and in this day and age that made finding anything quickly almost impossible.

"I'll stay. You can go."

"You sure?"

"Yeah. Get some sleep. One of us needs to be fresh in the morning." Max tried to keep his voice light in contrast to the terrible tragedy.

"What about the old guy? You think he'll make it?"

"I'll stop by the hospital first thing tomorrow and check," Max said. "Then I'll come out here."

Rich nodded. "Call me with your ETA. I'll meet you."

"Will do."

As soon as Rich left the scene, Max's friend, Trent Lawson, came over. "You okay? Heard one of the top floor windows exploded."

"Yeah. It's all good. You give Ed Hanson a call yet?"

"Ed?"

"Owner of the building."

Trent made a note of the man's name. "You're thinking arson here, right?"

"The color of the smoke and the markings on the wall make it a strong possibility. Rich said he spotted multiple source points, too."

"Crap. Hanson might have torched his own place for the insurance money."

Max shrugged. "It's possible, but he already submitted a

zoning proposal to tear this thing down so he could build a gym. Torching it would be a little obvious. A bulldozer would be less messy."

"Agreed. Got any other ideas?"

"The graffiti on the front of the building implies this might be gang related."

"Gangs? Shit."

"Whoever was responsible, I just wished they'd checked the inside first."

"Amen."

Max shook his head. "Christ. This is shaping up to be a long ass night."

Chapter Three

Around four in the morning, after Max was certain Detective Trent Lawson had everything under control, Max left the smoldering, wet mess, and headed home. Since he wanted to be back at the scene as soon as the sun rose, he quickly showered and changed into fresh investigative gear. Knowing he'd be covered in soot by day's end, he donned blue overalls and the last of his clean long sleeve shirts. This one scratched, but it would keep him protected from the hot debris.

He fixed a shitload of coffee that he hoped would clear the cobwebs from his mind, along with a simple breakfast of eggs and toast. As he was finishing the last of his meal, his cell rang. It could only be one person at five thirty in the morning. Christ, the sun wasn't even up.

"Hey, Rich." Max lifted his shoulder to hold the phone against his ear while he spread the jam on the remaining bite of his whole wheat toast.

"You won't believe what I found." Max's hand stopped in mid spread. Rich's voice actually shook, and Max swallowed hard, forcing back his alarm.

From the noise in the background, his assistant was at the warehouse. They must have just missed each other. "What is it?" Had they unearthed a body?

"I couldn't sleep, so I drove over to the scene. I think you'll want to see this."

His patience dried up. "Spit it out, dammit."

"There's a message, not just a bunch of swirls like on the front of the warehouse."

The tightness in his chest eased, relieved Rich didn't say there'd been another victim. "There's often been a message. What did it say?" Max wanted to strangle his assistant for not just telling him.

"It was spray painted on the back of the east side door."

That didn't answer his question. "Does it look gang related? Were the letters black with multiple colored haloes around each word?"

"Sort of. Just come and see for yourself." Rich's authoritarian tone seemed out of character, but Max chalked it up to his excitement.

"Be right there."

Other than needing to turn off the coffee machine and placing his dirty dishes in the sink, he was ready to go. When he arrived, cops and CSU techs were crawling all over the place, looking like ants at a picnic. The morning light had breached the horizon, but the sun had yet to make an appearance.

Rich was standing at the east end, waving him over. The sweet ember smell permeated the air, and while the smoke was gone, the heat still rose from the ground.

Max reached Rich but couldn't spot any additional graffiti. "Where's this message?"

"Let me show you. We didn't see it last night because it was too dark. It's on the outside of the door—the door Donner Pearson ran out of carrying the burned victim." Rich pointed to what was written in black spray paint.

Max said the words out loud. "You fucked with the wrong—," He tried to read the last word a few times, but the dark paint against the burned wood make it next to impossible. "I can't make out—"

"Guys, maybe?"

"That's it. Guys." Something seemed off. He read it again. "You fucked with the wrong guys. Hmm. Note how the whole phrase is outlined instead of each letter."

"Maybe he was in a hurry. Besides, the colors look similar to those used at the last fire."

"I agree."

Rich stepped closer. "I wish I knew why they'd leave such a personal message if they're only going to burn down the building."

"Because they can?"

"Maybe. We might be coming at this from the wrong angle."

Rich often had good instincts. "How so?"

"Could be the target was the interloper."

"Based on what evidence?"

"None." Rich scratched his nose. "Merely throwing something out."

They often tossed out theories. The first few were just that—guesses, but the more they dug, the closer they got to a solid lead. "I guess the trespasser could have been running from someone. When they found him, why not just kill the guy? What would be the purpose of torching the place? No one would have found the guy for weeks or months instead of a few hours. Any evidence would have been long gone."

"Beats me," Rich said.

"I'm going to ask Thad to compare the lettering to the other fires. When the lab comes back with the composition of the accelerant, we'll have a better handle on things."

"I know we kind of dismissed the owner, but I'm thinking he could be guilty. Maybe he hired some kids to paint graffiti on the side to throw us off."

Max glanced over at Rich. "You know the old saying. When you assume something, you make an ass out of you and me."

✧ ✧ ✧

Jamie drove toward the clinic the next morning, feeling almost like her old self. Zoey's words had made a big impact on her. Jamie liked the idea of doing something proactive, whether it be taking gun lessons, asking for a different shift, or even finding a new job.

All positive thoughts about having a lot of options disappeared the moment she caught sight of the travesty in front of her. Dear God. Her throat nearly closed. Not only were local law enforcement vehicles blocking the path to the vacant parking lot, the horror of the mostly collapsed warehouse had her heart slamming against her ribs so hard she almost lost her grip on the wheel.

She rolled down her window to draw in more air, but not only did the cold fail to relieve the sludge in her veins, the heavy scent of the fire made her gag. Stunned by the shambles, she shut the window.

Reality pierced her brain. The burned out shell of a building was where she believed Jonathan lived. *Oh, my God!*

Quickly nabbing one of the prime spaces in front of the clinic, instead of waiting to be diverted to a new lot, she jerked the car to a stop and jumped out. Leaving her food purchases in the car, she ran down the sidewalk. Cop cars, a CSU van, as well as an assortment of other vehicles, were spread out everywhere.

Where was her friend? Jamie frantically searched for Jonathan, and prayed he had the sense to find other shelter once the blaze started. As she glanced across the street, she spotted Larry and sighed. Thank God, he was safe. He might know where to find Jonathan.

Swallowing the ebbing panic, Jamie rushed across the street, holding her hand over her nose to keep the stench from entering.

"Larry. Have you see Jonathan?"

He looked up from the sidewalk with bloodshot eyes and shook his head. A giant claw of worry ripped a hole in her gut.

"It be bad, missy. Real bad."

Her stomach contracted as his ominous words found their mark deep inside her. Maybe he was talking about the state of the building and not about her good friend.

"What about Jonathan?" Blood pounded in her ears.

Larry wove his gnarled fingers together and refused to look at her. Then he shrugged. "Ambulance came for him last night."

She prayed Larry knew the difference between an ambulance and a coroner's van. "He isn't…dead, is he?" The word *dead* wedged in her tight throat.

"Tall man talked to him."

Tall man? Did he mean Max? "Did you see the blaze?"

He nodded. She waited for him to say he'd tried to help his friend or that he found someone to call 911, but she didn't want to push him. Larry often shut down when she asked him too many questions.

Jamie wanted to rush to the scene to find out about Jonathan's condition, but Larry probably needed her kindness more. Jonathan was his friend, too. "I'll be right back."

She jogged to her car, grabbed the snack bags with the fast food, and returned. She set the food next to him. "You might as well eat Jonathan's share. I'll see what I can find out and let you know. You take care now, you hear?"

"Yes, missy."

Larry refused to call her Jamie. He said it wouldn't be a sign of respect to use her first name.

She jetted back across the street, dodging the rubberneckers, and headed toward the carnage. A good head taller than the short squat man next to him, Max Gruden was easy to spot. He'd have the information she needed.

As she approached the yellow crime scene tape, a cop materialized as if out of thin air. "I'm sorry, ma'am. No one is allowed any closer."

Desperation flooded her system. Even if she explained she was a friend of the man who'd been burned in the fire, the cop would have no reason to let her speak with Max. Jamie had been raised never to lie, but desperate times called for desperate measures. "I need to speak with Max Gruden. He's my boyfriend."

✧ ✧ ✧

Trent strode up to Max. "Your *girlfriend* has asked to speak with you." He nodded toward Jamie.

"My what?" Max must not have heard Trent correctly.

He and Jamie had gotten along really well at the wedding until he started to preach to her about how thinking like a victim would hinder her ability to heal. Like she needed a lecture from him? Jesus. He'd been such a jerk. And she'd told him, too.

"Your dance partner over there tried to convince poor Bernard that she had to speak with you about something." Trent chuckled. "From the way she avoided you after dinner, I'm guessing she's exaggerating about your blossoming relationship."

Max glanced over at her. Blonde hair whipping around her face, Jamie stood there with her hands clenched. With the way she was shifting her weight from foot to foot, she had something important to tell him. "I'll speak with her."

As he took a step to face her, his left knee and thigh sent out a stabbing ache from where he'd landed after the blast, and he worked hard to suppress a groan.

"I can get rid of her if you want," Trent offered. The detective must have misinterpreted his grimace.

"I got this. I'll chat with her over there." It was a mud bath where they stood.

Not only did he want to know what she had to say, he wanted to make sure she was okay. Trent had told him about the clinic break-in last night.

Max recalled his last conversation with her. After an enjoyable meal with the rest of the wedding party, he and Jamie had gone for a short walk. While they were chatting outside the owner's farmhouse, he'd come at her with some very sensitive questions about her plans to get her life on track. No surprise, Jamie immediately retreated into her shell. He never should have pushed her so hard. *Stupid, stupid.* His dating skills really needed work.

He turned to Rich. "I'll be right back."

Walking toward her, Max couldn't help but notice how her jacket was several sizes too big. For a split second, he was tempted to drag her to breakfast just to make sure she had a good meal, but she'd accuse him of pity, and he of all people knew about that emotion.

When he neared, she planted her hands on her hips as if she was pissed that Bernard hadn't allowed her to cross the yellow crime scene tape. There was a reason for it being there. Not only might the soles of her nursing shoes suffer some damage walking over the occasional hot ember, crime scenes were off limits to civilians. If they weren't, there'd be no need for the tape.

"Jamie? Nice to hear I'm your boyfriend. I guess you've forgiven me for my attempt to push my values on you." He hoped she took his comment as a quasi-apology. When her serious expression didn't change, he smiled to help put her at ease.

She pressed her lips together. "I'm sorry about lying. I had to make sure I could speak with you."

Her desperate tone sobered him. "I'm listening."

"I want to know about Jonathan Rambler." Her gaze bored into him as if she were trying to extract all of the information in his head.

The name wasn't familiar. "And he would be?"

Her eyes widened, and he thought he caught a glimpse of hope. "He was the homeless man who often sits on the steps in front of this building. Larry said he was the one burned in the fire."

Larry? He could be the vagrant from across the street Max had seen this morning. "Is Jonathan a friend of yours?" He hoped he wasn't someone more important.

After finding an old mattress, some cans, and a heap of old clothes stashed in the building, the burned victim appeared to be homeless. Given her caregiver nature, Max wouldn't be surprised if she'd become friends with the man on her way to and from work.

"Yes."

"Then you know he *lived* in this abandoned warehouse?" Max was fishing for confirmation, but she didn't have to know that.

"I suspected." Her slight hesitation implied she'd never been a guest inside Jonathan's humble abode.

Max saw no harm in telling her what she wanted to know. All she had to do was go to the hospital and find out for herself. "I'm still investigating, so I'm not at liberty to divulge all the details, but from what I can tell, your friend, Jonathan, was asleep when the building caught fire. By the time the flames reached his side, a piece of burning wall fell and landed on him."

She clamped a hand over her mouth and squeezed her eyes shut. Empathy seemed to ooze out of her and he fought the urge to comfort her.

She straightened her small shoulders, appearing to get her emotions under control. "Did he say anything? Like why he didn't get out of the building?"

People often burned in their beds—especially if they were drunk—but now wasn't the time to give her a lecture about alcohol abuse. "No. He was in shock when the fireman brought him out."

She planted a hand over her heart. "Did they intubate him?"

"I didn't stay long enough to see, but given the amount of smoke, I imagine they would."

Jamie bit down on her bottom lip, looking quite young. "I need to see him. He might be stable now." She tilted her head a little before turning to walk away.

From her clenched hands, she was barely keeping it together. "Jamie?"

She stopped and slowly rotated around. "Yes?"

"Are you going to be okay? I'm really sorry about your friend."

"I will be."

Max had to warn her. "I'm not saying it was arson, but if someone was pissed enough to burn down the warehouse they won't take kindly to you asking too many questions, you know."

She strode back to him, her eyes wide once more. "I just want to help."

"I know you do. And you can. If you speak with Jonathan, and he tells you something about the fire, can you let me know?"

Jamie cast her gaze downward. "Sure. I won't get in the way. I promise."

She turned and headed back to the road. He felt sorry for her. She had two shocks in one day. Not only might her friend die, the clinic break-in would have rattled the strongest person. If the perpetrators had waited another minute until she was farther from work, they might have caught her. Steel hardened his body at the frightening thought. He wanted to reach out to her, but he wouldn't yet. Not until he was sure it wouldn't cause a bigger chasm between them.

Tired and frustrated, Max strode back to the fire, more determined than ever to find clues that would locate the perpetrator.

Chapter Four

As Jamie made her way back to the sidewalk, her head swam. The best explanation for why Jonathan hadn't roused would be if he'd been drunk. But when she'd left each night and passed him, she'd never seen him with any kind of alcohol. Larry, however, was a different story. It was possible the two had shared a bottle. Regardless of Jonathan's condition, her heart ached for her friend.

Too confused to think straight, she headed over to tell Larry what she'd learned, and to ask if Jonathan had been drinking. When she stopped to cross the street, she searched for Larry. Damn. He was gone. Again. Seemed anytime there was trouble, the guy vanished.

Talk about vanishing—that was what she needed to do. Her boss was an understanding lady, who no doubt had seen, or at least smelled, the terrible fire three blocks away. After Jamie had practically staved off the break-in at the clinic last night, she bet Yolanda would grant her an hour to visit Jonathan.

Jamie stepped inside the clinic and wrinkled her nose at the pervasive scent of smoke. For the sake of the patients, she hoped the air filters would do their job soon. Given half the seats were already occupied, it was going to be a busy day. Some of the people were regulars, but others were new to her. She visually scanned the condition of those present to make sure

Admitting hadn't missed someone in serious need of aid. No one appeared to be in dire pain, so Jamie headed into the back to look for her supervisor.

Yolanda Withers was in the hallway checking an X-ray. While Jamie didn't want to ask for the favor, she had no idea how long Jonathan might last. If she'd been in a bad fire and woke up in a hospital, the depression would surely add to her anxiety. From the few things Jonathan had told her about his war experience, being in a small room brought out his PTSD. At least, he'd be blissfully unaware while he was intubated.

"Yolanda?"

Jamie's boss whipped around and placed a hand over her heart. "Oh, Jamie. Are you okay?" Her gaze ran from head to toe and back again. "By the time I got the call about the attempted robbery, the policeman said you'd left the clinic."

"Yes, I'm fine. Really." In the last six months, those words had become her mantra.

"I'm so glad you're here. I thought you'd take the day off."

She'd considered it. "I'd rather be busy."

"I understand. Layla called in sick. Some upper respiratory infection seems to be going around."

That still left Nathan, Amanda, and Sasha to see the patients. Guilt and need collided. "I hate to do this, but I'd like an hour to visit someone."

Her boss set down the X-ray and sucked in a big breath. "Can it wait until the first wave passes?" The clinic had an ebb and flow to it. The mornings, and around five, were their busiest times.

Jamie wanted to give in, but she might never see Jonathan again. "There was a man burned in the warehouse fire. He's in critical condition." She didn't know that for sure, but from Max's description of the injuries, she suspected that was true. "He was a good friend." Even if she couldn't speak with him, seeing him would give her some peace of mind.

Yolanda bit down on her lip and glanced around. "I'm so sorry about your friend. Of course. Check on him, but do hurry. Today is shaping up to be crazy."

It might have been her anxiety kicking in, but Jamie gave her boss a quick hug. "Thank you. I'll be fast."

Jamie charged down the hall and hurried out the front door. It was only a ten-minute drive each way, which would give her plenty of time to visit. She climbed into her car and before she headed in the opposite direction, Jamie gazed at the fallen warehouse once more. Max Gruden was an intense man, driven to find answers. She prayed he'd find the culprit who set the fire.

A few minutes later, Jamie entered the Lucy Ambrose Center for Excellence (LACE) hospital parking lot, and a heavy weight settled in her bones.

It's okay. Benny's not here. The pharmaceutical tech was behind bars, where he needed to be.

After gulping down her now lukewarm coffee to settle her nerves, and taking a big bite out of her ham and cheese croisant, she slipped out of her car. Every day since leaving LACE, she'd thanked the health gods that Amber had convinced her to quit her job. Walking those haunted halls for those three months after the shooting had dragged Jamie down and caused endless suffering. She'd finally admitted that the bad memories would forever reside there.

Stealing herself from further bad thoughts, she entered. At the information desk, she forced a smile for Janice Greenwald, a woman who'd always offered a friendly wave.

"Hey, how are you doing? I've missed you," Janice said.

"Good. I miss a lot of people here, too." That wasn't a lie. Feeling good was another story. As much as she'd like to catch up with Janice, Jamie didn't have the time to chat. "I'm here to visit Jonathan Rambler."

Janice pecked at the keyboard then looked up. "I don't have anyone here by that name."

Duh. If Max didn't know Jonathan's name, neither would the paramedic who brought him in. She doubted her friend carried ID. "He was the John Doe from the warehouse fire last night."

"Let me check." More keys clicked, followed by a smile from Janice. "Ah, yes. He's in ICU, room three."

"Not in the burn unit?"

"Apparently, there wasn't room."

That wasn't good. Keeping her gaze on her destination, and not on anyone she passed, Jamie jogged to the bank of elevators and waited forever for one to arrive. When she reached her floor, her friend, Becky Andrews, who manned the nurse's station, was chatting on the phone.

She held up a finger and disconnected a few seconds later. "Jamie!" She walked around the counter and gave her a hug. "What are you doing here?"

Jamie told her about her friend. "Can I see him?"

"I'm sorry, but only family is allowed."

Jamie should have called ahead and asked about his condition, but she'd hoped she could have peeked in. "How is he?" She saw no need to say the homeless man might not have a family—other than Charlotte.

"Stable. He's intubated for smoke inhalation, but the doctor is hopeful that we can take him off the machine soon."

"And his burns?"

"Shoulder and neck. I didn't treat him though."

Poor man. If he lived, the rehabilitation would be extensive, and the skin grafts painful. Her heart nearly broke in two.

"Do you know when he'll be moved to the burn unit?" He'd get better care there.

"Again, we're hoping for a vacancy later today."

"Thanks." It was probably for the best that Jamie not see him all bandaged and helpless.

When she returned to the clinic, the waiting room was packed. In a way, that was a good thing. Running around helping one patient after another would keep her mind from thinking about Jonathan.

She wasn't the only one working hard today. Yolanda seemed more stressed than usual. Not only was one of the nurses sick, but the second doctor, Shane McDermott, was on vacation. Several of the doctors from LACE volunteered a few hours a week, but they usually came on the weekends or in the evenings.

Jamie took her time with each patient, but she didn't chat as she often did. About the time she was ready to go home, another wave of people arrived, so she didn't feel right leaving.

Jamie caught Yolanda in between patients. "Do you want me to stay late? I owe you an hour."

"No, Jamie. You go home. I'm locking up tonight."

"Not to sound paranoid, but what if those men return? You shouldn't be here by yourself."

Yolanda smiled. "Don't worry. I've hired security to walk the nurses to their cars and stay around while I lock up. The cop I spoke with said the RHPD would be driving by on a regular basis until nine."

"That's wonderful, and thank you for the added security."

Even though Yolanda suggested Jamie leave at five, she stayed until seven to help out. When she finally got out of there, even though it was still light, the guard insisted on walking her to her car.

Because she hadn't slept well last night, on the drive home, Jamie had to shake her head repeatedly to keep awake. While she had enjoyed being with Zoey at her house, Jamie looked forward to sleeping in her own bed.

Tomorrow before work, she'd call to see if the doctor had removed Jonathan's tube, and if he'd moved from the ICU. If he had, it meant leaving extra early for a visit. She couldn't in all good conscience leave Yolanda stranded again, especially if Layla called in sick.

Sometime tomorrow, she had to remember to contact RHPD and ask if they find the location of Jonathan's daughter, Charlotte. Wouldn't she want to see her dad one more time? Jamie would give anything if she could have spoken with her father before that drunk driver took his life.

Chapter Five

The sun had just dipped below the horizon by the time Max arrived home. It was no wonder he was hungry and exhausted. He and Rich had surveyed every frigging inch of that building, noting the burn patterns, and testing for chemicals. While they couldn't be positive without lab corroboration, it looked like the arsonist had used butane to start the fire—the same kind of hydrocarbon based fuel the Blood Rights gang used. Besides Jonathan's mattress and an odd assortment of clothing, the forensic team had unearthed all sorts of electronic equipment. Between the gear and the accelerant, he should get some answers.

The warehouse owner, Ed Hanson, had shown up and, when he found out about someone being injured in his building, he'd freaked. From his sincere reaction, the owner didn't seem like a likely suspect.

He also mentioned again how he'd planned to tear down the building soon, but that his small amount of insurance wouldn't do more than aid in clearing up the rubble.

After Ed left the scene, Max asked Trent to look into Ed Hanson's insurance claim to see if it was the paltry sum he'd claimed. Max also asked Trent to check with Thad about whether he'd heard any gang rumblings about the fire.

Max needed a shower bad and headed into his bathroom. As

he stood under the steaming water and let the warmth soothe the ache in his thigh and knees, he wondered if Jamie had found out anything from Jonathan Rambler.

Max had called the hospital to check on the man's status, but after ten minutes on hold, he'd given up. Tomorrow before work, he'd stop by LACE, though given the man's condition, Max wouldn't be surprised if he was still intubated. Smoke inhalation could be deadly.

He rubbed his face to banish the image of the homeless man's haunted eyes that seemed to have been reaching out to him, pleading for help. There was something about Jonathan Rambler that made him want to help the guy. Hell, maybe it was the full moon exerting some extra lunar force on him, or else the memory of his own family's death by fire had come back to haunt him. He blinked back the remembrance, shut off the water, and stepped out to dry.

The evidence told him Jonathan might have awoken only when the burning board fell on him, so Max doubted the guy saw or knew anything. Still, Max had to check.

A flickering memory of his wife reappeared. She was pointing to something high on a shelf. It had been too long since he'd had to retrieve something for anyone, lift a heavy suitcase, or unscrew the lid off a jar because it was on too tight. He missed doing that for someone. Then the memory disappeared, and try as he might, he couldn't bring it back. Every family photo had burned in the fire, and the wonderful times they'd shared were disappearing one by one as the years rolled on.

Move on, man.

He had. Sort of. The only thing he could never put behind him was that if he hadn't been a cop, his family would still be alive. That guilt would never wash away.

Max stepped into his bedroom and dressed. He forced his mind back to the crime scene to make sure he hadn't missed some clue today. As he sorted through the facts again, something about Jamie showing up didn't sit right with him. Was it all about helping her friend? Or did she know more than she was saying? If she'd heard scuttlebutt from the locals about wanting the eyesore gone, why not tell him? Had she thought the attempted clinic break-in was related to the warehouse fire, and she feared some kind of retribution? There could be a connection, but hell, if he knew what it was.

Max strode toward the kitchen for some food. With renewed energy from the shower, he yanked open the refrigerator. Empty. Crap. Guess he'd forgotten to shop. He shouldn't be surprised. Ever since his recent promotion, his life had been hell, and the coming month didn't promise a respite either. He sure as hell wasn't looking forward to sorting out the issues left to him. The amount of liquor licenses alone that had never been renewed was daunting.

With keys in hand, Max jumped in his car. He ate at Italiano's almost every night because he liked to go back to the office after dinner and work. No reason not to grab a bite there now. It was a place where he could think, in part because the staff knew to take his order and leave him alone.

As soon as he stepped inside the familiar restaurant, a bit of tension eased out of him. He slipped into his usual table next to the window that faced the door. While he wasn't interested in who showed up, he didn't like to be taken by surprise in case someone did. Having been a cop, his old habits never died.

Elissa, his usual waitress, hustled over. She always flirted with him for a bit, not because she liked him, but because he tipped well. He saw through her ploy, but she gave good service, and that worked for him.

"Trout or baked chicken tonight, handsome?"

"Chicken, and bring a pot of coffee." It was going to be a long night of thinking.

She grinned. "You got it."

Elissa quickly returned with his drink and he settled back in to go over the facts. He brought the cup to his lips and savored the strong rich scent before tasting it. The aroma of the beans alone helped defog his mind. Tomorrow, he planned to canvas the neighborhood to see if anyone had seen anything suspicious around the time of the fire. All during the investigation today, Max kept his eye out for Larry, but the guy never made an appearance. Damn. Jamie said Larry had seen something. The question was what?

Before Max had a chance to clear his mind of the fires and the investigation, Elissa delivered his meal. "Need anything else?"

"I'm good. Thanks."

She disappeared, just the way he liked it. Max had taken all of three bites when a shadow blocked the overhead light.

"Thought I'd find you here." The deep gravelly voice could only belong to one man—Dan Hartwick, his former boss and mentor.

Max glanced up and motioned for his friend to take a seat. He liked the man. Dan might only be two years older, but his honor, work ethic, and knowledge of the criminal mind spoke of a man with a lot of experience.

Dan waved to Elissa, and she trotted over. Dan requested coffee.

"You got it."

Max lifted his mug. "I trust your visit has to do with the warehouse fire, and not because you missed my happy face?"

Dan smiled briefly. "It does." He leaned forward. "Trent showed me the photos of the graffiti."

"Did he tell you that when Thad compared the message to the other arson cases, the lettering didn't match?"

"He did."

Elissa set Dan's coffee down then slipped away.

Max sipped his drink. "I asked Trent to look into the owner's story, but he hasn't gotten back to me." Research took time.

"I ran into Trent on the way over here. He told me to tell you that Hanson seems to be telling the truth."

"Damn. The owner torching his own building would have made things nice and easy." He wanted to ask Dan why he was there, but his mentor had his own style. He'd tell Max when he was ready.

Dan sat back and wrapped his hands around his mug, his lips pressed together. "I'm thinking the fire had something to do with the homeless man."

Dan sounded like Rich. "You do know this isn't your case?"

"I'm not here to interfere, but our departments do work together, and Trent works for me."

Thankfully, Dan's tone held no argument. "Is there something you know about Jonathan Rambler that I don't?" Why else would Dan have brought up his name?

"Yes. He's not Jonathan Rambler."

Max was sure he'd remembered the man's name. "Then who is he?"

Dan shrugged. "Not sure exactly, but something's off. His fingerprints aren't in the system."

Max thought about the implication. "That's not unheard of. That just means the old guy might never have been arrested. He still could be Rambler."

Dan leaned forward. "Here's the thing. He ain't no old man."

"I'm not following you." Max must have been more tired than he realized.

"The emergency room doctor called the precinct. Said the nursing staff told him that in the process of cleaning up the fire victim, they found the man was wearing a wig, wore a plastic retainer to make his teeth appear stained, and was covered in a ton of makeup to age him. Even wore padding around his middle."

Max's mind spun. "He was working undercover?" It was the

only logical explanation.

Dan waved a hand. "Pretty sure that's the case. About six weeks ago, RHPD got a courtesy call from the FBI stating they'd sent a team of agents to Rock Hard."

"Here? How many are we talking about?" Rock Hard didn't have an FBI field office.

"They didn't say."

Excitement lit up his blood. Max loved a puzzle more than anything. "There's another homeless man Jonathan befriended. His name is Larry. I've been trying to track him down, but he seems to have disappeared into the wind."

"You think he knows something?"

"He might." Max explained what Jamie told him. "It sure would save time if the Feds owned up that Rambler was one of their own."

"No kidding. Why bother calling the mayor when they don't tell him shit?"

"Do you think the mayor knows more that he's saying?"

Dan nodded. "Anything's possible."

"Bureaucracy at its finest." Max went over the few pieces of the information he'd found. "The message on the door said, 'You fucked with the wrong guys.' That could have been a warning to this Jonathan Rambler. His cover might have been blown."

Dan nodded. "That was my first thought."

Max's juices flowed. "To cover our bases, I'll ask Trent to check if Hanson pissed off some potential business partners."

"Could be someone doesn't want another gym in the area."

"Hanson aside, let's assume this so-called vagrant question is an FBI agent. The Feds should at least warn us if someone in our town is involved in the drug trade again, weapons accumulation, or human trafficking."

"Agreed." Dan brought his cup to his lips as if he had nothing better to do than sit and chat.

"Anything else you found out?"

Dan smiled. "Trent mentioned your *girlfriend*, Jamie Henderson, knew this Jonathan guy."

"She was friends with him."

"Have you asked her about him?"

Max couldn't figure out why Dan was butting in. "Not yet. I'm waiting for the appropriate time, but I will."

"Once the mayor gets wind of what's going on, he'll be riding not only my butt, but the fire chief's ass to find the arsonist."

"We don't have conclusive evidence it is arson."

Dan lowered his chin. "Multiple source points? Come on."

Max couldn't get anything past his former boss. "Fine. I still need to wait for the lab results."

"Do what you must, but in the meantime can you speak with Jamie about Jonathan Rambler or whatever his name is?"

Max blew out a breath. When they'd spoken at the crime scene, Jamie appeared to have forgiven him for what he'd said at the wedding.

"Fine I'll ask her, but there's no guarantee she knows anything. Jamie stopped by this morning, and seemed pretty shaken up. Not sure if it was because of the fire or the attempted robbery at the clinic last night."

"Heard about that. Trent's on it. Until we can confirm this man's identity, Jamie is all we have."

We? Max owed Dan his sanity. His boss had been there when Max's home had burned, and Dan had been the one who had brought him into the conference room to tell him his wife and son were dead.

"We might have better luck if Thad picked her brain. Jamie's good friends with his fiancée."

"It was Thad who suggested you talk to her."

"Jamie's not the most forthcoming person." At least she hadn't been at the wedding when he'd practically brow-beaten her into admitting she needed to take control of her life. Trying to extract information from her wouldn't put him on her good side.

Dan leaned forward. "I have faith in you."

"She probably knows nothing. Maybe we should call the mayor and ask him to find out who Jonathan Rambler is. You're good friends. How about you calling him?" If Dan had a job to do, he might leave the rest of the investigation alone.

Dan nodded. "Already did. He doesn't know, though he said he'd put in a call to the FBI. He's worried, too, about what their presence might mean to our town." Dan pushed back his chair and tossed down enough money to pay for five coffees. "Rock Hard is counting on you."

Chapter Six

When the alarm went off early the next morning, Jamie placed an arm over her face. She groaned, knowing she had to get up. After taking a few deep breaths, she tossed off the covers, placed her feet on the floor, and forced herself to rise. Wanting to look presentable in case Jonathan happened to be awake, she washed up then drew on her newest set of scrubs before heading into the kitchen to fix her coffee and down a bowl of Frosted Flakes. Before she made the trip to the hospital, she texted Becky. Her friend would know whether Jonathan had been moved to the burn unit floor yet.

Becky immediately shot back her reply: *Yes. Tube's out, but he's heavily sedated.*

Jamie thanked her, and stuffed her cell in her pocket. As soon as she finished her meal, she shrugged into her coat and left. It wasn't until she passed the fast food drive-through that an ache the size of a wall crumbling during an earthquake, crept up her body. Would she ever need to buy an extra cup of coffee and breakfast for Jonathan again? No doubt another homeless person, besides Larry, would find a space near the clinic to call home, but there was a wily intelligence behind Jonathan's pained eyes that had drawn her.

Jamie supposed she could get in the habit of buying a meal

for Larry each morning, but with his friend gone, he might find peace elsewhere.

When she stepped through the hospital doors, she saw that Janice Greenwald was manning the reception desk again. "Hey Janice. Could you check what room Jonathan Rambler is in?"

Janice typed the information into her computer. "Room 604."

"Thanks."

Jamie stepped off the elevator and wiped her damp palms on her pants, preparing herself for the worst. As Jamie rounded the corner, she ran straight into Max Gruden—literally. Reflexively, she planted her hands on his chest, and the solidness of his body stunned her.

Heat raced up her face and she lowered her arms. "What are you doing here?" She wasn't even sure how she'd managed to form those words.

✧ ✧ ✧

"Checking on your friend." Max kept his voice as sympathetic as possible, working hard not to mirror Jamie's defensive attitude.

A moment later, her rigid posture melted like ice cream on a hot day. Guess she couldn't believe he'd followed up. For a split second, a connection formed, but he was the one who broke it, not wanting to expose his own reasons for coming.

She probably thought he was here to pump her friend for information because he didn't trust her enough to tell him. She'd be wrong. Max was here because Jamie wouldn't ask the right questions. He believed she had no idea Jonathan was anyone but a homeless man.

Dan had texted Max this morning with some new information. Before finding out what Jamie knew, the mayor was able to get ahold of his contact at the FBI. He notified them of the fire and the severity of the man's injuries, but apparently, they already knew. They begrudgingly revealed that Jonathan was their agent, and that his real name was Vic Hart. His expertise was in domestic terrorism. That news made Max's blood run cold.

Two men in suits rounded the corner and strode past them, as if they were about to check on Vic Hart. They probably had been waiting at a distance for Max to leave the room. From their erect posture and trim physique, they looked like federal agents, but he couldn't be sure. The urge to question them burned inside him, but he didn't want to divulge Jonathan's identity to Jamie.

She twisted her lips as if she were debating whether to rush on by or ask him about his visit. "How is he?" Her neck stretched forward like she didn't want to miss a word.

"He was heavily sedated, so I didn't stay."

"I heard that." Her gaze lowered. Was she merely shy or was she hiding something?

"I'm about to speak to the ER doc who treated Jonathan. Do you want to come?"

"Do you think the doctor knows something?" The hope in her voice made her pain more real.

"Won't know until I ask him." He hadn't meant to sound flip. He was merely stating the truth.

She drew in her bottom lip as if she were trying to decide whether to join him, or stop in and see her friend. On second thought, it might be better if Jamie didn't come with him. The ER doctor might not say anything with her present.

"I want to visit Jonathan first."

"I'll let you know what I find out," he said.

She tossed him a quick smile, ducked past him, and strode down the hallway.

Man. He had it bad.

✧ ✧ ✧

Jamie should have thanked Max for visiting Jonathan, but she'd been stunned that he was there. She hadn't expected him to take time out of his day to check up on someone he didn't even know. *Wow.*

All last night, she'd thought about Max. He'd come on a bit strong at the wedding, but when she was finally able to be honest with herself, she could tell he was only trying to help.

With all that had happened, she realized she had to change her attitude or chance walking through life in cement-filled shoes. Starting today, she'd have a better outlook. Compared to Jonathan, her life was rosy. She had a place to live, a good job, and some amazing friends. She planned to reach out to others and to make more of an effort to get out.

Right now, though, she had to see her friend. Jaime inhaled and knocked on his room door, though he wouldn't be awake to answer. As soon as she stepped inside, she halted. Her heart cracked. His head, neck, and shoulder were heavily bandaged, and his breathing ragged. An IV stand stood next to his bed with the saline silently dripping into his body. The heart and blood pressure monitor beeped rhythmically.

Jonathan was probably pumped full of Ativan for his anxiety, and given morphine to ease the pain. She didn't want to rouse him just to say hello. He needed his rest.

She tiptoed over to his bed and softly called his name. Jamie waited a few beats, but as he continued to sleep, she studied him. Something was different about him. He looked younger, but how could that be? Maybe it was that his beard was cut short. Because his head was wrapped in gauze, his matted hair no longer showed. Had they cut that, too? The only reason would be if he had a head wound or was burned.

"Hey, Jonathan. It's me, Jamie. I brought you coffee and breakfast this morning, but when I couldn't find you, Larry seemed happy to take it off my hands."

Even though her voice shook, she hoped some part of Jonathan's brain could tell she was there for him.

His fingers jerked, but he didn't open his eyes. Her pulse raced.

Jonathan groaned. "No. No."

God. He was having a nightmare. Was he dreaming about the moment the board fell on him? Was he reliving the terror? She couldn't imagine waking up to smoke, fire, and disorientation.

Jamie placed her palm on top of his hand. "It's okay. No one will hurt you. You're safe now."

He shook his head. "Monster truck."

That was an odd thing to say. His jerking legs calmed. Hopefully, his nightmare had turned into a more pleasant dream. He might be remembering when he used to play with big trucks as a kid.

Jonathan's thrashing about suddenly increased, causing his heart rate to increase. "Forty-seven." His words were slurred, so she couldn't be positive she'd heard him correctly.

"Forty-seven? Is that what you said?" She didn't really expect an answer.

"Concut."

She barely made out that word. Could have been Connecticut, but she couldn't be sure. Jamie pulled up a chair and leaned closer to him. "Are you trying to tell me something?"

His movements became more agitated. "D."

When her hospice patients had been sedated, they'd rambled, too, but Jonathan seemed more distressed than any patient she'd taken care of. His fingers moved, almost as if he were typing. Her presence seemed to be aggravating him, so she pushed back the chair and stood.

"You rest now, you hear? Get well soon." Stomach churning, Jamie rushed out.

✧ ✧ ✧

After watching Jamie head off to Jonathan's, or rather Vic Hart's, room, Max took the elevator to the bottom floor. Dr. Randy Carstead had been the admitting physician on duty when the paramedics had brought in Jonathan Rambler. Max wanted to understand why a fairly healthy, trained FBI agent hadn't run from the fire. Something or someone must have stopped him. Also, if Max's assumption about the wall collapsing was wrong, he needed to know. It might affect his other conclusions.

He waited a good ten minutes for Randy to finish up with a patient. When the doctor made eye contact, he came toward Max, flipped off his gloves, and tossed them in a nearby receptacle.

"Long time, no see." Randy had been at Stone Benson's wedding a few days ago. "What brings you here?"

"Jonathan Rambler was brought in yesterday with burns to his chest and neck. I'm trying to reenact the warehouse fire on First Street. My data tells me a board fell on him. Does that line up with what you found?"

His eyes widened. "I'm impressed with your accuracy. The burn marks are consistent with a rectangular surface, but that's not all that happened to him."

Randy had his interest. "What do you mean?"

"From the size and shape, I'd say the butt of a gun did some damage to the back of his skull."

"So he was beaten?" Maybe that was why the agent didn't smell the smoke and get the hell out of there.

"Looks like it. With that kind of blow, he'd have been unconscious almost immediately. His knuckles were bruised, too, implying he'd put up a fight."

Fuck. Jonathan had grunted and thrashed about when Donner Pearson had placed him on the gurney, but all the jostling could have woken him up for a few seconds. "Thanks."

Randy held up a hand. "One more thing. I called the station this morning. Had I known you were in charge, I would have contacted you, too."

"That's okay. What did you find?" It was probably the information Dan had told him.

"The man was covered in stage make-up, a wig, and extra padding. Strangest damn thing."

From Randy's raised brows, his curiosity had gotten the better of him, but it wasn't Max's place to explain. "Interesting. Appreciate the help."

"Anytime." A nurse rushed over to the doctor and informed Randy that an ambulance had just delivered a car crash victim. "Gotta go. Don't be a stranger."

"You bet." Max hadn't socialized as much as he'd have liked in the last few months. While he'd played a game or two of darts and shared a couple of drinks with Randy, Max had been too busy finishing his fire science degree to do more.

He should probably go back upstairs and question Jamie about Mr. FBI Man, but she'd be less likely to talk about her friend with him in the room. Max decided to speak with her tomorrow.

He stepped outside. Crap. The air temp had dropped at least ten degrees. He'd hoped the cold front heading this way would hold off until after the weekend, but it didn't appear it would.

As he made his way to his SUV, he heard curses coming from the far end of the lot. Max stopped, looked around, and then spotted a raised car hood. He wove his way over to see if he could help.

When he neared the actual car, he stopped. Oh, no. Jamie had her head under the hood. That sucked. Poor girl had just experienced an attempted break-in at the clinic, seen a friend suffer a horrible fate, and now this. She'd have to be mighty strong to endure three setbacks in such a short period of time, but she didn't need his pity.

When he made it to her parking spot, Jamie was shifting her butt right and left. He swallowed a chuckle at her action. She didn't seem like the ass-wiggling type, nor did she seem like someone who would know a spark plug from a brake line.

When she planted her foot on her calf, an overwhelming rush of interest invaded his bloodstream. Damn, she was doing it again to him—just like at the wedding. Max had dated a lot of women over the years, but he hadn't been looking for someone special. He'd cut off that part of his brain, waiting until he'd found the arsonist who'd burned his family home. With that man in jail, he was ready to resume his life, only Max's emotional cells had yet to fire—until now. Too bad the timing sucked. Rock Hard needed him to do a job.

Max cleared his throat to let her know he was near. "Need help?"

She stiffened, shot out from under the hood, and turned around. Her long inhale implied she was warring with herself. "No." She paused. "Thank you. Grayson can be temperamental sometimes, but I've always managed to get him started."

A chuckle escaped. She named her car? "Grayson?" Max hadn't seen this whimsical side of her before, but he liked it.

Her chin lifted. "That's his name."

"Mind if I take a look? I'm rather handy with engines."

"Really?"

"When I was sixteen, I took apart an old clunker. Would have been able to put it back together again if my grandmother hadn't decided that my summer project took up too much garage space. She dumped all the pieces in one big bin. Never did get it to run properly, but I sure learned a lot."

She clamped a hand over her mouth and laughed. "Seriously?"

"I'm afraid so."

"Did she apologize?"

"Not my nannie. Said I should have known better."

Jamie smiled. "She sounds wise."

"Not to a sixteen-year old she didn't. So, do you want my

help or not?"

"I'm good."

Of all the women he'd ever known, he'd never met one who turned down help—especially when it came to cars. But if Jamie thought she could fix it without any tools, he'd stay for the show. Her decision to repair the car herself was a good sign. Her actions indicated someone who wasn't a victim anymore. Maybe their little talk had helped.

Folding his arms across his chest, he leaned against the car parked next to hers. Rich didn't expect him at the firehouse for another hour, but he bet Jamie had patients to treat at the clinic. If she didn't hurry, she'd be late.

God, but she was cute. Tiny, wiry, and with just the right amount of spunk. Now more than ever, he wanted to know who this woman was. She fascinated him.

Jamie continued to push and pull at the wires as if the car would miraculously start. "Would you like me to give you a jump?"

She kept her head averted. "If I jiggle the right wires, I can get it started. It's always worked before." Her focus and good intentions were admirable. He hoped she succeeded, but in his experience, randomly tugging on wires didn't solve many engine problems. When she seemed content with her attempt, she stood. "Let's see if that worked."

Her satisfied smirk sent another unwanted spark straight through him. What was it about this woman that pushed him off balance?

Don't even answer that.

Max zipped up his coat, fearing the dreaded storm might come sooner rather than later. She yanked open her door, hopped in, and cranked the engine. It made a grinding and freewheeling noise, like the starter or possibly the solenoid had gone bad. That would set her back both time and money.

Stubborn set to her jaw, she got out again, and ran her hands up and down her arms. Only then did he notice how thin her jacket was. He unzipped his coat, slipped it off, and placed his jacket over her shoulders.

"What the—" Her eyes practically crossed. "Now you'll be cold."

"You're welcome."

She smiled and her pretty blue eyes sparkled. "Thank you."

"I hate to bring this up, but if you don't call AAA, you'll miss work."

Her hands fisted. "Don't have that." She acted embarrassed, as if he'd judge her.

It didn't matter if she did. Not only did he have roadside assistance, he'd recently performed the inspection on their building, and had made friends with Emily, the woman in charge of towing. He bet she'd help. He pulled out his phone, made the call, and explained the situation.

"Let me see." He heard keys tapping over the line. "Carl is out on a job now, and it seems Pritchard hasn't showed up for work yet. As soon as Devlon gets back, I'll send him out."

"How long?"

"I'm guessing 'bout an hour if you're lucky."

"I'll be here. I need to run an errand, but I'll return before your guy arrives. Thanks." The whole time he chatted with Emily, Jamie continued to fiddle with the engine, but given the tilt of her head, she was listening to his every word. The big question was how she'd respond to his offer of help.

He disconnected. "Tow truck will be here in an hour."

"I heard, but I could have called someone."

Yes, but she hadn't. She had an interesting set of values. Given how she'd come early to the hospital, she didn't want to be late to work. On the other hand, he bet it bothered the hell out of her to let anyone give her assistance. He didn't know which path she'd choose.

He wanted to make it easy on her. "How about if I drop you

off at the clinic and come back here to wait for the tow?"

She finally faced him, her gaze shooting right then left. "You'd do that?"

"Sure. I like doing nice things for a beautiful woman." *I so didn't let that slip.* Shit. Now she'd think he was trying to pick her up. Which he was, in a way.

"You talking to me?"

Her very bad Al Pacino imitation hit some mental funny bone, and he dropped back his head and laughed. "You are something else, Jamie Henderson. I promise I won't take advantage of you on the short drive there." Max had no idea what was going through her head, but given her recent episode at the clinic, safety had to be paramount on her mind.

She nodded. "I appreciate it. But how will I get home without my car?" She held up a palm. "Never mind. I can call a friend."

"I'll give you a lift to your house. I have a feeling your car might need a new starter. If that's the case, it could be a few days for them to repair it. They might even have to order the part."

"Like I need this?" She bit her bottom lip. "How will I visit Jonathan?"

She'd given him the perfect segue to ask about the mystery man, but his cop instinct told him this wasn't the right time.

"Let's get you to work, and your car to the shop. After you find out what's wrong, you can come up with a plan."

She let out a large breath. "Thank you. Ever since yesterday, I've not been myself."

"I understand." He really did. Except he'd been out of sorts for years instead of days. Being able to help someone was like having a small hole in a fogged window wiped clean.

She handed him the ignition key, and then followed him to his SUV. He held open her door, and while the women he dated enjoyed the chivalry, he never had the sense they really cared one way or the other. With Jamie, he bet she'd like it. The woman had principles.

After meeting her in the hallway, and then watching her try to fix her car, Max was looking forward to finding out what made Jamie Henderson tick.

✧ ✧ ✧

Seeing Jonathan so injured had been torture enough, but having Grayson breakdown set Jamie's nerves on edge. She settled back in Max's car, crossed her arms, and rested her elbows on her purse. "If I'd had more time, I would have been able to fix my beloved car, you know."

He chuckled. "You couldn't have fixed a starter, Miss Car Expert."

"Oh, yeah?" Flirting with a man like Max was kind of fun. He'd been too serious at the wedding, but when he'd watched her work, there was something easy about him that she liked. She'd love to prove him wrong, but she had a feeling he was right about her car. That grinding noise did sound like a bad starter. Crap.

"Yeah." His smile widened.

"Does seeing someone in trouble always bring you such joy?" She kept her tone light, so he could tell she was teasing.

He pointed to his chest as if she were accusing him of some terrible deed. "No joy on my part. You looked like you had everything under control. I was there as backup."

"I know. I appreciate your faith in my talents." She would have been really late if he hadn't offered to wait around for the tow.

"Ever think of getting a new car?" Max asked as casually as could be.

She twisted so her back was against the door. He'd touched on a sore spot. "My car has another one or two hundred thousand miles left on him."

His Adam's apple bobbed. "That might be, but at what cost? First it's the starter then it's the timing belt, new tires, and new brakes. And don't forget the clutch, assuming it's a stick shift."

His concern had merit. Of late, Grayson had become more and more temperamental. But new cars cost money. "It is, but I'll take my chances."

He drummed his fingers on the wheel for a moment. "Why is this car so important to you?"

Max was good. Intuitive. He really seemed to listen, and to understand. "The car belonged to my dad before he died."

Like a cloud passing over the sun, his face darkened. Darn. Max might still have issues of his own, but she never intended to remind him of his own loss. *Way to go.* He had been so nice driving to the hospital before work to check on Jonathan, and then offering his aid. She needed to think before she spoke.

Max's gaze remained unerringly on the road ahead, even when they'd stopped at a light. *Talk to him.* "Did the ER doc tell you anything about what happened to Jonathan?" That was a safe topic.

His jaw tightened, as if he was debating how much to reveal. "Yes. Sorry. I meant to tell you, but I got distracted. Dr. Carstead confirmed that a burning board landed on your friend's shoulder. He also said someone hit him in the back of the head, which knocked him out." Max glanced over at her.

"Oh, my God. That was why they cut his hair. To clean the wound. It also explains why he didn't run out of the warehouse when it caught fire."

"I thought the same thing. Did Jonathan ever say if someone wanted to harm him?"

"No. We didn't talk much about personal issues." She looked out the window, trying to figure out if Jonathan's ramblings referred to what happened to him. "Do you think the owner of the building tried to evict him?"

"Doubtful. We interviewed him, and he kind of freaked

when we told him about Jonathan's injuries."

"Oh."

With nothing more to say, she kept quiet, trying to decide if Jonathan's strange words had been important. She never remembered anyone mentioning numbers in their sleep. What could forty-seven refer to?

Before she could come with even up one possibility, they approached the clinic. Only then did she realize she was still wearing Max's coat. She peeled it off and set it between them. The leather was old, but well loved. It even had some burn marks on the sleeve. "Looks like someone else likes to keep things for a long time." Two could play at the game.

"My wife gave that to me." The tension in his voice was as taught as a steel wire.

Fuck. Now she'd done it. "It was really, ah, warm. Thank you."

Admit it. *I suck at interacting with someone new.* Not that she was looking to date Max in particular, but she was tired of putting her life on hold. After the incident with the break-in, she wanted to be more proactive. Too bad the whole idea of starting again was not only unsettling, it was downright scary.

Chapter Seven

Max stopped right in front of the clinic, and put the car in park. "You should consider wearing something more substantial next time. Your jacket looks thin."

Max reminded her of her dad. Every time she went out to play in the snow, her father would insist she wear her mittens and hat.

"I was in a hurry this morning and didn't think about the forecast. I do have warmer gear."

"Bundle up tomorrow. There's supposed to be a storm coming."

"I will, thanks." Max was a kind man. And a considerate one, too. He was also really good looking, and the combination of compassion and physical appeal had her senses reeling.

Max nodded. "Once I make sure your vehicle has been taken care of, I'll give you a call when it's on its way to the shop."

"Thanks, again." This Max Gruden was different from the man at the wedding. This side of him she liked. A lot.

The tension across his face eased. "I'll also let you know when I hear what's wrong with Grayson."

His use of the Subaru's nickname spiked her pulse for a second. "I appreciate it."

She should be calling the shop, but since she didn't know where her car would end up, she'd let Max help one more time.

Jamie pushed open the car door and hurried into the clinic before he had the chance to set up a time to pick her up. If she could find someone else to take her home, she wouldn't have to inconvenience him. Hell, she probably should just call a cab, but the fifteen-dollar fare would eat into her budget. The free clinic didn't pay like the hospital did.

As soon as Jamie stepped into the waiting room, the familiar surroundings brought her some peace. With a quick glance at the few patients who were waiting, she headed into the back, and tried to push aside thoughts of the enigmatic, but intriguing Max Gruden.

Her first patient needed some blood work, the second antibiotics for an infected toe, and the third a few eardrops. The simple chores helped center her again.

The rest of the morning continued as usual, for which she was grateful. Max had called around eleven, but she'd been with a patient and hadn't been able to talk. His voice message said her car was at Richardson's Automotive, and that they'd have an estimate by the close of today. She had hoped they would have repaired her car by then, but she wasn't holding her breath.

Around one, she finally had the chance to take lunch. She was halfway to the door when she remembered she didn't have her car. Crap. She blew out a breath and spun around.

Her coworker, Sasha Langley, was standing there, purse in hand. She raised a brow. "Forgot you don't have Grayson?"

"Unfortunately, yes."

"I'm on my way to lunch. I can drive."

"That would be great."

They managed to get the same lunch hour about twice a week and usually ate together. Jamie had wanted some solitude to think about the break-in, the terrible fire, her broken car, and Max Gruden, but she'd have to put that off until tonight. Jamie would have suggested a drive through, but when Sasha was on one of her diets—which she was right now—she refused to stop at one. "Where do you want to go?"

"Valley Café?"

"Sure." Jamie loved the place. They left, hustled across the street, and slipped into Sasha's car that she'd parked in front of the recently shut down bookstore. "Valley Café will be crowded, you know."

Sasha shrugged. "Every good place will be."

Jamie was about to suggest Italiano's until she remembered Zoey had said that was where Max liked to dine. Running into him might look like she was chasing him, which she most definitely was not. "Valley Café it is."

There wasn't much traffic until they reached town, where finding a parking spot was harder than walking on ice in heels. The best Sasha could do was find a spot a few blocks away. By the time they reached the inside of the restaurant, Jamie's hands and feet were nearly frozen. "Brr. I thought spring was on its way."

"It was, until a big cold front decided to visit us from Canada."

That was what Max had said. "Great. Snow's pretty to look at, great to play in, but horrible to walk in when you're not bundled up."

"This is Montana, girl. Get used to it."

They snagged the last available booth. Once they ordered drinks, Sasha dropped her napkin on her lap. "How's your friend Jonathan doing?"

They hadn't had a chance to catch up today. "Not so good. He's heavily sedated, but at least he's not intubated anymore."

Sasha reached out a hand and clasped Jamie's. "I'm sorry. I read the paper this morning, but I didn't see any news about whether they caught anyone."

"I haven't heard, but I doubt they have." If they had a suspect, Max probably would have mentioned it. "Finding an arsonist within twenty-four hours of the blaze is unreasonable, unless the person is trying to get caught."

The waitress delivered their drinks, and Sasha ordered a chicken Caesar salad, while Jamie went with an old-fashioned hamburger.

"Not that I was spying or anything," Sasha said, wrapping her hands around her steaming mug, "but I happen to glance out the window this morning, and saw some total hottie pull up in front of the clinic in a black SUV. Wasn't I surprised when you jumped out." She sighed. "You get all the luck. I mean—" Her eyes widened, then immediately drew in a breath.

"It's okay. I'm good. And Max is not my boyfriend."

It drove her crazy that everyone walked on eggshells around her. Benny had been a good person until he cracked. In his warped mind, he was only trying to take away her pain. Somehow, he never seemed to realize that even if the victims were close to death, it was still murder.

"Tell me about this handsome non-boyfriend." Sasha gave her that don't-deny-me-the pleasure-of-living-vicariously-through-you look.

That made Jamie smile. "Not much to tell. Max Gruden is the town's new fire marshal and arson investigator."

"Two jobs in one. Impressive." She glanced to side. "Max Gruden. I like that name. It's strong, aggressive, powerful sounding."

Jamie agreed. "He can be aggressive and strong, but he's nice, too."

His boisterous laugh when she'd done her bad Al Pacino imitation rang in her head. The sound was as deep as it was rich, which Sasha would no doubt label sexy as hell.

"But he drove you to work." Sasha winked. "Don't tell me you were coming from his place this morning."

"Ah, no." Jamie was too dumbfounded to explain.

"You can tell me. I'm happy that you have a new beau." Sasha placed a hand over her heart. "About time, too."

Jamie tilted her head. "You are so off the mark. Max was at the hospital this morning and happened to be checking up on Jonathan the same time I was. He stopped to speak with a doctor, and when he came out, he saw my car hood up. I couldn't get Grayson started, so he offered to drive me to work then wait for the tow truck. End of story."

Sasha sipped her coffee. "Aw. How sweet. Why can't I find a knight in shining armor like that?"

"You will someday. I have to admit he was rather princely. I was struggling with the car, and poof, he just appeared. A lot of men might have slipped into their vehicles and left, but not Max."

Sasha snapped her fingers. "Max Gruden. Now I know where I've heard that name. Wasn't he the groomsman you were paired up with at the wedding?"

Jamie sighed. She'd shared too much. "Yes."

"It's destiny. That's all I'm saying."

"Keep thinking that."

Sasha laughed. "For helping you out of a jam, you owe him dinner at least."

She did? Yes. Sasha was right, but it didn't prevent Jamie from scrunching up her nose. "I don't think he'd accept."

While he had been nice and quite the gentleman, both Amber and Zoey had said he wasn't much into the dating scene, though Jamie had heard rumors to the contrary.

"Then you have nothing to worry about." Sasha looked toward the middle of the restaurant, probably to see if anyone had overheard, as her voice had escalated. "It's the thought that counts."

Jamie couldn't take the chance of him turning her down. She'd then know he believed she was too damaged. Jamie had to make up something to keep Sasha from pressuring her into asking him out.

"He's not my type." That was partly true.

Sasha set down her drink. “Really? Not your type? You said that Benny was weak and lacked ambition. Max seems to be the opposite. He’s perfect for you.”

Her friend was right, but she wouldn’t admit it. Not yet. “I ran into Max a few months ago at Banner’s Bar. Zoey had invited me to meet her men. Amber, Stone, and Cade were there, too, as well as a few others from the fire and police department.”

“So? Was Max rude or something?”

“No. He sat at the other end of the table, and I swear the man didn’t say a word to anyone the whole time.” She shook her head. “I dubbed him Robot Man.”

Amber had explained that right after that party, the cops, along with Max, had caught the arsonist who’d murdered his family. Only then did Max come out of his shell.

“You didn’t.”

“I did. He was there, but not there, if you know what I mean.” Seeing him now, she found it hard to believe Max had been so withdrawn. He sure had changed a lot. She wanted to believe that if Max could do it, so could she.

Sasha rotated her cup so the handle was parallel to the edge of the table. “All of the men I’ve gone out with have been there, but not there, so I know where you’re coming from. Was he stoic this morning when he came to your rescue?”

Jamie was botching this. “No. He was actually quite charming. Flirty even.”

“There you go. Then why not go after him, girl?”

Sasha was like a woodpecker—determined, unceasing, annoying. “He tries to get into my head.” Actually, he had the uncanny ability to see right through her. It was quite unsettling.

“That’s called interest. I wish I could find a man who wanted to know what I was thinking.”

“I guess.” Jamie sipped her coffee and her insides warmed. Sasha lips pursed. “What?”

Her friend downed the rest of her drink. “For starters, you’re closing yourself off again. You have to let those emotions out."

"Yeesh. You're as bad as Zoey."

"Bad, huh? Well, if you don't want him, direct him my way."

Before Jamie could respond, their meal arrived. She blessed the waitress for the distraction. The first bite into the juicy meat made her remember how good food could taste. "Mmm."

Sasha dug into her salad then leaned back. "Seriously, you have the perfect opportunity to land this guy. I bet he offered to drive you home today. Am I not right?"

"Yes, but I hate to inconvenience him, and secondly, I don't want to *land* him. Besides, he experienced a trauma when his family died in a fire. He doesn't need to be around a basket case like me."

Sasha shook her head. "What are you talking about? You're a catch, girl. You need to believe that and start living again. If you don't, I swear you're going to blow away. Every day you get tinier."

"I'm not that bad. I've been working long hours, and sometimes don't have time to fix a meal."

Sasha's eyes widened. "I thought you said you passed through the denial stage a while ago? Seems to me, you need to take a trip around the board again. This time, make sure to pass Go and collect your two hundred dollars."

"Funny." What Sasha said was true. "If you must know, after what happened at the clinic the other night, I've decided it was time to take charge of my life. So there." But was she ready to dip her toe into the dating pool? The memories and betrayal were still raw.

"Good for you. I say, ask him out. What's the worst thing he can say?"

"No?"

Sasha shrugged. "At least you'll know where you stand."

"You're right." She exhaled. "I'll do it."

Sasha grinned.

Dear God in Heaven.

Chapter Eight

For the rest of the afternoon, Sasha's advice reverberated in Jamie's head. She did owe Max for helping her, but his rejection would hurt. She could hear the conversation now. She'd ask him to a thank you-dinner, and he'd say that she didn't really owe him. Then she'd feel like a fool. Not asking him, however, would make her look ungrateful.

Because Max knew all about her history with Benny, he might not be interested in a woman who dated a man with emotional issues. It wouldn't matter that she hadn't realized Benny had been so unstable. She'd dated him in part because when she moved to Rock Hard, Benny had been there to pick up the pieces. Jamie's relationship with her mom had been rocky after her dad died, and they'd only gotten worse with time.

God, but she was so confused. Even if she decided to pursue Max, and if he wasn't put off by her past, was he willing to have a woman in his life? Seemed to her, if he wanted one, he'd have found someone already.

"Jamie?" The Admitting nurse called to her and waved a folder. "Your next patient."

"Thanks."

For the remainder of the afternoon, Jamie pushed aside thoughts of Max Gruden and focused on her job. Her shift was almost over, and she needed to let Yolanda know about her need to leave on time.

Jamie found her boss in the hallway, studying a chart. "Hey, Yolanda. I need to leave at five today. Would that be okay?" Her boss's brows knitted together for a moment, then relaxed. Jamie rarely left when her shift ended. The long hours kept her mind from thinking, but tonight Max's schedule came first.

"I heard about your car. I'm so sorry. You catching a ride with someone?"

"Yes."

Yolanda placed a hand on Jamie's arm. "I forgot to ask, how is your friend doing? Burns are scary."

"He's heavily sedated. With my car out of service for a while, my visits will have to wait." Jamie didn't feel right asking Max to stop at the hospital on his way to her house. She'd inconvenienced him enough.

Her boss nodded. "I can attest to how hard it is without having a ride. Do what you need to do."

"Thank you."

At four, she texted Max: *Is your offer still good to drive me home? I can be ready by five, but can stay here until nine if that's better for you.*

Seconds later, he replied: *5's fine.*

Jitters raced up her spine. It was dumb to be nervous. She was just hitching a ride home. Nothing more.

During the last hour of the day, Jamie rushed around like a madwoman in an effort to avoid dwelling on her impending conversation with Max. She'd decided since he seemed to care for Jonathan, he might be willing to ask his cop friend, Trent, to help locate Charlotte. Jamie couldn't decide if she should ask for her favor before or after she asked Max out. When she'd decided to take the plunge and see if he'd have dinner with her, she didn't know. But now that she'd made the decision, she was almost excited. She hoped he said yes.

Not long after his text, someone knocked on the office door. It was Sasha.

She leaned against the doorframe and smiled. "A handsome man is in the waiting room for you."

Was it really five already? Where had the hour gone? "Tell him I'll be there in a sec." Damn. She shouldn't have made him get out of his car.

"You got it." Sasha rushed out.

Jamie ducked into the bathroom to make sure she didn't have some random pen marks on her face. The dark circles under her eyes appeared more pronounced than this morning, but there was nothing she could do about it now. Once she refreshed her lipstick, Jamie hurried out to meet him.

Here goes. She pressed her hands down her jacket. As soon as she spotted Max, an overly strong visceral reaction shot up her body. With effort, she tamped it down. She had a favor to ask him and a favor to repay. That was all, or so she wanted to believe.

Max's face was heavily shadowed, but it intensified the bad boy look. The brown leather Bomber jacket, straight-legged jeans, and boots added to the image. What really wasn't fair was that he looked better after working eight hours than when he'd dropped her off.

Eyes straight ahead, she strode toward him. "Thanks for the lift." She sounded confident and in control. Good. His lips tilted up for a second as if he found her attempt at normalcy amusing.

"Ready?" he asked.

"Yes."

Like before, he held open the clinic door for her. "Had to park a block away. Sorry."

"No problem." She stepped onto the sidewalk and a car whizzed by on the street. She didn't know what it was about this time of year, but the streets had more traffic than usual.

When they reached his vehicle, Max made sure she was seated before rushing to the driver's side. Now came the hard part—asking the favor.

She waited until they'd turned off First Street before broaching the topic. "Can I ask you something?"

He glanced at her. "About?"

"Jonathan Rambler has a daughter named Charlotte. They haven't spoken in years, but I think she should know about her father's condition."

He winced. "I agree. What can I do?"

His willingness was a relief. "I thought maybe you could ask Trent to look into her whereabouts?"

"I'll be happy to try. Where does Charlotte live?"

"I don't know. Jonathan never said."

Max turned on Nugget Road. "The RHPD's data bases are rather extensive, but mostly for criminals. Can you give me anything else to go on? Trent won't be able to spare much manpower for this search."

"I understand. Jonathan said his daughter's my age." Max raised a brow, and she didn't miss the slight jerk of his head. "I'm thirty. Did you think I was eighteen or something?" Probably because she was so short and thin, most people told her she looked younger.

"More like twenty-five." It looked like he was working hard not to smile.

That was better than eighteen. "Jonathan said he grew up in Montana, if that helps."

"It might. Is his daughter married?" His serious demeanor returned.

"Divorced, I think."

He tapped his fingers on the wheel. "I'll pass the request onto Trent, but I can't promise anything. If you can think of something else that might help let me know."

She didn't know much more. "We didn't talk a lot. He mostly told me knock-knock jokes, and that was about it."

Max seemed to be fighting another smile. "My grandfather used to tell them to me all the time when I was little."

"That's sweet. Sounds like you had a happy childhood."

She hoped that wasn't too personal, but he'd spent a large portion of the wedding delving into her life, and now Jamie wanted to know more about him.

"It had its ups and downs. We didn't have much money, which stressed out my folks. They always worried they couldn't provide for us kids. My grandparents, on the other hand, had less money, but it didn't seem to bother them as much. They were always happy. That was why I loved visiting them."

"Did they live far from you?"

A dreamy look crossed his face for a moment. "Nope. Just down the street."

She leaned back her head, picturing Max running over to his grandmother's house for a snack and watching her cook. "I never knew my grandparents."

He glanced over at her. "I'm sorry."

"Me, too." She turned her attention back to Jonathan, trying to think what other clue he might have given about his daughter. "Jonathan did mention he'd served overseas. He has some shrapnel in his calf from unfriendly fire. Maybe the military has a listing of his family."

"Outstanding. Did he say which branch of service?"

Jamie searched her mind. "Army, I think, but I can't be certain. Sorry."

"That might help, but over the next few days, try to remember if he mentioned Charlotte's last name, what she did for a living, or even what her husband might have done for work."

"I'll try." Jonathan's ramblings surfaced. "This is probably nothing, but when I was visiting him this morning, he was talking in his sleep."

Max's grip tightened on the wheel. "What did he say?"

"I'm sure it was meaningless babble, but he mentioned *forty-seven*." She didn't know why she even brought it up. It didn't relate to Charlotte.

Max glanced over at her. "Just *forty-seven*?"

"As opposed to what?"

"Maybe it's an address. Like 47 Arbor Way or 47 Emerson Street."

Those were streets in Rock Hard. "He just said the number. I think I asked him what he meant, and then he said the word *concut*. At first I thought he might have been trying to say Connecticut, but I have no proof."

Max tapped his fingers as if he thought her friend's ramblings really had meaning. "Anything else?"

"Just *no, no*. And then *monster truck*."

He shot her another look. "Monster truck?"

"Yes."

"Did you know there's a Monster Truck Rally coming to Rock Hard in a few weeks?"

She leaned back. "No, I didn't, but that might be it. Maybe he dreamed of going." Like she did. A wistful memory washed over her. "My dad used to take me to all kinds of automobile shows when I was little. My favorite was demolition derby."

Max chuckled. "Is that how you became interested in fixing cars?"

"Yes. My dad was good with engines, too."

Since Max seemed to be in a good mood, she contemplated asking him to dinner right now. Or would it be more appropriate to wait until they were at her house? She pictured both outcomes, and decided it would be less awkward if she waited.

As soon as he passed SR25, she wiped her damp palms on her legs. He'd never been to her home, so she gave him directions. "That's my street."

Once she pointed to her house, he pulled in front, put the SUV in park, and jumped out. Benny never opened the door for her, but she found she liked it. The door opened and she stepped out.

Max was inches from her, and she had to look up. "Once

again, thanks."

"My pleasure." He held up a finger as if he'd forgotten something. "I spoke with the mechanic, and he told me your starter was bad. I hope it was okay that I gave him the go ahead to replace it. I knew you weren't planning on purchasing a new car."

"That's fine. I would have said yes, too. But the starter? That's going to cost a lot."

"Probably. The mechanic also told me they had to order the part given your car's age."

"Damn. How long will that take? Did he say?"

His lips pulled back. "He estimated three or four days."

She groaned a bit too loudly. At least he hadn't gloated about recognizing the problem while she'd been in denial. Most guys would have rubbed it in. "Not good."

"I'll be happy to pick you up in the morning. I only live about three miles from here, off Mountain View, south of Silvermine Way."

He did live close, which helped lessen her guilt about him having to drive out of his way. Until she could set up something with one of her neighbors, she'd have to take him up on his offer. By the time she got Grayson back, she'd have to give him her firstborn.

"I appreciate it, but only if I can treat you to dinner." The words surprisingly didn't stick in her throat, though her stomach tightened, and her pulse soared.

He hesitated. Damn. He was probably trying to come up with a polite way to say no.

"There's no need to repay me. I'm glad to help."

"O-kay." Even though she'd anticipated he'd turn her down, the disappointment cut deep. She told herself that his refusal was for the best. The less time she had to be with him the better. She was already starting to like him too much.

"I have a better idea. How about if I take *you* to dinner on

Friday night?"

"What? I just asked you out and you said no."

"Right. I'm old fashioned. You don't owe me. I'm happy to help. Date?"

Excitement mixed with confusion, but she'd think about it later. "Great."

He smiled. I'll pick you up at seven thirty tomorrow morning." He winked and strode back to his car.

So he wouldn't see the elation on her face, Jamie spun around and hurried inside.

As soon as Max drove away from Jamie's house, the image of his rejection skating across her face surfaced, causing a sharp twinge in his gut. Fuck. He should have accepted her offer to take him to dinner, but she couldn't afford it. And secondly, the man should be the one to ask the woman to dinner.

Given how Jamie didn't like to owe anyone, he should have expected she'd offer to pay him back. When she'd shared something about Jonathan, and then told him that tale about her dad, he should have seen her request coming. Shit. He never should have gone all macho on her. Where had his head been?

Frustrated at his own stupidity, he dialed Dan, who'd texted him twice today, asking about his progress on the case.

His mentor answered on the first ring. "What's up? Jamie tell you something?"

Max chuckled. "Can't I call an old friend?"

"I know you too well. What did she say?" They didn't call Dan, the bulldog, for nothing.

Max relayed the sparse information about where Vic Hart had grown up and that he'd been in the military.

"That doesn't surprise me. What we need to know is Vic's take on homegrown terrorists. Did he mention a name or anything to Jamie?"

Normally, Dan was totally level-headed. Now he seemed almost driven, like Max had been for all those years. "Easy there. Why would you think an undercover FBI agent posing as a homeless man would tell Jamie sensitive information?"

"Shit. I don't know. Just hoping, I guess. The idea of an extremist group in our neck of the woods creeps me out."

"You and me both. Jamie did say that Jonathan was mumbling rather incoherently. He mentioned the number *forty-seven* and then the word, *concut.* Does that mean anything to you? I thought it might be an address. Or possibly the name of someone."

"Want me to check it out?"

"That would be great." It would be one less thing Max needed to do. Ringing phones and noisy chatter sounded in the background. Dan must be at the station.

"Did Vic say anything else?" Dan asked.

"Monster truck."

"Like the rally?"

"Yup."

Someone called Dan's name. "I'll check that out, too. Gotta go. I'll let you know if I find out anything."

"Be careful. Terrorists are dangerous people. They're already paranoid. Don't stir up the hornet's nest."

"I'll try not to. If Vic's other agents would just step in and let us know what the hell was going on, we could help instead of possibly hinder the investigation."

"That's the FBI for you. I'll touch base if I learn more, too."

Max had work to do at the office. Just because there had been a fire to investigate, didn't mean he could let the rest of his job slide. Not having found a replacement for his old job was dragging him down. He never realized what his former boss went through each day with juggling basically two positions.

Max called in a to-go order from Italiano's, requesting one of the specials. He figured it would shorten his wait time. As soon as he stepped inside the restaurant, Elissa walked out of the kitchen with his bag in hand. "Here ya go. Put it on your tab for next time?"

Max did enjoy the service there. "Sure thing. Add on a tip for yourself."

She grinned. By six, he was seated at his desk, ready to eat the delicious smelling food. As soon as he made progress on the building inspections that were way past due, he wanted to check out the conspiracy sites in the hopes of learning something about the location of any possible cells near Rock Hard. He also wanted to see if *concut* meant anything.

First order of business was to give Trent a call before he left for the day. His friend answered right away. "What's up?"

Max explained about the need to locate Jonathan Rambler's daughter.

"You want to know because Jamie asked you to find her, or because you think the daughter might spill the beans on her old man?"

"The former."

"You and Jamie getting close?"

He didn't need any interference from his friend. "We're going out to dinner tomorrow."

Trent laughed. "Oh, yeah? It'll be good for you to cut loose. It might help that sour ass personality of yours."

"Thanks for the psychological profile, dickweed. I'm well adjusted, in case you haven't noticed."

Trent laughed. "If you say so."

Max refocused his attention. "So, you'll look into the whereabouts of Charlotte Rambler? I mean Charlotte Hart. Hell, if she's been married, she'll have a different last name anyway."

"If Vic was a member of the armed services, we might be able to track her down."

"I wish the FBI would lend a hand."

"Good luck with that. I doubt the Feds trust anyone in Rock Hard, which is why they're keeping a low profile. This daughter may not even exist, you know. An undercover agent would have a fabricated background."

"You have a point." They talked a bit more and then said goodbye.

Max had a ton of work to get done. At least he could cross one thing off his list. He'd promised Jamie he'd ask Trent for the favor, and he had.

Max almost didn't know where to begin. When Rich came in tomorrow, Max would ask him to work on the new building inspections. That would be one less thing Max would have to deal with. He was thankful his assistant was capable of handling the day-to-day work, so Max could concentrate on the warehouse fire.

He needed to bug Margaret, the owner of All Professional Employment, about her progress on finding him a replacement for his old job. Just as he pulled up his newly created spreadsheet, his cell rang.

"Margaret! You're working late. Please tell me you've found someone." His heart jerked hard in anticipation of good news.

She giggled. While she was in her late fifties and had this wonderfully upbeat attitude, she often sounded like a teenager. "I did, indeed."

He glanced to the ceiling in silent prayer. "Tell me about him or her." He didn't care who the applicant was as long as this person was competent. Hell, he'd hire a cat if the animal could get the job done.

"His name is Brandon Caulfield. He's thirty-two, and from Billings. He's a fireman looking for advancement."

Being from Montana was a plus. "What's his education?"

"He's a civil engineer."

"That's almost too good to be true." Perhaps Max could pass off the building inspections and subdivision reviews to the new guy. He had the education for it. "Why isn't Billings doing everything in their power to keep him? Something wrong with Caulfield?"

She laughed. "Nothing that I can tell. He has glowing recommendations."

Maybe there weren't any openings in Billings or bad karma existed there. As long as the man knew his shit, Max didn't care what demons were chasing him. This guy was the first qualified candidate Margaret had offered them. "Invite him for an interview, though I'm tempted to take him sight unseen."

"I'll set it up."

After he disconnected, a hint of satisfaction seeped in. If Caulfield worked out, when Max wasn't searching for answers to the arson, he could concentrate on the feisty Jamie Henderson. He couldn't wait.

Chapter Nine

The next morning, Max picked her up at precisely seven thirty. Not wanting to make him late for his job, Jamie had waited by her window. As soon as she'd spotted his SUV, she'd dashed outside. Before he even had a chance to open her door, she'd jumped in his car.

He slid back into the driver's seat. "You're mighty energetic this morning."

"Didn't want to keep you waiting, that's all."

"Appreciate it."

Max twisted around to back out of her drive, and the muscles around his collarbone bulged. It was an impressive sight. The man was all strength and sinew.

He faced front again. "Spoke with Trent yesterday about Charlotte Rambler."

That was good news. She waited for him to continue, but he turned onto Nugget Road without another word. "And? What did he say?"

"Not much other than he'd try to locate her. It's going to be tough without more to go on."

"I imagine it will be, but thank him for me for trying."

"Will do. If you remember anything Jonathan said about his daughter, even it's the color of her hair or what she liked to do on weekends, let me know."

Max really seemed to want to find this woman. "I'll keep thinking."

For the next few minutes, he remained silent either because he was legally bound not to discuss the progress of the warehouse investigation, or because he had nothing to say to her. Yesterday, when he'd driven her home, they'd chatted so easily. Perhaps he'd had as little sleep as she had. She'd spent hours searching for clues about what Jonathan's words might have meant. She had no idea why she thought they were clues, but her sixth sense told her she needed to look.

"By any chance, did you give anymore thought to Jonathan's enigmatic words?" she asked. Max seemed like the type of person to check out everything. "I thought maybe he knew who'd set the fire and was reliving it."

"I did check, but I couldn't find anything." A slight tic manifested itself on the side of his mouth. Did that mean he was lying or that he was fatigued?

Couldn't be a lie. Max was too honest.

He glanced at her. "I know he wasn't conscious, but did he seem agitated or calm when he spoke?"

"I should have mentioned that. He was quite agitated, thrashing about, and groaning."

"Interesting."

She waited for him to continue, but he didn't. From the way his lips were slightly moving, he was thinking. After a few minutes of silence, she decided to change the subject. "Amber texted me and said their honeymoon in Hawaii is amazing."

His grip on the wheel loosened, as if he were glad for something to talk about besides the case. "I'm happy for them. I've never been. Have you?" He seemed interested.

"Once, when I was younger." *Before my father died.*

"Did you like it?" His level of enthusiasm increased.

"I liked the island of Kauai the best. Oahu was too crowded for me, but the scenery and water were incredible."

"I've never been outside North America."

The heaviness in his voice saddened her. "Does that mean you've been out of Montana?"

He laughed. "Yes. Do I come across as being a country bumpkin?"

Fortunately, he didn't seem offended. "No."

The lines around his eyes softened. "My family didn't travel a lot when I was a kid, but Marie, my wife, and I liked to drive across the country. I loved seeing all that America has to offer."

They talked about her favorite states, and then he gave his list. Before he finished telling her about his trip to Canada the year Maria found out they were expecting their first child, Max pulled up to the clinic door.

"You're spoiling me."

"Why do you say that?"

"Because I don't have to walk the four blocks from the parking lot to the clinic in the chilly morning air."

He smiled. "I'll pick you up at five."

Those dimpled cheeks transformed his face, but Jamie dismissed the funny feeling in her stomach. It wouldn't do to think about him all day.

"Uh-oh. It's Thursday. In the chaos, I forgot it's my weekly girls' night out. I could cancel." She didn't know why she said that. He'd be happy not to be her transportation.

"No. You should go. Be with your friends. Remember when I told how much of a difference it made for me when I reconnected with my pals?"

"Yes. You're right. I guess I won't be needing a lift home then. I'll hitch a ride with one of my friends."

"You sure? I can pick you up and drive you home if need be."

Max was too nice. She placed a hand on his wrist, and she swore sparks burst on her palm. She left go quickly. "I'll be fine."

"Friday morning, then?"

"Perfect." She met his gaze. "If I haven't said it enough, I really appreciate you going out of your way to help."

"No need to thank me. I enjoy being with you, Jamie."

Her stomach flipped. Heat flooded her face at his admission, and she scooted out before he had to the chance to open his door.

Once Jamie stepped inside the clinic, she turned to watch him drive away. The man was sexy as hell. There was more depth to him than what she first thought. Despite all of the emotional setbacks life had thrown his way, Max Gruden had figured out a way to move on. She wanted to believe she was on her way to healing, too.

Her first patient arrived, and she led the gentleman into an exam room. Trying to figure out how to help those in need with the limited supplies the city provided made her day go by fast. For the most part, poor nutrition and lack of funds to buy their medications were what sent them to her in the first place.

A few hours later, Sasha tapped the office door where Jamie was catching up on her paperwork. Her friend had a devilish glint on her eye. "Is Mr. Wonderful picking you up again this evening?"

"Not tonight. It's Thursday. I'm heading over to Banner's for happy hour. I wish you could come."

"Me, too, but it's my bowling league tonight."

Jamie smiled. "You know you're always welcome."

"I appreciate that. As soon as the league finishes, I'll join you. I don't need to be at bowling until seven if you want me to drop you off at the bar on my way."

That was so nice of her to offer. "That would be great."

Sasha smiled, leaned against the doorframe, and crossed her feet at the ankles. "You know, if you want to pay me back for my generosity, you can always see if Max has a brother or a hotter-than-sin cousin for me to go out with. Hell, I'll just take a sexy fireman."

Jamie laughed. "I'll have to ask if he has any brothers. He said he had siblings, but I never asked their sex, age, or marital status."

"You do that." Sasha pushed off from the doorjamb and went back to work.

For the rest of the day, Jamie tried to kick Max out of her head, but she failed miserably. She was falling for him. No man, Benny included, seemed to put her needs ahead of his. For a split second, she debated cancelling the date with the girls so she could see him, but Max wouldn't approve. Sharing her terrible week with her friends would help her cope.

Jamie snapped her fingers. She had to remember to give Becky the present she'd found for her last week. It was a pin of a bear dressed in nurse's garb. Becky was crazy about bears, whether they were stuffed bears, real bears, or even fictional bear-shifters. As long as it had fur, she was in heaven. Jamie had spotted the small piece of jewelry at one of the shops along First Street, and knew she had to get it for her friend. If Jamie had been thinking straight, she would have given it to Becky yesterday when Jamie had visited Jonathan, but she'd been a bit preoccupied.

Close to six, Sasha found Jamie in the break room stuffing her change of clothes in a bag.

"Ready to be chauffeured?"

"Absolutely." Jamie grabbed her purse and gear, said goodnight to the women on the late shift, and followed Sasha out.

The guard who'd been escorting the girls to and from their cars was there. He walked at a discreet distance behind them, probably to afford them some privacy. Once they were in the car, he waved, and headed back to the clinic. What had the city come to? She hoped they found those goons soon.

"What are you going to wear to dinner tomorrow night?" Sasha asked.

Jamie had been tempted to dress up, but she was undecided. "You don't think it will be a little strange if I walk out of the clinic all dolled up, do you?"

"Hell, no. A date is a date."

"I'm not sure I have anything that really fits."

Sasha smiled. "You can't get out of it with that excuse."

Jamie chuckled. "Fine. I'll try my best."

"That a girl."

Sasha pulled a half a block from the bar, as there were no spaces in front. "Say 'hi' to your friends for me. I will make it soon."

"Will do. See you tomorrow."

Jamie got out of the car and headed toward the bar. When she spotted two black vans, the muscles in her stomach tightened. She thought she'd conquered her fears from the attack, but apparently she hadn't. It was dusk, and lots of people were around. Nothing was going to happen.

She hoped.

Jamie inhaled and walked faster, seeking the safety of the bar. Before she reached her destination, another black van drove down the opposite side of the street, causing the hairs on her neck to rise. Why did every vehicle seem to be a black freaking van? Her imagination was out of control. She couldn't help it. As she reached for the door to Banner's, she turned to see who was driving that van. It was a man wearing a baseball cap. Shit.

Stop it. She couldn't let her imagination run wild or she would lose her mind. Most men around here wore caps. It was damn cold out. Yeesh. It had been bad enough when she thought everyone in the hospital was a killer. She didn't need another few months of nightmares.

Just as Jamie was about to step inside, a shout sounded behind her. She spun around. It was Becky, and the tension in Jamie's shoulders released. Perfect timing. Handing the small gift to her friend in front of the other girls would be tacky. Jamie dug her hand into her pocket and extracted the gift.

"Hey, girlfriend," Becky said as she gave Jamie a hug. "I stopped in to see your friend before I came over, and he's resting peacefully."

"That was so sweet of you to check. Above the call of duty, actually." Jamie held out the gift. "For you."

Becky's eyes widened. "For me? Why?"

"Because you're a wonderful friend. As soon as I saw it, I knew I had to get it for you." Jamie spotted Lydia Sayers, the owner of Naughty Desires, head their way. All of the girls had suggested she join them, and Jamie was happy Lydia was finally able to make it.

Their friend was a bit out of breath when she arrived. "Phew. I actually got away from the store on time."

"Awesome," Jamie said.

Becky pocketed her gift without opening it. She, too, must have realized unwrapping the present in front of others wouldn't be cool.

"Ready for some fun?" Jamie put as much enthusiasm into her tone as possible.

"You bet," Lydia answered.

Jamie pushed aside her anxiety and yanked open the door. While the inside smelled of beer mixed with the tangy scent of peanuts, Jamie basked in the familiarity. She glanced to their usual spot. "Melissa and Zoey are here."

As soon as they reached the table, both women stood and gave Jamie a hug. Zoey pressed her lips together. "How are you holding up, sweetie? I heard about your car."

"Car?" Becky asked.

Jamie loved Becky, but when it came to gossip, the girl never seemed to be on the receiving end. "Let me get a drink and I will tell you all. My life has been anything but dull."

Just as Jamie and the girls pulled out chairs and sat down, their waitress, Abby, rushed over. "What can I get you, ladies?"

They each ordered, and Abby hustled to the bar.

"Start from the beginning." Melissa said.

Jamie retold the story of the break-in, the tale of the horrible fire and finding out that her friend had been seriously burned, before ending with her car breaking down.

"Oh, my God. Who did you piss off?" Melissa asked.

That brought a smile to Jamie's face. "I keep asking myself the same question."

Zoey sipped her drink. "You know the old saying. What doesn't kill you, makes you stronger."

"If that's true, you'll be able to call me 'Iron Girl' pretty soon."

They all laughed.

"How are you getting around?" Melissa asked. She was a nurse at the hospital where Jamie used to work.

"Remember Max Gruden, the tall man, from Amber's wedding?" Jamie asked. Melissa nodded. "He's been driving me to and from work. He lives near me."

Everyone smiled. She knew if she told them of her date tomorrow, the girls would fuss too much.

Becky, the romantic, leaned forward. "He really seemed taken with you at Amber's wedding."

"He's a very nice man. He even gave me some pointers on survival."

Becky's eyes sparkled. "He's not just nice, he's freaking hot. Doesn't he get your motor revving? I know mine would be if I were around him."

Jamie laughed. "It's too soon to tell, but I'm keeping my options open. End of story."

Becky grinned, acting as if she'd gotten more information than she'd hoped for. "Good for you."

Zoey stared at her for a moment, acting as if a miracle had occurred. She then directed a question at Lydia. After all, this was Lydia's first time at their happy hour.

It didn't take long before everyone turned their focus to the newcomer, asking her about her business, and what was new in her love life. Happy hour seemed to be geared toward making sure everyone was on the right path to true love. That was one of the many things Jamie liked about meeting with her friends. They were all so supportive.

After they all filled up on finger food, and shared more gossip, Zoey pushed back her chair. "If you'll excuse me, ladies. I have a dinner date with Pete and Thad. Jamie, can I give you a lift home?"

"That would be fantastic." While she would enjoy seeing Max again, he deserved a break.

They said their goodbyes and left. It seemed as if the other women wanted to hang out for a while, so the timing worked for her. Zoey pointed to her car at the end of the block. "So, how's it really going with Max?"

Jamie had wondered if she'd bring up that topic. "He asked me out to dinner tomorrow night."

Zoey's face lit up. "And?"

"I said yes."

Zoey stopped and gave her a hug. "I'm proud of you."

Jamie chuckled. "I finally got it through my thick skull that I needed to move on."

"I'm happy for you."

"Me, too."

Zoey dropped her home and wished her luck with Max tomorrow. It was getting late, and Jamie wanted nothing more than to soak in the tub and think positive thoughts. She'd snacked on a ton of the pita chips and mozzarella sticks so she wasn't really hungry.

Once inside, she headed into the bedroom. She lifted her top over her head, and was about to toss it in the dirty clothes bin, when her cell rang.

"Ugh. Who's calling me?"

Not that she didn't like to chat, but now wasn't a good time. She bet it was Max, checking to see if she needed a ride home. Jamie smiled. He was one of a kind. She prayed she didn't blow it at dinner tomorrow.

Jamie grabbed a bathrobe and slipped her arms in the sleeves as she raced to the kitchen to retrieve her cell from her purse. It was Becky. Disappointment raced through her.

She slid her thumb over the screen. "Hey, what's going on?"

"Oh, Jamie. Can I come over?" Her voice cracked.

A ton of adrenaline blasted her. Jamie pulled out a chair and sat. "What's wrong, hon?"

"A man. He was wearing a baseball cap. Like the one after you. He followed me down the street. If I hadn't parked so close. Oh, my God. I think he might have caught me." Her words whooshed out in spurts.

The image of the men chasing Jamie toward the clinic slammed into her mind. "Was he tall with brown hair?"

"No. Blond. My height, maybe."

If Jamie had a car, she would have driven to town. Road noise made it hard to hear. "Are you in your car?"

"Yes." Poor girl sounded scared to death.

"Did you call the police?"

"No."

"Are you positive he was following you?" The thought gave Jamie the creeps.

"Yes. As soon as I got in my car, he stopped. In my rearview mirror, I saw him call someone. I'm totally shaken." A horn sounded.

"Had you ever seen this man before?" Now she sounded like Trent.

"No. Never."

Jamie searched her mind for the right thing to say. "I don't need you talking on the phone and driving. I'll be waiting for you."

"Okay."

As soon as Becky hung up, Jamie rushed back into the bedroom to change. She couldn't help but compare her near attack to what happened to Becky. Jamie needed to call someone. If she knew Trent, she would have contacted him, and while Max was no longer with the department, he might be willing to call his friend for her.

There were cameras on every corner in Rock Hard, which might mean the cops would be able to identify the man. Scaring women to death should be illegal.

As Jamie drew on her jeans and a warm top, she tried to put herself in Becky's place. When Thad and Trent had showed up at the clinic, she was glad to have the support. Becky sounded quite upset. Being able to tell her story to a professional would help calm her. Jamie was sure of it.

Damn. Zoey said that she, Pete, and Thad were going out to dinner, and Jamie didn't want to disturb them. She rushed back to the kitchen and called Max. Jamie paced, waiting for him to pick up.

"Jamie? You okay?"

Why did he have to assume the worst? Was it because she was a magnet for trouble? "I'm fine, but my friend isn't." She explained about Becky walking toward her car and some guy in a cap following her.

"Could it have been one of the men who followed you?"

She'd thought that, too, until Becky described them. "No. The man after Becky had blond hair and was rather short. The men after me were both tall. Unless Becky stole some drugs from the hospital and was waving them around, this guy was after something else." In the background she heard an engine start.

"I'll be over there in ten minutes," Max said. "And I don't want you saying you have everything under control."

He knew her well. "Okay, but why not call Trent?" She had

to admit that just knowing Max was coming to the rescue evened out her racing pulse.

"I'll listen to what Becky has to say and if need be, I'll contact him."

"Thank you." In the short time she'd known Max, she'd come to rely on him. He'd become her sounding board, her friend. She prayed she wasn't making a mistake by opening her heart.

Chapter Ten

With the few minutes Jamie had left before Becky and Max arrived, she threw a bag of popcorn into the microwave. She found finger food comforted a person, especially when the anxiety level was off the charts.

Becky arrived just as the microwaved dinged. She immediately threw herself into Jamie's arms. For the first time in a long time, she was able to give support, instead of receiving it. The sensation was wonderful.

"Come and sit down. I made some popcorn."

Becky's eyes were red and her breathing ragged. Her friend fortunately didn't reek of alcohol. The girls were good about not overdoing it.

Becky hiccupped. "That's awesome. Can I have a glass of water, too?"

"Sure, hon." Jamie dumped the popcorn in a bowl and filled two glasses with water. Since Max might want coffee, she prepared a pot.

Jamie entered the living room carrying a tray of their snacks and drinks. "Can you start from the beginning?"

The briefest of smiles formed. "That's what I always say."

"I know. By the way, I called Max. He insisted on coming over."

"Why?"

"If this guy scared you that bad, it must be serious. Don't you want to know who he is?"

"Can Max help?"

"He has friends in the department. He used to be a cop. I know Banner's has security cameras, so the police could check them, too."

"Okay. Do you really think those surveillance cameras are good enough to get an identification?"

"I don't know. If, as you said, this stalker had his cap low enough, no, but we have to let the police do their job."

Becky stabbed her hand in the bowl of popcorn. "They'll think I either made it up, or tell me they can do nothing because the man didn't harm me."

"Possibly, but if this guy does the same thing to another woman, there might be a record of him being a stalker."

Becky stuffed the popcorn in her mouth. "You're right."

"So, tell me again what happened." Becky's story over the phone had been quite disjointed. Before her friend could tell her tale, tires grated on the drive. "Hold on. That must be Max."

Jamie jumped up and peered out the window. When she spotted his car, she let out a long held breath. While Becky didn't know Max that well, they had been introduced at the wedding.

Before he rang the bell, Jamie opened the door. "Thanks for coming."

She had this urge to hug the man, but refrained. If Becky hadn't been there, she might have.

Max looked frazzled, like he feared this person had followed Becky there. "Hope I can help." He stepped over to the sofa and sat next to Becky. "You want to tell me what happened?" Max had a way with making a person at ease.

"I made coffee," Jamie said. "It's decaf. You want some?"

He looked over at her and smiled, the connection between them strong. "Sure."

"Becky, how about you?" Jamie asked.

"Yes, please."

Jamie ducked into the kitchen for the drinks, but she could hear the conversation. She hadn't expected the rush of excitement at having Max here. The more time she spent with him, the more comfortable she became. By the time she filled the cups and carried them out, Becky seemed a bit more composed.

Max turned toward Becky. "If Trent can pull up some mug shots, do you think you could identify him?"

"Maybe. Do you think he'll come after me again?" The fear in Becky's voice caused Jamie's gut to twist.

Max shrugged. "I want to say no, that you were some random, pretty woman that this man targeted, but I can't be sure. If I had to guess, he might have been debating asking you for a ride. Once he got you alone, there was no telling what he might have done."

Becky visibly shivered. "I would never give a stranger a ride."

"I'm glad."

They each picked up their coffee mugs and sipped their drinks. Becky placed a hand on Max's arm. "Thank you for coming out here. You didn't have to."

Jamie hoped Becky wouldn't say something to embarrass her—like how lucky Jamie was to be with Max.

"I'm always happy to help."

For the next half hour, Max asked Becky and Jamie questions, and they did their best to answer.

Jamie set down her cup. "Could there be a correlation between the clinic break-in and Becky's stalker?" Jamie asked.

Max shook her head. "The only similarity is the fact all the men had caps covering their faces."

Damn.

Becky wiped her hands on her napkin. "Jamie, we might be friends, but that doesn't mean anyone would know that. We no longer work at the same place, which would make our connection even more tenuous."

"You're right."

Max leaned back and tapped his leg. "Are you ladies positive this man wasn't some jilted boyfriend of yours?"

Jamie sat up straighter. "I'm sure. He wasn't Benny, and I haven't dated anyone else."

Max took another sip of the coffee then set it back down. "We must be missing something. Becky, can you go through it one more time. Leave nothing out. Not even the slightest detail."

Jamie guessed his request was to see if there were any inconsistencies. Max had definitely been in his element, asking intelligent questions and never badgering Becky.

After an hour, Becky's energy began to wane.

Max slapped his thighs. "I think I've picked your brain enough. I'm glad you called Jamie. I'll follow up with Trent, and let you know if the police find out anything." He stood.

Becky's smile was weak, but she no longer appeared to be as scared. "Thank you. Jamie is right. You are a good man."

Max's face turned a dull red. She was happy Becky said that. If Jamie had more courage, she would have told him she liked him.

Max helped Becky up. "Get some rest. For the next few days, make sure you ask the security guard at the hospital to escort you to your car."

Becky nodded. "Trust me, I will."

Jamie got up and hugged Becky goodbye. "The cops will find the guy. Don't worry."

"I hope."

Max pulled on his coat. "Do you want me to follow you home?"

Becky looked over at Jamie as if she needed her permission. If Jamie were in Becky's position, she'd feel better knowing some creep hadn't found out where she lived. Jamie nodded.

"I'd like that."

Jamie walked them to the door. Once more, Max had come to her rescue. This time she wrapped her arms around him without hesitation. She expected him to stiffen, but he didn't. He hugged her right back. His warmth seeped deep into her. "I don't know how I can repay you."

He smiled down at her. "You know I don't do things to get something in return."

He'd shown that side of him time and time again. "I know. I agree with what Becky said. You're a good man, Max Gruden."

He tapped her nose. "So are you. A good woman, I mean. See you tomorrow."

She smiled. "You bet."

What that man did to her body should be outlawed. Tomorrow was going to be an exciting day.

✧ ✧ ✧

Jamie had a hard time waking up the next morning because she'd barely slept. Not only did she relive the delicious feeling of hugging Max, but she'd stayed up late doing some research on the Monster Truck Rally coming to Rock Hard, as well as on *concut*. What she found made no sense. Tomorrow on their date, she'd have to ask Max what his take on it might be. She decided not to mention her find during her morning ride, since there wouldn't be enough time to discuss it in detail.

With a cup of coffee in her system, along with a bowl of Frosted Flakes, Jamie trudged to the window to wait for her ride. She should be elated she wouldn't have to rely on Max for transportation anymore, only she wasn't. The relying on him part she could do without, but not seeing him after today would be hard. She'd come to enjoy her time with him. This past week had been rather special. Amber had paired up Jamie with Max at the wedding for a reason. Now she could see why.

Admit it. I'm falling for him. Hard.

Max's SUV pulled into her drive, and with her change of clothes in a tote bag, she rushed out to meet him. Before she could pull open the passenger side door, Max opened it for her.

"Thank you."

Max's jaw slightly hardened. "Have you heard any more from Becky?"

He was the last one to see her. "No. I'll call her later today to see how she's holding up."

"Good." Max slid into his seat and pulled his car out of her drive. "I contacted Trent this morning. He said he'd look at the surveillance tapes to see if he could get a possible identification of the man following Becky. RHPD has good facial recognition software in place."

"Speaking of which, did RHPD ever come up with the names of the men who tried to break into the clinic?"

He shook his head. "No. Those scum seemed to know where the cameras were located, and kept their faces averted the whole time."

"Damn. Did I mention my boss hired a guard to watch the clinic? I know Trent said they'd have a cop drive by a few times, but I don't think Yolanda thought that was enough."

"Excellent. Will this guard be there during all operating hours?"

That would take a few men. "No. The clinic is open thirteen hours a day. This man will escort the workers from their car to work, and then he'll return for another four hours from five to nine."

"I'm glad the workers will be safe."

"Me, too."

"I'm also glad that I'm your chauffeur. It means you'll be extra safe."

She placed a hand on his shoulder. "You are too good to me."

He grinned, as he pulled up in front of the clinic. "Keep

thinking that."

"I'm looking forward to our date tonight." Her pulse sped up.

"So am I. I'll call the garage and text you if your car is ready."

"*If* it's ready? You don't think it will be?"

He shrugged. "Old parts are hard to find."

Damn. "I can call if you want. It is my car."

"Jamie." He gave her his sternest look.

She laughed. "That's right. You're a man. You like to do things like that."

"You got that right." He winked.

She'd never met a man who seemed to care so much about her needs. She liked it. "Bye."

Jamie slipped out of the SUV and rushed inside for her shift. Yolanda was off today. With Dr. McDermott still out, a new physician from LACE hospital was substituting. Sasha had told her that when that happened, it was up to the nurses to basically run the show. Unfortunately, Sasha also had the day off, making the clinic feel a bit more frantic. Lucky for them, they had fewer patients than usual, and Jamie managed to make it through the day without too much stress. She was even able to push aside the incident with Becky, and almost succeeded in not fretting about her date with Max.

At four, her cell dinged. It was a text from Max. Excitement filled her until she read his message: *Sorry. Car's not ready. Next Wednesday for sure. I'll pick you up at five.*

"Something wrong?" Mr. Sanders asked. Her patient was sitting on the edge of the exam table waiting for her to take his blood pressure.

She shook her head. "My car's still in the shop for almost another week, but it's all good." There was an upside. It meant more time with Max.

"I know how that can be. Had me an old Ford truck. I babied that thing for over two hundred thousand miles, but at the end it was in the shop more than it was out."

He sounded a lot like her dad. "I like the part about the car lasting."

Close to five, Layla said she'd take the next few patients so Jamie could change for her date. She'd tried on several outfits last night, and in the end, went with black jeans, pumps, and a knit top. After her usual application of lipstick and blush, she added a light layer of eye shadow and a smoky gray liner. A quick dab of concealer under her eyes, and she was quite satisfied with the result. Instead of dragging her change of clothes with her on their date, she left them in the break room. She had more scrubs at home.

As Jamie headed toward the waiting room to meet Max, Layla stepped out of an exam room, folder in hand. She looked up and her eyes widened. "Wow. Hot, girl. Max is going to drool."

"It's not too much?" Jamie hadn't been on a first date in years.

"No. You're gorgeous."

"Thanks." Not wanting to keep him waiting, Jamie stepped outside a minute before five.

The air had a bitterness to it, forcing her to tug her collar closed. Right on time, Max arrived. She opened the door to the SUV before he could get out.

"You're giving a guy a complex."

She stilled. "What are you talking about?"

"You don't let me open the door for you anymore." He sounded like he was flirting more than acting offended. Or maybe it was wishful thinking on her part.

Jamie never considered he did it for himself, but rather to be nice to her. "It's cold," she said.

"Just pushing your buttons, honey. Buckle up."

Honey? She liked it. They were actually on a real date and she couldn't wait to get started.

Chapter Eleven

Max looked over and smiled. "I guess I should have asked. Is Italiano's okay?"

"Perfect."

With the car heat turned to high, Jamie was actually toasty by the time they arrived. This time, she waited for him to open her door. Max held out his hand and, when she placed her palm in his, the skin-to-skin touch sent a delicious sizzle up her arm. From the glint in his eye, he just might have felt the attraction, too.

When they stepped inside Italiano's, only about five tables were occupied. She'd eaten there a few times, but only for lunch. The red checkered tablecloths and candles stuffed in the Chianti bottles screamed the seventies, but the atmosphere was cozy. Without waiting to be seated, as the sign prominently displayed on the stand requested, he escorted her to a table near the window. Max didn't seem to be a rule breaker, so what was going on?

"You eat here often?" Zoey told her he did, but Jamie wasn't sure if her friend had been exaggerating.

"Almost every night."

Really? He looked so fit. She thought she'd become a creature of habit by eating her frozen dinners all the time. He was worse off by far.

"Do they save your table for you?"

"They do."

Must be nice. Elissa, the waitress who'd served her a few times came over. "My, my." She grinned, acting like she'd uncovered a safe hidden behind a painting. "*Two* for dinner?" She raised her brows almost if she expected him to explain Jamie's presence.

"Very good, Elissa," Max shot back. "Two is the correct number." The genuine twinkle in his eye implied this banter was common between them.

Elissa laughed. "What can I get you *two* to drink?"

Jamie liked how she emphasized the word *two*. It meant she wasn't offended. "Coffee for me." She wanted to keep her wits about her.

"Coffee for you, too?" Elissa asked him.

"As always."

The last time Jaime had been to Italiano's she'd ordered the homemade ravioli with the tomato basil sauce. Because it had been so good, she opted for it again. Seconds later, Elissa returned with their drinks.

"You ready to order?"

"Ladies first," Max said.

That was new for her. Benny often ordered before her. "Number seven." She pointed to the menu item.

"Excellent choice."

"I'll have the lasagna," Max said.

Elissa's brows rose. "You're in a good mood." She smiled, made a note on her pad, and scurried toward the kitchen.

Jamie leaned forward. "Do you normally order the same thing?"

"I always have some kind of chicken or fish, but I'm in the mood for a change tonight."

Was it because of their date? She could only hope. "You don't eat red meat?"

"I do, but when I'm at Italiano's, I like how they prepare their non-red meat dishes better. If I go to the Steerhouse, I'll have steak."

What an interesting man. As much as Jamie enjoyed learning about him, her mind was buzzing with what she'd found out about Jonathan. Once she got that off her chest, she could relax and focus on Max. "I, ah, did some research on what Jonathan said."

Max's brows rose. "Do tell."

"Your explanation of his mentioning *monster truck* made total sense to me. Jonathan probably was referring to the upcoming event. I'm thinking that perhaps when he was in the service, he went to a rally. When he heard a show was coming to Rock Hard, he was thinking about it."

"Sounds reasonable. Go on."

Elissa brought over the wonderful smelling coffee, and Jamie took a sip, even though it was piping hot. "I figured the number *forty-seven* didn't mean anything in and of itself, so I moved on to *concut*."

Max centered his mug in front of him, but he didn't drink it. "And?"

"When I put that word in a search engine, nothing came up, but then I remembered what you said."

"Me?"

"That it might be an address. I went to the map function and typed in 47 Concut. A couple of places showed up, but only one with a D in the state's name."

Max's fingers tightened on the coffee mug. "D? You never mentioned a letter."

His interest seemed to have peaked. "I forgot Jonathan had mumbled it at the end. I didn't think it meant anything at first. Guess what came up?"

Max shook his head. "I have no earthly idea. What?"

"It's a street in Washington, D.C. When I went to the street view, I found it was the FBI building."

He whistled. "Really." He studied her for a moment. "So what do you plan to do with your information?"

"Go back and talk to Jonathan. Find out what's really going on." She picked up her napkin and placed it on her lap. "From the moment I met Jonathan, I knew there was something different about him. He was smart. Well spoken. I figured he had PTSD or something, and that was why he was homeless. When I visited him in the hospital, he looked quite different. I know they had to cut his beard and shave part of his head because of the wound, but his skin tone was more olive and…and he was thinner." She sucked in a big breath. "Something's going on. I actually thought he might be some undercover FBI agent."

Max pressed his lips together. "There is something going on." He shook his head and glanced to the ceiling, indecision crossing his face. Max reached out and clasped her hand. "I'm sorry, Jamie. There are some things about him that you don't know. I want to tell you what those things are, but I'm in the middle of an ongoing investigation, and that limits what I'm allowed to say. I'm going to ask you to trust me for the next few days while I file the appropriate paperwork. Then I can tell you something. In the meantime, can you not visit Jonathan or ask around about him?"

She stilled. "You think it could put me in danger?"

"That's exactly what I'm worried about. And it's precisely why I need you to trust me."

She sank back in her seat. "Oh, shit. Do think those men who chased me, knew about Jonathan? That they saw me stop and chat with him every day? They might think he told me something." Dread oozed through her.

"Did he?"

"No." She glanced around to see if anyone was looking over at her. Her voice had escalated. "I told you. We only talked about his bum leg, the weather, and knock-knock jokes."

His face relaxed. "Are you sure you are hiding something? For all I know, you're some super villain, like Cat Woman. Or maybe even an underworld mob boss. Huh?"

She let out a nervous laugh at his attempt at humor. She then sobered. This was worse than she ever imagined. "I'm scared, Max."

He squeezed her hand. "That's a good thing. I need you to be cautious."

She inhaled. "Okay. Message delivered. No contact. No talking."

"That a girl. Thank you."

Elissa delivered their meals. "Here you go. Can I get you anything else?"

Jamie was happy for the distraction. "How about a triple vodka, straight up?"

Their server's eyes widened. "Really?"

"No." Jamie glanced at Max. "Perhaps just a glass of Merlot."

"You got it." Elissa looked at Max. "How about you?"

Max looked up at her. "I'll stick with coffee."

Elissa winked at him, and strutted away with a definite swing to her hips.

Jamie glanced in their server's direction. A wave of jealousy slammed into her, but she forced it back down. Jamie liked Max. A lot. Even more so, now that he'd been straightforward with her. His need to protect her brought much comfort. "She seems taken with you."

A slight color raced up his face. "Hardly. I tip well, that's all. Besides, I'm old enough to be her father."

Elissa looked close to twenty-five. Jamie wasn't sure if that was Max's way of saying he thought she was too young, too, or if he was fishing for a compliment. "What are you? Thirty-six?" Amber said he was a little older than Thad.

"Forty-three if you must know."

He didn't look it. But forty-three was hardly old. "Ancient by anyone's standards." Flirting with him partially eased the fear that had been rekindled with the news he had almost shared.

"I feel ancient." He reached down and rubbed his thigh. But then he winked. "Careful with the old man jokes. I'm falling apart at the seams."

"Aren't we all?"

Max leaned forward. "Okay. Serious stuff aside, I want to know more about you."

Jamie was happy for the change of topic, and she was thrilled that he liked her enough to ask. He already knew the bad stuff. "What do you want to know?"

"What made you go into hospice care?"

"How did you know I was a hospice nurse?" She held up a palm. "Amber told you, right?"

"Bingo. Trust me when I say that when I found out what you did for a living, my respect skyrocketed."

No one had said they'd respected her because of her career. Not even her mom. "Because I was a nurse?"

"Yes, but especially for being a hospice nurse. I don't think I could be around death day in and day out and keep my wits about me. How did you do it?" His sincerity warmed her insides.

She'd often asked herself the same thing. "I guess I got used to it, but I won't deny it was hard. I first became a nurse because I wanted to help people. Hospice came later." She drank some of her coffee.

"Do you like the clinic work better?"

"It's a nice change." She wanted to take the focus off herself. Actually, she needed it. "Now, it's my turn. Tell me why you decided to go into law enforcement."

When he didn't answer right away, she took the opportunity to stuff a large ravioli in her mouth. *Mmm.* The rich taste of basil and warm tomatoes was divine. Elissa placed her wine on the table, smiled, and drifted away.

"It's a long story. You sure you want to hear it?"

"I don't have to be anywhere." Jamie really enjoyed this lighter side of Max. Hell, she liked everything about him. Whether he was serious or trying to be humorous.

His eyes brightened. "It's boring, but you asked for it. I went into law enforcement, partially for practical reasons." Max leaned back in his seat, but kept his gaze on Jamie's face.

"Practical, huh? Sometimes it's more fun to think with your heart. I loved to help people, so that's how I ended up being a nurse. If I'd been practical, I probably would have entered academia, and made more money." Damn. She hadn't meant to turn the conversation back on herself. "Sorry. Interrupting was rude. Go ahead with your *logical* reasons for going into law enforcement."

From the way his lips began to curl upward, he got her jab. "I graduated from high school with so-so grades, probably because my folks never pushed me to do well. They assumed I'd work in the paper mill like my dad, and saw little need for an education. Which was why my family was poor. Dad had no real ambition. Anyway, I tried the assembly line for six months, and decided there was no way in hell I could take the daily grind, so I chose college instead." He waved his fork, as if he wanted to duel with the spoon she was gripping.

Jamie set down the utensil, and picked up her wine glass. His dilemma hit home. "I bet that was hard, having parents who didn't support your decision to pursue an education." There had never been any doubt that she'd go to college.

"It was, especially since I had to pay for it."

"Ouch. That sounds really tough. I couldn't imagine having to support myself at that age. My mom was a psychologist and could afford to send me to school." Jamie held up her hand. "Suffice it to say, she was a big proponent of me getting a degree or two."

"You were lucky."

Jamie saw college as a way to leave home, but she was fortunate her mom had paid for it. "I was. Did you work your way through college or save first?"

"A bit of both. I got a job working for a guy who had a snowplow business. Cleaned people's driveways during the winter. It was a good gig, until spring arrived. Though, with the money I had earned, I could afford a few classes at the community college."

"I thought you had a four-year degree." Maybe her information had been wrong.

"That came later. Much later. At RHJC, I stumbled onto a criminal justice class I found fascinating. Near the end of the semester, our professor brought in a guest speaker by the name of Detective Dan Hartwick of the RHPD."

Jamie smiled. "Cade and Thad's boss. Did his little talk convince you to go into law enforcement?"

"It did. He told me if I got my AA degree, to come see him for a job. And the rest is history."

"I like it." Amber had told her that after Max's police career he'd moved over to the fire department, but Jamie didn't feel right asking for the details of the switch. Amber said it had something to do with the fire that killed his family. The last thing they needed more of tonight was serious talk.

When he didn't say anything more, both of them dove into their meal as if they hadn't eaten in months. She was sure it was to keep from having to discuss his family or the investigation.

She washed down dinner with her wine. "From all the television shows I've watched, I can guess what a detective does day-in day-out, but I'm not really sure what a fire marshal does. I know you investigate fires, but there can't be that many blazes in Rock Hard to keep you busy, right?"

He smiled. "Right. It's a good thing only a portion of our job is taken up with actual fire investigation. Because of my police background, I was able to become an arson investigator. To me, it's the best part of the job. When we're not trying to figure out what started fires, our time is spent dealing with code enforcement, like liquor licenses and building construction. We also supervise fire drills, give training on fire safety, and even give general safety puppet shows to first graders."

She huffed out a laugh. She couldn't picture Max in front of little kids. "You do that?"

"Don't look so amused, young lady. Actually, Rich is amazing with the little ones. I work with the older, at risk kids. I counsel them about the hazard of setting fires."

"I had no idea."

"That's why I work all the time. But I'm in the process of finding a replacement for my old position. In fact, Rich should be interviewing him right now." He drained his coffee and ate the last bite of his lasagna.

"I'm glad. You work too hard."

He smiled. With all that he did, Max never acted stressed out. He was amazing, really. He also really liked helping others—like herself. Not only that, but Max said he enjoyed working on cars. Even though she tinkered with Grayson, Jamie was more into watching cars race, but either way, they both appreciated automobiles.

Before she could find out what else they had in common, a short, round man in an apron waddled out from the back holding a white take-out box. His eyes sparkled as he made a beeline toward them. He placed the item between them on the table. "Max! How wonderful to see such a happy couple."

Max's neck flushed pink. "Jamie, this is Giuseppe Buscemi, the owner."

Mr. Buscemi lifted her hand and kissed the back. "My pleasure. So glad to see you're keeping this lonely man company."

Max's brows pinched together. "Giuseppe." Jamie had to swallow a laugh at Max's growl.

"What, my friend? It's not right to always eat alone. Life is too short."

Max's gaze shot to what the owner had set on the table. "What's this?"

Giuseppe planted a hand over his chest. "Can't a man bake a pretty woman a small dessert?" He stepped back and winked. "Enjoy." He was gone before Max could answer.

What a delightful man, but his actions seemed to embarrass Max. She was tempted to see what was inside, but decided to finish the last ravioli instead.

"Sorry about that. My good friend can be a bit over zealous." Max waved for the check.

"He's Italian. Besides, he seems really nice."

The left side of Max's mouth hitched up. "He can be. He can also be nosy. I bet he came over just to check you out." Elissa hustled over with the bill. Automatically, Jamie picked up her purse to pay for her half, but Max handed the waitress his credit card before she had the chance. "It's on me."

While he sounded rather insistent, it was hard for her to always be on the receiving end of his generosity. "I should be the one paying. You chauffeured me to and from work for the last few days."

"Sorry, honey, that's not the way I work. I asked you out, remember?" His voice might have held some lightness, but his eyes were piercingly serious.

Arguing seemed to be futile, and the use of the nickname melted her insides. "I appreciate it, then."

Elissa returned, and he signed the receipt. Max lifted the box and handed it to her. "This is for you."

She accepted the gift. As soon as she was seated in his car, she opened the lid, and the Tiramisu made her mouth water. The design on top was beautiful. "Oh, my."

He looked over. "What is it?"

She held it up. "A heart made from the cocoa. How cute it

that?" She pretended that Max had ordered it for her even though she suspected differently.

"Giuseppe's an old flirt."

"I like that he is."

On the way back to her house, they both kept quiet, no doubt thinking about the danger she might be in.

He turned into her drive, stopped, and put the car in park. He twisted toward her. "I have an idea. Would you be interested in going with me to the Monster Truck Rally in two weeks?"

A rush of excitement slammed into her. Any kind of car event thrilled her. "I'd love to." Jamie thought he might have asked her to dinner because she'd asked him first. Now, she believed he really liked her.

"Fantastic."

While doing her research, she'd actually checked out the upcoming event. "I can't believe I'm going to see Ghost Ryder and the Monster Medic in person."

Max laughed and the sound shot straight down her body. "You really are into cars."

"And trucks."

Max eased out of his seat, came over to her side, and pulled open her door. She grabbed the dessert and stepped out.

Max slipped the box from her fingers, set it on top of the hood, and wrapped his arms around her waist. Her heart almost stopped when he pulled her close.

"I had a really nice time tonight, Jamie."

"Me, too."

His lips slightly parted.

Oh, my God. He's going to kiss me.

Chapter Twelve

Max couldn't believe how perfectly Jamie fit against his body. She was so sweet and warm. If anything happened to her, he'd be devastated. He thanked his good luck she was willing to listen to his warning. She sounded sincere when she said she'd be careful. Her trust in him meant a lot to him.

Jamie placed her palms on his chest and looked up at him with expectation. God, what she did to him. He prayed he wasn't rushing her, but he needed her badly. Max dipped his head, and when she didn't pull away, he kissed her—slowly at first, then with more intensity. The moment she leaned into him, desire swamped him.

He wanted her so fucking much. Max teased open her lips, and when she dipped her tongue into his mouth, his cock hardened. He loved her strength, her convictions, and her passion.

Jamie moaned then wrapped her arms around his neck. That did it. If he didn't stop now, there was no telling what might happen. Max broke off the kiss.

She looked up at him with slightly swollen lips. "Do you want to come in?"

Her plea undid him. "Yes."

More than she could know, actually, but he wasn't ready to

tell her. He didn't want to assume her request was an invitation for sex. If it wasn't, he hoped to hell, he could keep his distance. Damn, it was going to be so fucking hard not to touch her. To kiss her. To make love with her.

Jamie picked up her box off the car hood and led him up the steps to her front porch. She fumbled with her key, but managed to open the door a few seconds later. She didn't look at him as she led him inside, and he hoped she wasn't having second thoughts about the kiss.

She faced him. "Can I get you some coffee?"

"Sure." It wasn't coffee that he wanted. It was Jamie.

Max followed her into the kitchen. She peeled off her coat, and he removed his, too. He liked watching Jamie pour water into the coffee maker, then measure out the grounds. He thought by putting some distance between them that his need would diminish. Fact was, the opposite had happened. The domestic scene had broken his resolve, and he wanted her more than he had a second ago.

Before she was able to turn on the machine, Max stepped behind her and twisted her around.

"Max?"

She wet her lips, and all thought fled. He walked her backward toward the entrance. "Ever since the wedding, I haven't been able to get you out of my head." He inhaled her delicious scent, a scent that reminded him of fresh linen.

She drew in her bottom lip, and glanced up at him with hope. "I've been thinking a lot about you, too."

He inwardly groaned. He wanted her to understand exactly what she'd be getting if she agreed to be with him. "I'm forty-three, and have had a lot of bad shit happen in my life, but one thing I know, is that when I'm with you, I feel whole. Good. Happy."

Jamie ran her palms down his chest. "You make me feel safe. And happy, too."

That was as close to an admission that she liked him as he'd probably get. "I won't lie. I want you, Jamie."

"I want you, too."

If this were any other woman, he might have stripped her right there, but this was delicate Jamie. She'd only dated one other man in the last few years. Max held out his arms. "You want to do the honors?"

Her eyes widened. "You mean take off your clothes?"

He chuckled. "That's as good a starting point as any."

She grinned. "But in the kitchen?"

He lowered his arms. "Not romantic enough, right?" What had he been thinking? Jamie was classy.

"How about the bedroom?" she asked.

Her chest expanded as if she was holding her breath. "Works for me."

She smiled, clasped his hand, and led him through the dining room and down the hallway. He wanted to assure her that if she changed her mind, he'd stop, but why put that terrible idea in her head?

Her bedroom was at the end of the hallway. She flicked on the light, and a pretty little lamp lit up the small room.

She turned to him. "Sorry. I didn't get the chance to make the bed this morning."

He never made his. "It's perfect."

"It's pink."

He had yet to even glance at the bed, as Max hadn't taken his gaze off her. "Honey, it could be purple polka dots and I wouldn't care. This is all about you and me, not whether you'd make a good maid." Once more he raised his arms. "I promised you could take off my clothes. I don't let just anyone do this, as it's not my normal style. So if you want, have at me."

She moved closer and pressed her lips together in concentration as her tiny fingers pushed the top button through the hole. Already, he could tell this was a mistake. He'd never last. Her knuckle brushed his chest, and a trail of fire shot downward. She undid the next two, and his desire strengthened too fast. "Need help?"

"Hold your horses. I'm getting there." Her brows pinched.

Max looked over her head to help calm his growing urgency. She tugged on his shirt and lifted it out of his jeans, then finished opening it. The second she was done, he slipped the material over his shoulders and let it drop to the hardwood floor.

She bent down and retrieved it. "Don't want to get it dirty."

He so didn't care what happened to his shirt. She could have stomped on it. Jamie folded his shirt and placed it on her dresser. All the while, his imagination ran wild about what he planned to do with her luscious body.

"You're killing me, girl." He lifted her up, and she squealed in delight.

Max gently placed her on the heap of sheets. The woman couldn't have weighed more than a hundred pounds. He then toed off his shoes, shucked his jeans, and tossed off his socks. He'd leave the briefs to her.

"Holy shit." Her mouth opened wide.

He froze. "What's wrong?"

"You're...perfect."

Relief washed through him. He thought she'd tell him that she wasn't ready. He wasn't sure what he would have done. Max crawled on the bed next to her. "I'm glad you find me appealing."

"More than appealing."

Max chuckled at the surprise in her voice. He dragged her on top of him, loving the feel of her body on his, and kissed her hard. Jamie clasped his face and returned the kiss with as much passion. Holy crap, but he hadn't been this turned on in forever. They kissed, nibbled, and then kissed again. Sometimes, it was slow and sensual, and other times hard and fast.

As much as he wanted to spend hours making love to her

lips, there was so much more he wanted to explore.

"I'm feeling a bit underdressed here." He nodded to her fully clothed body. He kept his tone joking so as not to pressure her. She was fragile in many ways.

"Then maybe you should take off my clothes."

Whoa. He loved this bold side of her. "I'll be glad to."

He lifted her off him, and slid his hands under her knit top, loving her smooth silky skin. He slipped the knit fabric over her head, and her blonde hair flew everywhere. She patted it down, as if what she looked like mattered to him.

Max caught sight of her pretty white bra and sighed. It was simple, but perfect. "Nice."

She clasped her hands over her chest. "I'm kind of small."

"Nonsense. You're *perfect.* In fact, everything about you is perfect." He liked using the same word she had.

He lowered Jamie's hands before he slipped the straps down her shoulders. With a quick release of the back clasp, he lifted off her bra and gazed upon her nakedness. Amazing. He leaned over slowly, giving her time to stop him. When she didn't, he dragged his tongue across the tip of her pert nipple. She moaned, and a second later, the tiny bud hardened. On the next pass, he sucked on the taut peak.

She gasped and grabbed his shoulder. "Yes. That feels so good."

He never dreamed she'd be so sensitive. Just as he lowered his hand to cup her pussy, his cell rang. The ring tone belonged to Trent. *Fuck.* He didn't want to answer it, so he let it ring.

"Aren't you going to get that?" The worry in her voice made him think twice.

"God help me if there's another fire." He sat up, pulled the phone from his pants pocket, and pressed the on button. "This better be fucking important."

"Sorry, man. Something bad has happened. It's really bad."

Max had never heard Trent come close to losing control. His

friend never let emotion color anything he did. "Tell me."

He glanced at Jamie. Her hands were fisted. Shit.

"A group of five men stormed the free clinic where Jamie works. The security guard is dead along with one other."

All he could think of was that maybe the men believed Jamie was inside. His heart squeezed at yet another close call. He wouldn't say anything in front of her. "What can I do?"

"I need your help."

Trent wouldn't have asked him if he didn't require Max's expertise. "Are you there now?" Max didn't want Jamie to suspect anything, so he didn't ask for any details.

"Yes."

"I'll be right there."

Max disconnected the call and tossed his cell back on the floor. "I am so sorry. I've got to go."

She picked up her shirt and pulled it over her head. "Is it another fire?"

"No. There's been a murder." He didn't want to lie to her.

She clasped his hand. "Who?"

"Trent didn't say." That was the truth. "Jesus, Jamie. Trust me when I say I don't want to go."

"I understand."

Max hugged her close, kissed her, and then stood. As quickly as he could, he dressed. "I'll call you tomorrow, okay? Maybe we could go to a movie or something."

The joy that had been on her face a moment ago, disappeared. "Sure. I'd like that."

Jamie walked him to the door. If the murder hadn't happened at Jamie's place of work, Max would have told Trent to handle the situation alone.

"I'll be in touch." Before he changed his mind about leaving, Max hustled out of her house.

As he neared the clinic, about ten police cars were blocking the way. A few residents were standing on the street watching, their necks craned. Dear God, what had happened inside? He hoped Trent planned to question these people. Someone might know something.

Max did a quick scan for a short, blond man in a baseball cap, but no one fit the bill.

Given a terrorist cell might be in Rock Hard, and Vic Hart "worked" nearby, this terrorist cell might be closer than he thought. Could agent Hart have pulled out a phone to call his contact and been spotted?

Damn. That was pure speculation, which was something Max never liked to fall prey to. He hoped that when he saw what happened inside, he might have a better idea what they were dealing with.

He parked and slipped out of his car. As he made his way toward the carnage, his heart grew heavy for Jamie. Whatever happened here tonight, she'd have to face it. Poor girl just might crack.

Max had to protect her. At all cost.

He held up his badge and made his way inside the clinic. He detected no odor of smoke, so this wasn't fire related. No door or window had been broken either, implying the shooters had arrived before the clinic closed, or had gotten hold of the key. The waiting area looked untouched, giving credence to their initial suspicion that theft of drugs might be involved. He wished he knew what they were after.

Nick Rogers, a detective who'd been on the force with Max, was standing at the hallway door. "Hey, Max." He let out a long exhale as if the scene in the back would give nightmares to anyone.

"Trent called me. He inside?"

"Yes, but it ain't pretty."

Murder never was. "Thanks for the warning." The farther Max went down the hallway, the louder the chatter became. The exam room doors were open and everything inside had been trashed. His gut soured. What had they been looking for in those rooms? Drugs weren't usually kept in the exam rooms, but maybe the free clinic was set up differently from the walk-in clinics.

At the end of the hallway, he found Trent, the coroner, and two detectives.

"Trent?" Max's voice caught.

His friend turned around, his face ashen. "The security guard didn't stand a chance."

The method of death would be important. "How?"

"A bullet to the head. Close range."

"Fuck." Jamie said the guard escorted the workers to and from their cars. "Where was he?"

"In the side alley, smoking a cigarette. Whoever did this must have snuck up on him."

Totally senseless. "They could have just as easily hit him in the head and knocked him out. Why did they have to kill him?"

"Stop him from sounding the alarm I suspect. I doubt he had a key to the place."

Max didn't want to ask who the second victim was, but for Jamie's sake, he needed to find out. He nodded to the woman sprawled on the floor in what once was a white lab coat. Her chest was covered in a dark red stain. "And her?"

Chapter Thirteen

"That's Dr. Yolanda Withers," Trent said. "Took two gunshots to the chest, but from the cut on her lip and the red marks on her neck, it appears as if they roughed her up first."

"Jesus. What did they take?" Max was sick to his stomach. Apparently he'd gotten soft in his old age.

"That's the thing. We don't know. This is where I'm hoping you can help us. Come with me."

Max followed Trent to a back room where the drugs were kept. The refrigerated section was still locked, and the glass untouched. Boxes on shelves had been tossed aside, but anything in a vial was left alone.

Nothing made sense. "What about the narcotics? Could they have been after only one type of drug?"

"Not that we could tell. We'll need someone who has the inventory list to confirm that."

"You thinking this was personal against Dr. Withers?"

"That was my first thought, until I went into the break room. Let me show you." Once more he followed Trent who pointed to the destruction.

Max stopped in the doorway. Three officers were taking pictures and cataloging the mess.

"Holy shit. What do you think they were looking for?" The

cushions were ripped, and everything in the cabinets was dumped on the floor. Max didn't dare enter, not wanting to mess with the crime scene.

"Beats me. Did Jamie mention anything about storing something important at the clinic?"

So that was why Trent had called him. "Not that I recall. She mentioned their limited supplies, as well as their inadequate drug supply. I can't imagine what would be so important that it would require five men to storm the place. I'm guessing you looked at the camera footage?"

"Yes." Trent's head lowered.

"What? They have baseball caps over their eyes?"

"Worse. They had infrared LEDs under their caps. All we could see was five people with big glowing heads."

"Crap. You let Hartwick know?"

"He came by earlier. He's speaking with the mayor now."

"Sounds like a professional hit."

Trent nodded. "That was my guess."

"What can the mayor do other than find another doctor to take her place?"

Trent stepped out of the room, away from the crime scene. "This might sound crazy, but do you think there's anything in here domestic terrorists might use to make a bomb or a deadly virus?"

A band tightened around Max's chest at the thought that kind of destruction could cause. "I can tell you how to make a Molotov cocktail, but that's it. You'll need to ask a chemist for what goes into a bomb. My knowledge is rather limited, though I do know that bombs require a lot of chemicals, and none of the boxes in here are large enough for what they'd need. Unless there's a cleaning supply cabinet with, say, a shit load of drain cleaner and rust remover, they won't have enough for something substantial. They can buy what they need at a local store, so why come here? They'll need to find a way to make nitroglycerine, but a few ten-ounce bottles of hydrogen peroxide won't do it. For that, they'd be better off with a pool sanitizer. I think you're barking up the wrong tree if you think this is chemical related."

Trent dragged his fingers through his hair. "I'm having my men do a background search on Dr. Withers, but I doubt I'll find anything."

"I trust the clinic will be closed tomorrow?"

"For a few days at least. If the mayor suspects terrorists, he'll want every inch of this place processed."

Max dreaded having to tell Jamie. "What can I do?"

"Talk to Jamie. See what she knows."

Max glanced over Trent's shoulder at the dead woman. "The men couldn't have mistaken Jamie for Yolanda Withers. Jamie is blonde and petite. This woman is much taller with dark hair. Besides, the men after Jamie didn't have on infrared caps."

"There has to be a connection."

"Got any ideas?"

✧ ✧ ✧

When Jamie's cell rang, it took a second to figure out what the noise was. She cracked open her eyes, and spotted the glowing phone. The bedside clock read eleven. None of her friends would be bothering her at this hour. She sat up with a jerk. It must be Max. He might have finished with the crime scene, and perhaps wanted to continue where he left off. How he could see a dead body and then be in the mood to make love was anyone's guess.

Jamie quickly picked up the phone, and when she saw who it was, her heart raced. "Hey. You okay?"

"Yes."

She waited a beat for him to continue, but he didn't say anything. Oh, shit. "Was Jonathan murdered?"

"No. No. May I come over? I need to speak with you." His

voice was measured, controlled, and tense. There was also a decided sense of urgency.

"Of course." The last time he said they needed to talk, he told her about Jonathan being involved in his investigation.

"I'll be there in ten minutes. Is that okay?"

Jamie swallowed hard. "Sure, but what happened?"

"I'd rather tell you in person." Max disconnected the call, and Jamie sat there stunned.

It was a good minute before the blood returned to her limbs, and she could move again. He'd said there hadn't been a fire, that someone had been murdered. Who was it?

Oh, no. Amber was still on her honeymoon. Had she, Cade, and Stone left the island early and their plane went down? Her ears pounded. No, that tragedy would have been blasted all over the news.

She prayed it wasn't Becky. The person who'd been following her could have come back and attacked her. Acid burned Jamie's throat.

"Stop it." She'd fall apart if she kept up with what ifs.

She hurried to dress. If she had to leave for some reason, she wanted to be warm. Just as she yanked on her boots, the doorbell rang. At the sound, bile tinged her mouth. She wasn't sure she could take another blow. Jamie rushed to the door, peaked out to make sure it was Max, and opened up.

He looked like shit. "Jamie." His voice sounded like gravel.

She stepped to the side to let him enter. His hair was tousled, looking as if he'd plowed his fingers over his scalp a hundred times. Even his coloring was pale. "Come in."

Max hugged her, and then kissed the top of her head. "Got some coffee?"

"I'll make some." The familiarity should have calmed her stomach, but it didn't.

Max followed her into the kitchen. "Jamie, I'm afraid there was an incident at the clinic."

Jamie's hands shook so hard, she feared she might drop the cups if she reached for them. "Mugs are on the top shelf of the cabinet next to the sink." Jamie nodded to the correct one. "Want to get down two?"

The door squeaked open and two cups scraped across the shelf.

She measured the coffee grounds and dumped them in the container, spilling a portion of them. Then she added the water. "Cream or sugar?" Shit. She knew better. "I forgot. You like it black." Jamie wiped her palms down her pants. She didn't want to know anything. If only she could wish everything away.

"Black's good."

She faced him. "You said someone was murdered."

"Yes. The security guard."

She slumped against the counter. "Oh, my God. Why? Were those same men trying to break into the clinic? Did they get mad when he didn't have the key?"

"We can't be sure, but it probably was to stop him before he stopped them."

Her mind raced. "Do the cops think it was the same men who came after me?"

"Let's get our drinks, and I'll tell you what I know."

"Why are you dragging this out? You can tell me." Her words squeaked out.

"Jamie. Let me do this my way. Please?" His in-control tone softened, as if he knew she'd need to sit down.

She blew out a breath, knowing she couldn't shake the news out of him, even though she wanted to try. The coffee finished dripping, and she filled their cups. "Shit." She'd spilled almost half the contents. Jamie was about to get the paper towels to clean up the mess when he gently clasped her arm.

"Go sit. I'll wipe up the counter and bring in the drinks."

Jamie set down the carafe, stepped around him, and went into the living room, shaken to the core. Her stomach was churning, and her throat felt as if it was on fire. She dropped onto her usual place on the sofa and closed her eyes, needing to find some calm.

Max came out with two mugs and placed hers on the coffee table in front of her. He sat on the cushion next to her. Her mouth was too dry to ask him again what had happened.

"Around nine this evening, after one of the men killed the guard, five men stormed the clinic."

Her mind spun. He'd said the crime occurred at nine. "Oh, no. Yolanda would still have been there." Jamie clamped a hand over her mouth to stop the slight keening sound from leaking out.

"I'm sorry, Jamie. They killed her, too."

Her whole body shook. Knowing the details wouldn't make it any easier, but she had to ask. How?"

"Two bullets to the chest."

Jamie dropped her head in her hands and wept. His cup smacked against the wooden coffee table a second before his arm wrapped around her shoulder. She leaned into him, but her mind refused to process anything but the tragedy. Jamie normally wasn't a crier, but Yolanda's death was too much to bear.

Be strong. She sat up, and a handkerchief appeared under her gaze.

"Here."

She blew her nose and wadded the cool material in her hand. Thinking more logically would help. "What did they take?"

"That's the thing. We can't tell."

Her heart lurched. "No drugs? Isn't that what they were there for?"

"Nothing in the refrigerator was touched. Many of the boxes on the shelves were moved or tossed on the floor, but for the most part, they left the storage room alone."

"That doesn't make any sense. Were they after Yolanda?"

Her breath hitched. "Did they think I might be there?"

"I never said the crimes were related. The first attack might have nothing to do with the second."

"You don't believe that any more than I do. Two attacks, one right after the other, suggests they might be."

He studied her for a moment as if he wanted to wait until she'd calmed before asking her more questions. "Were you wearing a hat the night of your attack?"

That seemed so long ago. "No. I had on my thinner coat because I'd forgotten to check the weather forecast. I didn't think to bring a hat. The day before had been much warmer."

"I remember."

His question registered. "Without a hat they would have spotted my blonde hair and known I wasn't her."

"Yes."

The sadness and pain blocked out her thoughts. "I realize this is an ongoing investigation, but if my safety is a possible issue, I should be told what the police think."

"We believe these men were looking for something besides drugs. Trent thought you might be able to help."

"Me? I go to work, deal with patients all day, and then come home. I usually don't have much time to socialize with anyone. I might have lunch with Sasha, and occasionally Layla, but that's it."

"Hmm."

Jamie thought that when Benny had killed all those patients, nothing could be worse. Now, she realized she'd been wrong. The people he killed had little time left on earth. Yolanda wasn't yet fifty. Jamie's body shuddered. Max scooted closer and pulled her into a hug.

She choked back another sob and looked up at him. "What happens now?"

Chapter Fourteen

Max clasped Jamie's hands, and the warmth of his touch shot straight to her heart.

"For starters, the clinic will most likely be closed for a few days. Trent and his men need to do some cleanup, as well as finish processing the scene."

Jamie was having a hard time understanding why this tragedy had happened in the first place if no drugs had been taken. "Will the staff be notified?" she asked, her voice shaky at best. "I can't imagine coming to work only to be met by police cars and unanswered questions."

"Trent said he'd contact Dr. McDermott, who's supposed to be back at work tomorrow. He's hoping the doctor will help him make the calls. The terrible news might be better coming from someone they know."

"It would." She squeezed his hand and looked up at him. "I want to do something for Yolanda's family."

Pain crossed Max's face. "That's nice of you. Does she have children?"

"Not that I know of. She's divorced."

"I'm sure her family will appreciate anything you decide, but until we know who was responsible and what they want, I don't want you to be alone with her family. I can't guarantee you'll be safe."

"I don't want to be alone either. I'll invite Sasha over here, or else go to her house."

Max let go of her hand, picked up his coffee, and brought the mug to his lips as if he needed a moment to figure out how to respond. "I was thinking more along the lines of you staying with me. You can come to the firehouse during the day. That way, I can make sure nothing will happen to you."

"I appreciate the offer, but is that really necessary?" She huffed out a breath, sorting through her options. "I guess you can't know what these killers will do next. What about Becky? Her man could be involved somehow."

Max nodded. "I'll see what Trent can do about offering her protection. If she's at the hospital, and stays with a friend, she should be safe. Trent might suggest she leave town."

How terrible. "Just so you know, Zoey was at her office in the hospital when one of her clients nearly killed her."

Max looked off to the side. His thoughts were probably as jumbled as hers. "Christ. I wish I had the answers. It's driving all of us crazy." He told her about the men having LED lights under their visor caps, making identification impossible.

"Did one of the men limp? He couldn't have hidden that."

Max's jaw hardened. "You saw someone who limped?"

She explained about one of the men who ran after her. "I told Trent."

"I'll follow up with him." Max set down his coffee. "Look. I understand that you want to be with your friends tomorrow. Hell, I'll invite them all to the station if you want, but I won't let you out of my sight."

She appreciated he cared about her. "What about Sasha, Layla, Nathan, Hannah, Donna? Could they be targets, too?"

He pulled out his phone. "I'll suggest to Trent that he ask them to go someplace safe. I know that RHPD doesn't have the resources to protect all of them."

This was more depressing by the minute. "What is to prevent these from coming to my house tonight?"

"It won't matter. You'll be with me. Go pack a bag. While you're doing that, I'll call Trent and see what he can do about protecting the others."

The independent side of her wanted to say she'd be fine, but her intelligent half said she was way out of her league. "Thank you. I would feel safer being with you."

✧ ✧ ✧

Jamie woke the next morning to an empty bed. She was in Max's bedroom. Because she'd barely slept, her brain was still a bit groggy. Adding insult to injury, she had a headache. Sleep had been fleeting because she'd kept replaying that first night at the clinic when the men had chased her. As hard as she tried to jog her memory, no other details surfaced. She desperately wanted to put a reason behind everything.

Max was puttering around in either the living room or kitchen. It was Saturday morning, but she bet he'd go into work. Crimes needed to be solved. Poor Max. She bet he didn't get much sleep either. Every time she rolled over, she bumped into him and woke him up. He'd been so sweet, never complaining. He'd kiss her, and then tell her to go back to sleep, that no one was going to get past him.

Frustrated and deeply sad by the two senseless murders, Jamie sat up. When the pain in her head lessened, she stood. Whoa. Her world spun. She sat back down and grabbed hold of the blanket. She inhaled deeply to get the blood flowing again.

She couldn't stay in bed. If Max went into work, she'd have to go in with him. He said he wouldn't let her out of his sight. That meant she needed to get dressed. Jamie eased out of bed and stood for moment to make sure she wouldn't falter. When she was confident she was steady, she got readt. No telling how cold the men kept the fire station, which meant layering was her best option.

Once she washed up, she headed to the kitchen. The aroma of coffee filled the air. Max stood at the sink. His beard growth was substantial, and his eyes were bloodshot, proving she'd kept him up all night.

"Good morning," she said with as much enthusiasm as she could muster.

"Is it?" His normally even temper seemed to have vanished.

She rushed to his side. "I'm sorry I tossed and turned. I know you didn't get much sleep."

His face softened. "Oh, honey. My restlessness had nothing to do with you. I swear I kept hearing sounds outside."

She lightly punched him. "Way to calm me down. I'm devastated over Yolanda's death, and I'm petrified that I might be next. You really think they'd find me here?"

Max yanked her to his chest. "Shh. Nothing is going to happen to you. I promise."

He was too wonderful. She didn't even want to think about why he had such a strong protective streak. He still might feel guilty about his wife's death.

She lifted up on her tiptoes and kissed his cheek. "Thank you."

She then stepped over to the counter and picked up the lone coffee cup. Max had his in his hand.

He nodded as if he understood this was equally hard for her. "I'm going to take a shower, and then we can hit a drive-through for some breakfast."

"I'd like that." She sipped her coffee. She wasn't sure how long he wanted her to stay with him. Was last night it? Or would she be here until this case was solved?

"You want me to pack my things?" She held her breath, hoping he said no.

"It'll be safer if you stay here until we figure out what's going on." With that, he went back toward the bedroom.

That made her feel better. Max was so much more experienced than she was.

He rushed down the hallway, and Jamie took a moment to look around. Last night, she'd been too upset to notice much. His kitchen wasn't any bigger than hers, but it was a lot neater. Maybe it was because he didn't fix many meals in there.

The shower turned on, and Jamie wandered back into the living room. She expected to see some pictures of his wife and child, but there weren't any. What a shame if his photos had burned in the fire.

Not wanting him to think she was snooping, she plopped down on the sofa. His place wasn't overly big, but there was enough room to enjoy a movie and have friends over. She liked that the furniture wasn't the typical black-leather-bachelor style stuff. The colors were muted and serene, almost as if a former girlfriend or sister had chosen the furniture. Jamie didn't see Max the type to take the time to pick out pieces that matched. He was too much of a guy. No artwork was on the walls either, which she found curious. Why did only some parts of the house look like a decorator had a hand?

The water stopped less than five minutes later, and she cut off her musings. He hadn't been kidding when he said he'd be quick. Two minutes later, Max emerged with wet hair, looking like he'd come from a photo shoot. In the short time he'd been gone, he'd managed to shave. Max had on a black button-down shirt, dark jeans, and cowboy boots. The man certainly wore clothes well.

"Ready?" he said.

Jamie jumped up. "Yes."

She slipped on her coat that she'd tossed on the chair last night, and slung her purse over her shoulder. Once he locked up, she trudged behind him to his car. The wind was whipping hard through the trees, but the cold wasn't affecting her like it normally did. She was too numb to feel the biting chill. It was as if she was a drone, moving in whatever direction Max told her to.

She knew the symptoms. She could feel herself sliding into the abyss of despair. Between Jonathan's injury, being chased by two bad men, having her friend scared out of her wits because of a stalker, and then two people she cared about be murdered, Jamie was losing the battle to keep in control.

She forced herself to remember the last time her anger had grabbed hold. That had been a good feeling. It had meant she was alive. Damn, but she couldn't find that emotion. Fear and confusion were now her constant companion. But she couldn't give up. She had to claw her way to the surface, one breath at a time.

"Jamie? Get in, please."

Max had opened the door, and yet, she hadn't realized he'd even touched the handle. Not being aware of her surroundings could be her downfall. She had to keep focused. "Sorry."

Not that she had any intention of even trying to solve Yolanda's murder, but if she could help in some small way, she wanted to try. Max climbed in the car and started the engine. As he pulled away, she took the time to study his house. It appeared to be situated on a couple of acres backed up against a forest. The one-story, wood-framed house had a wide front porch, but there were no chairs to make it look cozy. The grass was winter brown, but the evergreens along both sides gave the place life.

Once he turned onto the main road, his gaze darted between the side view and rearview mirrors. While she understood he was only trying to protect them, it wasn't helping to calm her stomach.

As promised, Max stopped at the fast food place for some breakfast, and he insisted they dine inside. Jamie tried to eat everything, but her stomach wasn't in the mood. Fortunately, Max didn't bug her about her lack of appetite. It was if he'd been in her shoes before.

Once they arrived at the station, the hustle and bustle of the place helped settle her wild thoughts. The men's laughter sounded good to her ears. They were joking with each other as they cleaned their truck, seemingly oblivious to what had happened at the clinic last night.

"Do you want to sit in the break room, or at a desk next to my office?" Max asked.

The men might feel self-conscious talking if she were there. "Near you."

"Come this way." With his hand on the small of her back, he led her toward the rear of the building.

Her worry eased knowing so many men were around to keep them safe. When they stepped through a door, silence surrounded them. A glassed-in room lined the back wall with two desks in front. One had a ton of paper on it, the other sat empty.

Max nodded toward the empty desk. "Make yourself at home. This was my old desk, but Brandon Caulfield will be arriving next Monday."

She'd forgotten about the interview. "Rich must have liked him."

"He did."

Jamie sat in Max's former chair. It was too large for her, but she enjoyed that it swiveled and rocked.

He slid a hip on the edge of the desk. From his relaxed posture, it was as if he wanted to talk about something other than what had transpired last night. "Since you asked about the new hire, I thought you'd like to know that Brandon played pro ball for one season before he blew out his knee."

Jamie wanted to lose herself in the story—anything to forget why she was there. "I can't imagine working that hard all through school, only to have your hopes dashed in one second." Amber told her that Max had taken a bullet to his leg when he'd been a cop, and yet he hadn't let his injury stop him from pursuing his second career. She didn't know what a football injury had to do with being a fire inspector, but she was happy Max was willing to share. "What happened then?"

"After Brandon rehabilitated his knee, he quit the team. Decided to take a different career path—that of being a firefighter. Said his dad had been one, as well as had his father before him, so he wanted to join the ranks. It was in his blood."

"He sounds perfect. I bet you'll be glad for the help." When she changed jobs from being a hospice nurse to working in the clinic, there had been an adjustment. Max was probably going through the same thing.

"You can't imagine." His cell rang, and he stiffened. Max eased off his old desk. "Gruden."

He nodded then walked into his office where she couldn't hear the conversation.

"Damn."

Chapter Fifteen

When Max answered his cell, he wasn't sure he wanted to hear what his friend had to say. "Hey, Trent."

"We found the man who followed Becky." Relief filled his voice.

That hadn't been what Max expected Trent to call about, but he was thrilled. "Can you link him to a local cell?" Max twisted in his seat to make sure Jamie couldn't read his lips. The whole idea that domestic terrorists existed in town needed to be kept quiet.

"We know his name because he has a record, but we can't link him to any terrorist cell. The mayor said he'd send the information to his FBI contact, and let them tell us whether the man is dangerous."

"You're detaining him, I trust?"

"Yes, and he's demanding a lawyer, so there's little hope we'll learn much. We don't really have anything to hold him on since the man didn't speak with Becky or touch her. It's her word against his. I'm just hoping the FBI comes through for us."

"Me, too. What about the clinic workers? Are they going to be safe?"

"Yes. We've got that covered. Hold on a sec." Voices sounded but Max couldn't tell what they were saying. "That was Dan. Seems our invisible FBI team is going to pick up this dude.

He's one of the men that Vic Hart had previously pointed a finger at as being involved. This was the first time he'd surfaced."

Max slumped back in his seat. He wasn't sure if that eased or increased his anxiety. If this terrorist cell had targeted Becky Andrews, it seemed more likely that Jamie was involved, too. Only how? "Does Becky know?"

"I'm about to call her as soon as I hang up."

"Good. I'll speak with Jamie again about what she and Becky did that night. Since a few days have passed, her memory might have cleared."

"Good. Let me know."

"By the way, I asked Jamie to stay with me to make sure she remains out of harm's way."

"She was okay with that?"

Max hadn't discussed their new intimate status. "Yes. Let's leave it at that." Trent whistled. Right now, Max's concern was Jamie. "Did the Feds give you any odds on the likelihood these men might attack again?" He hoped the FBI had told the mayor something.

Max glanced through the office window at Jamie sitting at his desk, reading. Her presence helped him stay focused.

"So far, the Feds haven't been forthcoming with shit, but we can always hope. My men and I plan to speak with the other clinic employees, but I'm not getting my hopes up that they know anything. Was Jamie able to give you any insight?"

"No. She's stunned right now. It seems as if she and her boss got along well. Jamie's torn up about her death."

"I'm sorry. You planning on her staying with you until this stuff is over?"

"Yes."

"Good. I'll keep pushing from my end. We'll get the bastards." Trent rang off.

Because Jamie had glanced his way a few times, he needed to

tell her the man after Becky had been caught. He pushed back his chair and strode out. "I have the tiniest bit of good news."

She straightened. "I'll take a crumb."

Since Rich hadn't come into work yet, Max pulled over his chair and sat next to her. "They caught the man following Becky."

Her face brightened, but it wasn't enough to erase the tension lining her eyes. "That's wonderful. Who was he?"

Jamie had guessed that her friend might be an undercover agent, but she hadn't hinted that she knew anything about why Jonathan was in Rock Hard. Max needed to keep her in the dark a bit longer.

"We know the man's name, and that he has a record, but that's all. He's lawyered up. The important thing is that he can't hurt Becky anymore."

Jamie closed her eyes for a moment. Max didn't like the deep shadows under her lids, or how her skin pulled tight across her cheeks. They'd stopped at a fast food place for breakfast, but she'd only picked at her food. When he'd been in the depths of despair, food held no interest for him either.

"Does she know the good news?" Some life filled her face.

"Trent is about to call her. That was him on the phone." Max leaned forward, his elbows on his knees. "Can you take me through the evening from when you arrived at Banner's Bar to when Becky called you that night?"

"We already told you everything."

He hadn't meant to cause her more anxiety. "I know, honey, but can you go through it again? For me?" The last two words did the trick. He saw the moment his plea caused her to relent.

"Fine, but there's nothing there."

He squeezed her hand once. "That's okay. Let me decide." When he was in cop mode, the malaise that seemed to follow him, lessened.

"I'll admit I was a little shaken from my car breaking down

and from the first break-in, so I was careful to watch where I was going. I even checked for black vans."

His senses sharpened. "Did you see anyone suspicious?"

She huffed. "The streets looked like a black van convention. I saw a few parked on the street and one or two drive by. One of the drivers even wore a cap. As if that made him different from the rest of the Rock Hard men." She huffed out a laugh.

Jamie didn't seem to think that was important, but he did. "Keep going."

"When Becky showed up, I gave her a present I'd found for her. Then another friend, Lydia Sayers arrived, and we all went in."

"Did you recognize any of the men in the bar?"

That got a laugh out of her. "I was there to talk with my friends, not scope out the place for a date."

Her comment made him feel better. Jamie was just trying to survive.

"Then what?"

"Then nothing. We chatted and Zoey offered to drive me home. She said she had a hot date with Thad and Pete."

He'd heard what happened after that. "That's good."

She leaned forward. "Does it help?"

"That's one thing about police work. Nothing seems to help until the pieces come together. Then it can be the link that unlocks the case."

Rich came in and abruptly stopped when he spotted Jamie. He raised a brow. "Good morning. It's Jamie, right?"

"Yes."

Rich had seen her when she'd come to the first crime scene. Max gave the formal introduction. "Jamie's friend is Jonathan Rambler—the one who was caught in the fire."

Max raised his brows hoping Rich would get the clue to keep quiet. Max hadn't let his assistant in on the fact there were domestic terrorists in Rock Hard. The information would be doled out on a need-to-know basis.

"I'm sorry about your friend."

"Thank you."

Max stood and looked down at Jamie, who seemed so small and lost. He wanted to hug her and tell her everything would be okay, but he wasn't one to lie. "I need to get back to work. I didn't bring anything from home to eat, so we'll have to do lunch out."

Jamie's lips lifted for a moment, clearly seeing through his lie. "Sure. I'll sit here and read."

On the way to lunch at Italiano's, she and Max agreed not to talk about the tragedy, believing anyone overhearing the conversation might become frightened. Their meal was a bit strained, as they both seemed lost in their own thoughts. Jamie wanted to face what was happening, but she didn't know the whole truth. She understood Max couldn't tell her anything more about Jonathan's connection to all this crime until he'd filed some kind of paperwork.

The meal wasn't a total loss, however. One nice thing about Max eating the same restaurant every day was that people knew him. A few knew Jamie, too. Several stopped at their table and offered their condolences about the deaths at the clinic. It was nice to know so many people cared.

After they ate, he drove her back to the station, where she resumed her position at his desk. Being a lump on a log was okay for one day, but she couldn't sit and do nothing tomorrow. The silence would drive her crazy, not to mention the growing fear that these murderers were still out there.

Finally, five o'clock rolled around, and Max said they could leave. From what Rich told her, Max usually stayed at work until long after he was gone. She really appreciated that Max was willing put her needs above his work.

Assuming Max didn't have other plans, once they got back to his house, she wanted to sit with him and watch old movies—assuming he was into that kind of thing.

"Ready to chow?" Max asked, as he came out of his office.

"I'm not really hungry." Max lowered his chin. "Okay, okay. I'll try."

He smiled and her insides stirred. "That's my girl."

Ever since Max had come over to her house to listen to Becky's story, Jamie had begun to believe that Max just might consider her to be his girl. If she wasn't such a mess emotionally, she'd have been overjoyed.

"Italiano's okay?"

She laughed. "Yes, but someday, I'll have to break you of that habit."

"I like the someday part."

Heat raced up her face. She hadn't meant to imply they had a future, but she would be amenable.

They sat at Max's usual spot, and she ordered the ravioli again. The meal tasted okay, but Jamie didn't have much of an appetite and picked at her food. Max didn't eat with his usual gusto either.

As they nibbled, her mind kept darting between subjects. During her musings, she remembered Sasha asking her about Max's family, and if he had a spare brother. Jamie had called Sasha from the firehouse. Her friend wasn't doing much better than Jamie was. Perhaps if Sasha had someone to take her mind off her troubles, she'd heal faster.

Jamie washed down the food with her coffee. "I never asked, but are you from around here? I know you said your dad worked at a paper mill, and that your folks retired to Florida, but I never asked the name of the town." Just because he went to the junior college in town, didn't mean he was born and raised in Rock Hard.

Max hesitated, almost as if he wondered why the sudden interest. "I am a native."

Perhaps that was why everyone seemed to know him. "Do your siblings still live here?"

"Trying to see if there are any skeletons in my closet?"

Thank God he was back into flirting mode. It helped her cope. "Totally."

A small smile emerged, as if he might be pleased she was taking an interest in something other than the tragedy. "Sam and Amelia still live in town. Sam, who's thirty-six, works at the paper mill. He's in management now. Wouldn't be surprised if they make him manager of the whole damned place someday."

The pride in his voice was evident. "And Amelia?"

"Mel, as we call her, is the baby at thirty-three. She's been married and divorced, and only now is getting her life together. Despite some of her issues, she was a huge help to me after the fire."

Crap. Jamie hadn't planned for that topic to come up. "And your other brother?"

"Jack is forty-one. He never got along with the folks and moved out after high school. Twenty years later, he landed his ass in Mississippi at a pest control company. Doing pretty well, too. Has a wife and two happy kids." His voice trailed off as if he envied that part of his brother's life. Max set down his fork. "I never asked if you had siblings."

Jamie's throat constricted. "Only a half-sister. Let's just say Evelyn and I never saw eye-to-eye."

"A tale better told later, I take it?"

She liked that about Max. He seemed to know when to probe and when to pull back. "Yes."

Elissa came over with the bill, and Max paid. "Tomorrow morning, I'll drive you over to Richardson's Automotive so you can pick up Grayson." He stood and helped Jamie with her coat. "But don't think that means you're free to roam, young lady."

"You're a spoilsport." But he sure was a loveable one.

On the way to his SUV, she caught him glancing right and left, most likely checking for black vans or men wearing caps. That didn't help her anxiety level.

Max held open the car door and she slid in. Once he was seated, he drove toward his house. "As much as I love having a roommate, with the clinic closed for a while, have you considered leaving town for a few days until we figure out who harmed your friends?"

Harmed? Try murdered. She could tell from the sincerity that he was thinking what was best for her. "You mean like fly home? To California?"

"Would that be so bad? You'd be safe there."

She shrugged. "I guess, but it cost a lot to fly, and seeing my mom would be depressing." At least Evelyn had moved out of state a few years ago.

He glanced over at her. "You two don't get along? I didn't realize the animosity extended beyond your sister."

Jamie didn't want to get into it. "Being around my mom is like stepping into a pool of disappointment."

"That bad, huh? If you ask me, your mom is a fool. She should be very proud of all you've accomplished."

His words helped. "Thank you, but I think I'll pass on the sunny vacation."

"If you went, you could sleep without worry."

"You seem quite convinced that I need to hide." The food in her belly churned.

Max worked his mouth and gripped the wheel. "Here's the thing. We don't know what we're up against. If I knew for sure, I would warn you. The offer stands for me to be your temporary bodyguard."

"Thank you. I'd like that. Do you think we could stop at my house so I can pick up some more clothes? I only packed enough for one night."

He grinned. "You got it."

He turned off the road into her neighborhood. Once in her drive, he cut the engine. Once more he opened her door and she slipped out. Max was worming his way into her heart fast. Hell, he was already there.

As soon as they stepped onto her porch, she stopped. "Are you kidding me?"

He wrapped an arm around her waist. "What's wrong?"

She pointed to the broken living room window. "Someone broke my freaking window. I can't believe it." The porch light barely illuminated that side of the house, so it was difficult to tell the extent of the damage.

She'd taken but one step toward the damaged area, when Max stopped her. "Jamie, get in the car."

His words turned her stomach into knots. "You don't think this has anything to do with the clinic break-in, do you?"

"Now." With an arm around her waist, he half-guided, half-lifted her to the passenger side. He pulled open the door, hurried her in, and then closed it.

He ran to his side, jammed the car in reverse, and high-tailed it out of there.

Her heart jammed in her throat. "Shouldn't we see if there's any more damage? Someone could have robbed me." The words gushed out without much thought behind them. The ramifications scared the shit out of her.

Max fished out his phone and handed it to her. "Call 911. Tell them about the break-in."

Oh, shit. "Do you think the intruders are still there?" That seemed to be the only logical explanation. It didn't matter there was no car in the drive. "Are you thinking they're the same men who'd killed Yolanda?"

"It's possible."

With maybe more fear than when those men were chasing her down the street, she punched in the emergency number and relayed what they'd seen.

Max held out his hand. "Let me."

She handed him the phone. He pulled off to the side then told the emergency operator to contact Trent Lawson of the RHPD. He also gave her some code, which Jamie assumed meant it was a robbery-in-progress. The cops might get there faster if they thought the threat was still there.

He disconnected and punched in a new set of numbers. "I'm calling Dan Hartwick."

"Why?"

"I'll explain in a minute." He tapped his foot while the phone rang. "Dan. It's Max. Someone just broke into Jamie's house." He glanced over at her. "No. We called 911. Near her house, keeping out of trouble. Sure. Is that wise? If you think I should, I will." He clicked off his phone. "We need to talk."

Chapter Sixteen

With Jamie's life now possibly in danger, the FBI finally agreed with Max that Jamie needed to know about the terrorists.

"Tell me." The poor woman was shaking.

Max faced her, dreading the idea of heaping more bad news on her. "I'm not sure where to begin."

Her lips firmed. "How about at the beginning?" The crack in her voice tore at his gut.

"I thought you weren't practical?" This probably wasn't the time for levity, but seeing the fear in her face was messing with his head.

Some of her tension seemed to disappear, but she didn't crack a smile. "Max! Please."

"Okay. After the warehouse fire, Detective Hartwick came to see me—about Jonathan. He said there was something odd about the vagrant."

As expected, her body stiffened. "Odd?"

He told her about the makeup, the wig, the retainer, and the fat suit. "That sent up a red flag to the department."

She clenched her fist and pumped it. "I knew it."

"Jonathan Rambler's real name is Vic Hart. The FBI confirmed he's one of their agents. Just as you suspected."

"Why didn't you tell me before?"

"I couldn't. I take my oath to uphold the law seriously."

She shook her head as if she was trying to make sense of what was true and what she believed to have been true. "Do you think Jonathan only befriended me to make his homeless act look legit?"

The stress had to be screwing with her mind. "No. I think he was desperate for some normalcy, and you provided it. That's all."

She tugged on her seatbelt, and shifted to face him. "Why would an FBI agent be in Rock Hard? What was he trying to uncover?"

Max blew out a breath. *Here goes. Sorry, Jamie.* "That was my first question. Long story short, the Feds said Vic Hart was investigating a case regarding domestic terrorism."

She planted a hand on her chest. "Here?"

"Montana is a big state. It's easy to hide out. There's a lot of empty land, and people will leave you alone if you wish."

She slid her hand down to her lap and picked at the hem of her jacket. "I'm speechless. Did Yolanda's death have anything to do with these terrorists?"

"We can't be sure."

She chewed on her bottom lip. "This is so much to take in. If these terrorists targeted the clinic, what were they looking for?"

Jamie glanced up at him. Except for the rays from the quarter moon, he couldn't see her expression very well and he didn't dare turn on the overhead lamp. "I was hoping you could tell me."

She looked off to the side, then back at him. "Like I said before, I know nothing."

"I'm sorry to keep asking, but I thought if you knew these murderers were terrorists, something new might come to mind."

She was silent for a moment. "No. Nothing. You know I'd tell you if I could."

"I know you would, honey. Come here." Max unbuckled his seatbelt and slid over next to her. She crawled into his arms and hugged him tightly. Max kissed the top of her head. "I'm so sorry that you had to get caught up in this, Jamie."

"Me, too."

Flashing lights came toward them. "Cops have arrived."

She sat back up and swiped the back of her hand across her eyes. "Can we go back to my house now?"

He wanted to return to his home, but the police would need to question Jamie about the damage—assuming there was some. If these were the same men, and if they didn't find what they wanted at the clinic, Jamie's house might look similar to the clinic crime scene. God help her. She'd need him more than ever.

"In a bit. I want to give them a chance to clear the scene." Two patrol cars whizzed by.

Max hated to see anything else destroy the thread of control Jamie was clinging to. If there was something he could do to help, he would do so in a heartbeat.

✧ ✧ ✧

Jamie grunted. "What's taking them so long?"

Max had parked in front of her house over half an hour ago, but he wouldn't let her leave the car and ask about the progress of the investigation. He said they had to stay in the vehicle until one of the cops said it was okay to enter.

Finally, Trent traipsed down the porch steps toward her and knocked on the car window. Jamie pushed open the door and stepped out, her legs stiff.

His mouth was pinched. "You can come in, but be prepared. It's bad in there."

Jamie planted a hand behind her to steady herself on the car door. Her knees actually buckled, but she caught herself before falling. Her body was numb, as if part of her realized it couldn't absorb any more blows. "Did they take a lot?" She'd just purchased a television. It didn't matter it was used.

Trent shook his head. "Hard to tell. From the looks of it, they were searching for something."

Just like in the clinic.

Max came around the back of his SUV and placed his palm on her back for support then stepped next to her. "Trent knows about Vic Hart, so you can speak freely."

It took a second before the name registered. Jonathan was Vic Hart. How could she have been fooled by such a nice man? He'd seemed so sincere. "Tell him what? That I was nice to a man who betrayed me?"

Sympathy swamped his eyes. "Remember, Vic was undercover. It wouldn't have been safe to tell you he was an agent looking for terrorists."

"You're right." She turned and faced Trent again. "I swear Jonathan, or rather this Vic guy, never told me any secrets. Whoever did this didn't find what they were looking for because it wasn't there."

Trent dragged a hand down his chin. "Could Vic have handed you a paper cup or a bag to toss on your way back to the clinic that had information written on it?"

She ran their encounters through her mind, recreating her daily routine. "If he gave me some trash, I threw it out. I'm sorry, but I just don't remember that kind of exchange. I'd bring him food then leave. He didn't have time to eat it before I had to be at work."

Trent nodded as if he knew when he'd reached a dead end. "If you think of anything, tell Max. He'll let me know."

As Trent turned to go back inside, Max led her up the steps, and she leaned against him for support. When they reached the door, Max held it open for her. The moment she stepped inside, her heart stopped beating, and she grasped the doorjamb to keep upright.

"Oh, my God." Every pillow had been sliced open, and any item she'd placed on top of a surface had been tossed on the floor. Between all the food and junk strewn about the kitchen counters and floor, she didn't dare try to go in there. From where she stood, the cupboards and drawers were mostly empty.

A whisper of air finally entered her body and blood pounded in her ears.

Max leaned over. "Anything missing?"

She faced him, her emotions in total turmoil. Was he talking about a large ticket item? "Missing? It's too soon to tell. They didn't take my television, and I don't own anything of value, except for my computer." At the destruction, bile raced up her throat.

"How about jewelry? Or maybe some antiques? Thieves can sell just about anything at a flea market."

She stood on her tiptoes and tugged on his shoulder. He bent down. "I thought you said these were terrorists." She wasn't sure if she was allowed to mention that in front of the crime scene techs.

"Alleged terrorists. I'm hoping it's a random robbery, but I doubt it."

She understood that the cops were trying to be thorough. "I have a few rings that belonged to my mom, but I think they were costume jewelry. All the trinkets I've accumulated over the years seem to be on the floor." She spotted a picture of her grandmother. "Oh, no." Of all her relatives, her Gram was her favorite. Jamie rushed over to see if the photo itself had been damaged. The glass was broken, so she stepped around the debris.

As Jamie bent to examine the picture, Max clasped her shoulders before she could retrieve it. "We can't touch anything," he said.

Her heart broke as he helped her rise. Jamie turned and

faced him. "Did they have to break this?"

"I wish I knew the answer." Max gathered her in his arms, and she placed her head against his chest, the action giving her strength. As much as she'd like to stay there, she needed to see the rest of the damage. She stepped out of his embrace and studied the rest of the living room from where she stood.

"Why trash the kitchen and rip the artwork off the walls? It's stupid." Her pots and pans came from a discount store, and her patients had painted most of the pieces that had been hanging on the walls.

"Perhaps they were looking for something specific. Something hidden."

"What? Like a wall safe?" Her eleven-hundred square foot home with its broken shutter and loose front porch step didn't scream wealth. Jamie threaded her fingers through her hair. Her lip trembled, damn it. "I just want to yell. Scream. Stomp. Anything to make this go away."

Slowly, as if he feared she'd crumble, Max once more enveloped her in his arms. This time she didn't pull away. Instead, Jamie cried—for Yolanda, for Vic Hart, for her ruined belongings. She hiccupped and Max held her even tighter. The security he was offering made the tears flow hard and fast.

"Shh. It's okay." He patted her back like a child.

She didn't want anyone feeling sorry for her—especially Max. He'd been through a lot himself. Zoey claimed anger was good and Jamie had plenty of it. It was time to use it. She stepped back and swiped a hand across her face. "I need to look at the rest of the house."

Max nodded as if he recognized that her take-charge attitude was healthy. "Let's do it."

The first room she checked was her small second bedroom that she used as an office. When she spotted her laptop, she heaved a sigh of relief, until she realized something wasn't quite right.

Max placed a hand on her back. "Something wrong?"

"I always close it." The top was up.

He withdrew a clean handkerchief from his back pocket and wrapped it around his index finger. Max tapped the spacebar, and the screen shot to life, looking just the way she'd left it.

"You don't have this password protected?"

"I'm the only one here." He turned his back to her and scrolled through the file names in the finder. "What are you hoping to learn?"

"Not sure." When he appeared satisfied, he asked the man taking photos to have them dust the keyboard for prints.

"Won't that mess it up?" Jamie couldn't afford to buy another laptop.

"He'll be careful."

This was a nightmare. After the office, she stepped into her bedroom. If she had thought the kitchen was bad, this room was even worse.

Jamie's chin wobbled. "Assholes. The thieves didn't miss a drawer."

Clothes had been tossed all over the floor, the pockets of her pants and coats turned inside out. She should have been embarrassed that her underwear was in plain sight, but she was too upset to worry about propriety now. Christ. It was going to take forever to clean everything up.

"Fuck." Max dragged a hand over his head. "What the hell were they looking for?"

"Whatever it was, they didn't find it. If they had, the destruction wouldn't have extended to the whole house. They would have stopped when they located it."

"You're right."

"Do you think they'll come back, thinking they can beat it out of me?" Shivers of fear skated up and down her body at the possibility.

"They won't get the chance since you won't be here."

She'd be at Max's. Jamie looked up at him. "I don't know what I would do without you."

Max leaned close and kissed the top of her head. "I don't want to think about it."

She and Max were still in the bedroom surveying the mess when a tall man knocked and stepped in. Jamie recognized him from the wedding. He was Dan Hartwick, Cade and Thad's boss, and the man Max used to work for.

"Jamie," Dan said. "I'm sorry."

She nodded. Max placed a light touch on her shoulder. "Go ahead and gather what you can. I have a washer and dryer so you can recycle your outfits."

"How long before I can come back?"

"It could be weeks. If domestic terrorists are responsible for this, I think it would be wise if we lock down the house until this issue is cleared up."

"Weeks?" At least she'd be with Max.

"Or more, honey." Max tugged her close. "I'll keep you safe."

"I'm counting on it." While she knew very little about domestic terrorists, she bet they had military training and were experts at hiding. "I just hate that some crazy men get to decide how to run my life. Hell, we don't even know if the person or persons who broke in had anything to do with Vic Hart or the clinic."

"True, but I'm not taking any chances. Whoever was here was a bad person. That's all we need to know."

"You're right."

"First things first. Go pack."

This royally sucked. As soon as Dan slipped back out into the hallway, she dragged both of her suitcases from the heap on the floor, tossed the cases on the bed, and stuffed in as many clothes that would fit.

"Excuse me for a sec. I need a few things from the bathroom." Jamie stepped over the debris and trekked down the hall. Thankfully, the cop who'd been in there had finished taking photos.

Finding anything, however, proved to be more difficult than locating her clothing. Nothing was where she'd left it, but she did the best she could to gather her essentials. When she returned to the bedroom, Max was conferring with Trent.

She joined them, waving a Band-Aid box. "This person is certifiably crazy. He dumped the contents in the sink then threw the box on the floor. Was he just being vindictive or did he really think I kept hidden treasures inside?"

Max's brows rose. "Who knows what goes through a criminal's mind."

"If only I were a diamond thief, it might make sense. Could they have me mixed up with someone else?"

"I don't think it's smart to start thinking like that. Next thing you know, we'll be chalking this up to a random event, and that could put you in even more danger." Max tapped his chest. "Not going to happen on my watch."

She shook her head. "I should just put a sign on my door telling them I don't have whatever it is they want."

Max strode over to her and clasped her shoulders. "Don't even think it."

The urgency in his voice shook her. "I was only kidding."

When he lowered his hands down her arms, his touch brought her much needed relief. His protective side made her feel like she wasn't so alone.

"Sorry," he said. "It's just that we don't need people finding out about this. There will be chaos if the town learns of the danger of possible terrorists. The FBI needs to neutralize them first."

"I know, I know. You told me to keep my mouth shut and I plan to do just that." He held her gaze for a while. She couldn't handle any more bad news. "What is it?"

"What has me worried is if the perpetrators think you're working for the FBI, too."

Now Max had lost his mind. "That's ridiculous. I'm a nurse."

He lifted one shoulder. "It's not any crazier than a homeless man being a federal agent."

Max didn't need to say her fate might be the same if these men found her. She grabbed his arm. "Can we go? I don't want to stay here longer than necessary."

"Sure. Let's let Dan know." Max picked up both of her suitcases as if they weighed nothing.

Jamie reached out to grab one, but he gave her a look that told her to not even try.

"I want to take my laptop in case they come back. They could sell a working computer at a flea market."

In a way, she wished they had taken a few big-ticket items. Ordinary thieves would have been easier to deal with. These men might not want her possessions, but it made her feel better having the laptop with her.

Once she stuffed her computer in her large purse, Max led her into the living room where the cops were going to town fingerprinting every available surface. Black powder coated her precious possessions.

Jamie grunted. "If these thieves are the experts you think they are, I bet they wore gloves."

"Most likely, but it's hard to open small boxes and feel for what's inside if your hands are covered." He nodded to the Frosted Flakes on the floor.

"Did they think I'd hide something in the cereal?"

"People conceal things in the strangest places. We can only hope they made a mistake."

She had little confidence they had. Jamie shivered and looked over at the broken window. "It's freezing in here. I'll need to get someone to fix that. I don't want squirrels or other animals getting in."

"I'll take care of it. Hey, Dan? Can you have someone fix the window? Someone who you can trust to keep things quiet?"

"Sure. I'll also have a cleaning service come in and straighten up the place."

Not having to worry about this mess was a huge relief. "Thank you."

Dan picked his way over to them. "It's always the worst when an innocent bystander gets drawn into the fray." Dan looked over at Max. "Keep her safe."

"You can count on it."

Before they made it to the front, a knock sounded on the door, and a man of medium-height, with a dark crew cut, dressed in a black suit, entered. He flashed a badge, but closed the leather case so fast Jamie couldn't tell what agency he was with. Since Vic Hart worked with the FBI, Jamie suspected this man did, too.

The two cops taking photos continued to work, but they glanced his way. Max stepped in front of her as if to keep her from harm, and Dan moved quickly to greet the newcomer.

"May I help you?" Dan asked.

"I'm Special Agent Chuck Forbes of the FBI." The haughty man glanced over at Jamie then back at Dan. "Vic Hart worked with us." Agent Forbes straightened his shoulders as if he didn't like Dan towering over him.

The tension in Dan's face disappeared. "Thank God. Maybe we can finally get some answers."

Chapter Seventeen

"I'll do my best." Special Agent Forbes looked around and shook his head. "Someone wanted something badly."

"How did you know to come here?" Dan asked.

Jamie liked that Max's former boss was cautious. She'd wondered the same thing about the man.

"I first stopped by the station, and they told me about the break-in, but I didn't expect this." He waved a hand.

"You part of the team that's in town?"

"No. I work in Washington. The team here works for me. After the incident with Vic, I flew out."

"Did Hart suspect the terrorists were onto him?" Dan sounded very professional.

Forbes dragged a hand down his clean-shaven chin. "I'm not sure what Vic suspected. He was in touch nightly with the others, but he never hinted that his cover was blown." Forbes turned to her. "Are you Jamie Henderson?" She was pleased that his tone had softened.

"Yes."

He held out his hand and she shook it. A faint aroma of cigarettes clung to his clothes, along with the aroma of cherry scented gum. He must be trying to quit smoking.

"One of the men at the station said you were Vic's friend.

Did he say anything to you about being compromised?"

"Are you kidding? Until a few minutes ago, I thought Jonathan was a homeless man. Not some FBI guy."

Chuck's lips pressed together and glanced around again. "Seems someone doesn't believe you."

He might be right, but she didn't like the gruffness in his tone. "Trust me. I was totally in the dark here until a few minutes ago."

Chuck Forbes glanced at Max. She thought she caught a look of admiration, before he turned back to her. "I'm sorry. This must be a tough time for you. I heard you were close to Dr. Withers, too."

"Yes. Are you saying the men who harmed Vic are the same ones who murdered Dr. Withers? Do you think they are responsible for all this?" He couldn't know that for sure.

"Let's say, it's a strong possibility." He looked over at Max, raised his brows, and held out his hand. "Sorry. Chuck Forbes."

"Max Gruden. I'm investigating the warehouse fire where Vic was beaten and left to die."

"I'm glad you're here. I wanted to let both you and Detective Hartwick know that the FBI will be taking over all three investigations. I know you've been working on the warehouse fire, and we appreciate it, but it's necessary for us to consolidate the leads. If you could turn over your notes, it would save us time."

Max's fingers tightened around her waist. "I'd like to help, if I can." While he kept his tone even—friendly even—knowing Max, he wouldn't be happy being left out of the loop.

Trent came into the living room from the bedroom, and Dan introduced him as the lead on Yolanda's death. Agent Forbes repeated his request for all information on the case. Trent's face turned unreadable, but she bet he wasn't happy about the change of plans either.

"Gentlemen, I know no one likes to give up an investigation, but I assure you my men and I can handle it. Understand that our nation might be at risk." Forbes shifted his gaze back to Dan. "I brought a few agents with me from Washington. They're at the hospital now. When Vic wakes up, we'll need to learn what he knows."

Is that all he cared about? Information? "You need to protect him," she said. "Once they find out Vic is alive, they might want to finish the job."

"Young lady, I assure you, we will do everything possible to protect our agent. He's an extremely valuable asset."

His attitude was condescending, but she liked his willingness to make sure nothing happened to her friend. "Good."

Max stiffened. "Jamie and I will be leaving town for a while."

Forbes looked pleased. "That's a good idea."

Wait a minute. She and Max were leaving town? Chills crisscrossed her body. He'd said she'd be safe at his house. Rational thought returned. Now that he no longer had to work on the warehouse case, and the concept that the terrorists might think she had something that she didn't, it would be best to leave. She looked up at him. "What should I tell the clinic?"

Chuck stepped close. "Ma'am. Consider telling your boss that you have a family emergency. Or you could tell him the truth, that you're scared. You might have been targeted twice. Just don't mention the FBI or terrorists."

The agent was right. "I'll tell them I have a family emergency. They'd never believe me if I said I wanted to take a few days off because I was scared." This man didn't know her history. Because the clinic was already short-staffed, her friends would believe she'd abandoned them if she pulled the *scared* card. Yolanda's death was a terrible tragedy, but those in need would still require health care. "How long should I say I'll be gone? Do I need to ask Dr. McDermott to find a temporary replacement? If I do, do you think the city would spring for it? The clinic's budget is close to non-existent." She had a few sick days accumulated, but this might take longer.

"I'll recommend the mayor fund it. As for how long you'll be gone, I can't say."

Lying to her friends about what was happening would be hard, but Jamie's life was at stake. She had no choice. With this new development, she also needed to let the garage know she wouldn't be picking up Grayson for a while either.

God, but this was a cluster fuck.

Dan stepped next to them. "Max, don't tell anyone where you're going. I'm not sure who we can trust."

While Dan didn't glance at the federal agent, she bet Agent Forbes was on the list. If the government had been more forthcoming in the beginning, some things might have happened differently.

Max faced the agent. "I'll have my assistant send over my notes on the investigation."

"Thank you." Forbes fished out a card and handed it to him. "This has all of my information to contact me."

Max faced Dan. "I'll have my cell. Call me."

"Will do."

Max's features softened. He ran a knuckle down her cheek. "Ready?"

She'd never be ready, but she had little choice. "Yes."

As soon as Max closed the car door and slipped into the driver's side, Jamie needed answers. "Where are we going?"

"I have a cabin near Kalispell."

That was a good two hours from Rock Hard. She liked they'd be far away. "Is it safe?"

"A hell of a lot safer than here." He glanced over at her. "Don't worry, honey."

She knew the refrain—he'd keep her safe. She prayed that

was true.

Even after Max drove past Rock Hard city limits, Jamie still shook. Foolishly, she'd believed that after the men had chased her down the street and into the clinic, she'd figured out how to take back control of her life. Now, they'd resorted to murder and shattered her calm. She'd spent her life helping others—people like Vic Hart—and look where it had gotten her? Into trouble.

Jamie totally understood that she had to get away. Seeing first-hand how those terrorists would stop at nothing to get what they wanted, fear had settled in her bones. She failed to push aside the senseless deaths.

Max was driving only slightly above the speed limit instead of racing out of there. What was up with taking his time? Perhaps he didn't want to attract attention.

"Do you think these men know we've left town?" Her voice shook.

"Doubt it." His hands tightened on the wheel, failing to disguise his concern.

Jamie wanted to know her odds. It would give her something to chew on, to analyze. "What are the chances we'll be safe?" He wouldn't be able to say for sure, but she needed to ask the question. Her nerves were too much on edge to just sit back.

"Small. We left town too suddenly. When I was with the RHPD, Dan Hartwick brought someone in from the FBI to discuss homegrown terrorists. Unfortunately, there's no real profile for these men other than they are often under thirty and are unhappy individuals who seek revenge against someone or a group. They are self-recruited, self-trained, and self-executing, implying they think they're invincible. I doubt they even realize the cops suspect they were responsible for breaking into your house—assuming they were. They're probably telling themselves you'll stay with someone for the night before returning tomorrow to clean up the mess."

"Where they plan to beat me for some answers, then kill

me." Jamie squeezed her eyes shut and inhaled to settle her stomach. She sat up. "You don't think they were smart enough to plant a bug in my house for when the cops came, do you?" Then they'd know everything.

"Jamie. Don't do this to yourself. It will only drive you crazy. We're getting out of town. That's a good thing, okay?"

"Okay." There was no doubt she needed to leave Rock Hard, but was hiding in a remote part of Montana the answer? Would these men discover Max's cabin? His name would be on the property appraiser's website. "Who else besides Dan knows the location of your getaway place?"

"No one I work with. I've known Rich Egland for ten years and he doesn't know where my cabin is—just that I have one. As for the firemen at the station, I don't interact with them on a daily basis. We're kind of like tag teamers. They put out the fire and I come in to figure out what caused it."

That made her feel better. "Does Trent know where this place is?"

"Yes, but he won't say anything."

She wished there had been another option to ensure her safety, but there didn't seem to be one.

She pulled out her phone and called the clinic. As she'd hoped, she got the answering machine. Jamie left a message for Dr. McDermott. She told him that because the clinic would be closed for a few days, she wanted to visit her sick mother in California, but that she wasn't sure of her return date. Should her mom take a turn for the worse, she'd call and ask him to find a replacement.

Jamie believed it had been the right thing to do, but as soon as she hung up, she wasn't so sure. By going with Max, she was basically putting his life in danger, too. "Maybe you should just drive me to the airport. I can stay with my family."

"No."

"You suggested it."

He glanced at her. "Changed my mind. I'm not letting you out of my sight for any reason."

She loved his noble sentiment, but she wasn't his responsibility. "You don't have to put your life on hold for me."

He reached out and clasped her hand. "I want to."

Jamie placed a hand on his thigh. "You're the best."

The first smile of the evening emerged. "I try."

Being with Max was definitely the best choice for her. He'd not only be able to protect her, he'd keep her from doing something stupid. Benny and Jonathan might have fooled her, but not Max. He'd proven with his actions that he followed through on his commitments. No one had made him rush over to her house when she was consoling Becky, nor did he have to let her stay with him when he believed danger was near. The man was pure gold.

The problem was that while he might keep her body safe, what about her heart? Every cell in her body told her there was no place for romance right now, that she needed to give her full attention to staying alive, but Max was doing something to her equilibrium.

She was falling in love with him. There. She admitted it. Jamie sensed he cared deeply for her, too, but did he think about a future? Right now, he'd be focused on them staying out of harm's way.

"You okay over there? You haven't said a word in fifteen minutes."

"Just thinking," she said.

"My mom always told me that worry is productive only if you can do something about it. Right now, let me do the worrying. I'll make sure we're not being followed. Try to get some rest."

Rest. Right. He must have seen her check the side view mirror every minute. "I'll try." Even in times of stress, he was thinking of someone other than himself.

She glanced over at him. The light from the dashboard illuminated his strong nose and jaw, deep-set eyes, and powerful arms. He intrigued her. If she had to be protected by anyone, she'd have chosen Max Gruden—arson investigator, fire marshal, and all around awesome guy.

Following his suggestion, Jamie leaned her head back and closed her eyes, trying not to let the fear eat away at her. If these radicals hadn't killed two innocent people, she might have blessed them for forcing her and Max together.

Her friends used to accuse Jamie of finding the silver lining in all bad situations. Of late, she'd lost sight of that, and she wanted to try again. As terrible as this was, being with Max had shown her she could feel again. She couldn't pinpoint when she'd felt the tingling of life return to her soul. Was it when she found him visiting Jonathan? When he'd offered her his coat in the cold parking lot? Or when he'd held her tight against his strong chest and let her cry? Whenever the moment, Max had done her a big favor by proving to her that she wasn't dead inside. She'd be damned if she was going to let these bastards take away what little progress she'd made toward getting her life back.

The car slowed and Jamie jerked her attention to her surroundings. "Why are we pulling off? I thought your cabin was north of here." The sign they'd just passed said Kalispell was another twenty miles up the road. Had he spotted something?

"Easy there. My place is east of here. It's at the base of a smaller mountain range. I tell people it's near Kalispell because no one has heard of Marie, Montana."

"Oh." Jamie sank back against the seat, letting the adrenaline ebb. One thing seemed clear to her, she'd lost her ability to keep things in perspective. The town must be small. "Can you see any neighbors from your cabin?"

He'd said it was remote, but remote to one person might mean something else to another.

"Not unless their house lights are on, and the trees have lost their leaves. Most of us own ten to twenty acres." She didn't know if that was a good or bad thing. Max reached out and squeezed her arm. "Don't worry, honey, I won't let anyone get near you. Just so you know, I love to hunt and fish. That means I have several guns and rifles for game at the cabin. I also have a ton of fishing poles, but they won't do us much good in a standoff."

If he was trying to cheer her up, it didn't work. "These men are terrorists. They could have rocket launchers." All sorts of horrible images filled her mind, causing her stomach to sour.

"Jamie. A word to the wise. If you think about something too much, it might come true. You'll have to trust me when I say, I won't let them near you."

He sounded confident, but he was only one man. "Are you saying I'm supposed to think of this as a vacation and not worry about these bad men?"

He chuckled. "If you can, that would be great."

Like that was ever going to happen. Jamie grasped onto the seatbelt for some support and attempted to push aside the danger, but she couldn't.

Seconds after exiting the main road, he entered a vacant parking lot in front of a closed general store. "Why are you stopping here? They're not open."

"Not yet." He withdrew his phone from his pocket and called someone. "Hey, Hank. It's Max. Need a favor."

Chapter Eighteen

Max explained to this friend that he was on a mission for the FBI and needed not only supplies, but a lookout man. "Good. We're parked in front now." Max disconnected the call. "Hank will open up in a minute."

"Was it wise to mention the FBI? You didn't even tell your own assistant the truth when you asked him to send you report over to Chuck Forbes."

"Didn't have to. Rich is smart. He'll figure out something's up by the email address."

Max did seem to have thought of everything. He, too, used the same family emergency excuse to explain why he'd be away for a few days, and while she'd only heard Max's side of the conversation, Rich didn't question him much.

"Hank, on the other hand, is a different matter. If I want his help, I needed to tell him something. Note, I didn't mention anything about terrorists."

Once more, Max's logic prevailed. "I've never known a store owner to open up after hours."

"The town's small. We help each other."

Coming from near Los Angeles, Rock Hard was small to her. "How small is small?"

"I'd say maybe four hundred residents in the summer, but only a handful in the winter. Marie picked this place because of its name." Max looked out his window as if the memory was bittersweet.

Jamie could understand. "She sounds like someone I would have liked."

Max looked back over at her. "Yeah, you would have." The lights inside the store clicked on. "That's our cue. Come on."

A shot of adrenaline coursed through her. "Are you sure you can trust him?" Had she been the only person in the world to be fooled by others?

"I've known Hank for a long time. I trust him with my life."

She hoped he didn't have to test his faith. Max eased out then came over to her side. Jamie had already decided to wait until Max opened the door before getting out. More than ever, she had to remain vigilant.

He clasped her elbow to guide her down. "Watch your step." The parking lot was mostly gravel.

The inside of the store was bigger than what appeared from the outside. The shelving was at least six feet tall, and the aisles were rather close together. Only half the overhead lights were on, casting eerie shadows on the floor. Given the owner had just unlocked the place, she didn't expect anyone to be in hiding inside, but she studied her surroundings nonetheless. Not only were the shelves stocked with food, there was a section for ammunition, sporting equipment, and camping gear. It seemed to be a one-stop shop.

"Max!" Hank rushed over to them.

The owner looked to be in his sixties. He sported a barrel chest, thick forearms, and long, gray hair tied in a neat ponytail. The two men hugged.

Max glanced at the large man's belly. "Hank, you old dog. Need to get some exercise." While he sounded cheery, his tone seemed forced, as if he didn't want Hank to know the severity of the situation.

His friend laughed. "That's what the missus keeps saying. If she'd quit making her pies and all, I wouldn't have this problem." He looked over at her. "Who's this pretty thing?"

Jamie probably looked closer to a drowned rat who'd been left outside to dry than someone who was attractive, but she appreciated the compliment.

"This is Amelia Langford."

The breath she'd been about to inhale never went in as her mind raced. Why give a fake name if he trusted Hank with his life? What was going on? After giving the concept some thought, Max must not have wanted Hank to have to lie in case anyone came looking for her.

She relaxed, then held out her hand. "Nice to meet you."

"Likewise." He glanced back at Max. "She part of this FBI thing?"

"She is. Do me a favor. If anyone comes here asking for me, or us, give me a shout. I'd appreciate it if you don't mention I'm with a woman."

"They bad?"

"The worst. Amelia was an innocent victim, and I'm here to protect her."

Hank held up his left palm, and placed the other on his chest. "My lips are sealed. No one will take you by surprise. Want me to let Sheriff Duncan know?"

"Wouldn't hurt. Tell him there was a fire in Rock Hard, and the arsonists are looking for a way to keep the evidence from seeing the light of day. That is the truth."

"You got it." Hank sounded proud to be part of something important. She hoped he didn't ask why the FBI would be involved in a local arson case.

Max looked down at her. "I haven't been up to the cabin in a while, so we'll need food. Let's grab a cart and find what we need."

"Thought you said you were coming up last weekend," Hank said.

"Planned to. Got a bit delayed. The arson case kicked my butt."

She snagged one of the three available carts, and they went up and down each aisle, stocking up on staples. The normalcy of their actions wasn't lost on her, and she could almost picture herself shopping with Max all the time.

He stood in front of one of the refrigerator doors. "Do you drink milk in the morning or orange juice?"

They'd had coffee this morning. "Orange juice."

He grabbed a carton and moved down a few feet. "Eggs and bacon?"

"Please." Jamie had forgotten how nice it was to be with someone again, even if it was just for doing simple chores. She warned herself not to romanticize any of this. Her life was in danger, and that was what was important.

"Need some ammo?" Hank called from behind a shelf.

"I can always use more," Max answered. "How about a box of 9 mm hollow point for my Glock, and two boxes of 12 gauge shotgun shells?"

"You got it."

Max faced her. "I know all of this is hard."

"I don't like violence, but I know it's necessary."

He wrapped his arms around her for a second then kissed her forehead. "You're a real trooper."

"It's not like I have much choice."

He chuckled. "Got that right." Hank came over and handed him the ammunition. Max waved one of the boxes at her. "If this had been a few months ago, I could have caught us a deer or an elk for dinner." Max smiled, and suddenly her troubles seemed more distant.

"That's okay. Packaged food's fine with me." Benny wasn't into sports or anything else remotely manly, but Jamie liked knowing Max was so capable.

His lips quirked up. "Come on. Let's check out. It's getting late."

Jamie tried to pay for half the groceries since she didn't like being a burden, but Max wouldn't hear of it. "You wouldn't have bought so much stuff if I wasn't with you."

He laughed. "You eat like a bird."

That was true, but she should still contribute. "I want to help."

"Perfect. You can do all the cooking."

Now he'd stepped over the line. "You want to starve?" This time, they both chuckled.

Hank helped Max stack the groceries in the back of the SUV. "Be careful, now. We're expecting a bad storm tonight."

"I heard," Max replied. "We'll be ready."

That might have been why he'd purchased a ton of water jugs. He must think they might be holed up in the cabin for quite some time. In her dreams, she'd pictured being with Max. When they'd been almost naked in his bed, when he was kissing her, and sucking on her tits, she'd been in heaven. Jaime had never experienced anything like that before. Max had been gentle, but aggressive at the same time. No fumbling for this man. Now that they'd be together for days, excitement skated over her skin. Only this time, she wanted the intimacy.

As the men said goodbye, she jumped in the SUV. Not only didn't she want to be a target, it was damned cold outside. Max slid in and started the engine.

Jamie ran her palms up and down her arms. "How far is it to your cabin?"

"Fifteen minutes, maybe." He turned the heat on high. "It'll warm up in a sec."

In what seemed like no time, Max turned down a dirt road. Several hundred feet deep into the woods, his headlights illuminated a cute cabin.

"Home, sweet, home," he said with enthusiasm.

She hoped he wouldn't insist on sitting by the window, waiting for trouble. Jamie wanted to share in creating the meals, talking to him, and then exploring his body.

✧ ✧ ✧

"Wait here while I check things out. I don't want to assume we're safe," Max said. "I'll leave the engine running so you can keep warm."

"Thank you." Jamie crossed her arms over her chest and sat up straighter, as if she expected trouble.

Damn. He probably shouldn't have been so blunt, but when he was in protection mode, his instincts took over, leaving his tact behind. Even though Jamie seemed to understand the severity of the situation, he didn't want her taking any chances.

While the padlock on the front door was still closed, a good soldier would know how to break in without making it obvious. Not that Max thought anyone would be in the house, but with Jamie in his care, he had to do whatever it took to make sure she remained unharmed.

At least he didn't have to worry about someone cutting the line to the power grid. He wasn't hooked up to it. He ran his house on solar energy. If the weather didn't cooperate, the cabin had a back-up generator.

Max unlocked the cabin door and turned on the light. So far, so good. Nothing appeared disturbed, but that didn't mean his location hadn't been compromised. His rookie year, he'd walked into a crime scene and been surprised by a thief. Max had never made that mistake again.

He had no doubt the terrorists had figured out that Jamie was probably with him. If they followed her to the clinic, they would have seen him pick her up every day this week, which meant they probably had his license plate number, name, and who knew what else.

After he checked to see the windows were still locked and

that no one was hidden in a closet, he rushed back to her. Max yanked open her car door. "All good. Go on in. I'll bring in the groceries."

"I can help."

Damn. He kept forgetting about her caregiving nature. "Great."

From the back, he handed her the two lightest bags. Max gathered what he could and followed right behind her. The porch lamp shed enough light on the path, so she shouldn't trip. When she reached the front door, Max leaned around her, pressed on the door handle, and pushed it open. His arm brushed hers and unwanted heat shot through him. God, but he wanted to make love with her. He had to remember that Jamie would need time.

Seeing her house trashed then having the FBI step in, he bet she was too scared to let go and trust someone again.

Jamie rushed inside and glanced around. "I love it. The pine walls make it so rustic."

Until she'd squealed her delight, he hadn't realized he'd been waiting for her approval. "I love it here, too. The heat comes from a wood-burning stove in the corner over there, and the appliances won't quite be what you're used to, but they do the trick. About the only modern convenience I installed was the tankless water heater."

"It's more than I could have hoped for."

He was thrilled she felt comfortable here. "Put the groceries on the counter while I get your bags."

She spun to face him. "Uh-oh. You never went home to pack your things."

He was pleased she thought of his needs. "I have a second set of everything. I like that I can leave at a moment's notice. But thank you for thinking of me."

As he jogged out to the car, he paid close attention to the sounds of the forest. It was isolated here. Shit. Maybe coming to the cabin hadn't been the ideal solution he thought it would be. His only other option had been to choose a random town and a random hotel. They'd have to move nightly in order for Jamie to have the needed security.

Max had to go on the assumption that these men were sophisticated technologically, and that they could trace all credit card transactions, which meant he'd have to get cash that didn't come from a bank. He prayed they could stay put for a few days at least. He didn't want to go on the run. Jamie would be looking over her shoulder at every turn, and that was no way to live.

Christ. When they were shopping at Hank's, he should have gotten a burner phone. Then they could communicate without fear of detection. Damn. He wasn't thinking straight. Max gathered her suitcases and brought them inside. "I'll put these in your bedroom, then get the fire started."

She let out a small gasp. "Can't I sleep with you?"

Chapter Nineteen

Max's cock hardened at the thought of being next to Jamie all night. He rushed over to her. "Of course, honey. I'd like that. I wanted to give you the choice of where to stay. That's all. I know this is a trying time for you."

She smiled, and relief washed through him. "Thank you, you're a kind man."

"Just kind? I'm hoping you can come up with a few other adjectives for me later on." He smiled and turned around just as he caught her eye roll. He loved trying to get her to relax.

Once in his bedroom, he placed her bags on his bed, and then checked to see he'd left the bathroom in good condition. The refrigerator door banged shut, reminding him she was in the main room alone.

He hustled back out. "Find everything?"

"Yes. I like how you've organized the food the same way I would have."

"Good. Let me get started on warming up the place before we freeze." She hadn't removed her coat yet.

She looked up at him. "Do you have a specific place you want me to put things?"

"Wherever you like, but how about keeping a few of the non-refrigerated items in a separate pile?"

Her brows pinched. "In case we have to leave in a hurry?

For when they find us?"

There went her cheer. Damn. This uncertainty couldn't be good for her sense of control. "Yes." When Jamie's lip trembled, Max returned to her side and hugged her. "Don't worry. There's only one main road up here, and Hank will keep an eye out for us."

There was a back road, too, but it lead up and over the mountain. He doubted anyone would come that way, as there were numerous switchbacks and pitted roads that could snap an axle if one went too fast.

She looked off to the side. "Terrorists don't always come in cars, I bet. They're probably military men who would think to stash their vehicles somewhere, then hike in through the woods." Jamie's hands fisted at her side.

She was a smart one. "This isn't the movies, honey. I don't think a lot of them are highly trained military operatives who've gone to the dark side." He wanted to tell her everything was going to be okay, but he never was one to lie. "I know you're scared. Hell, I am, too, but if you think about all of the 'what ifs' too much, you won't sleep. Considering we're a good eight miles from town, and the undergrowth is next to impossible to get through, I don't think they'll come by foot."

He leaned over and brushed his lips against hers. When she moaned, he had to pull away for fear he wouldn't be able to stop. He tapped the counter next to her. "I'll leave it up to you how much you want to keep out. Then you need to hit the hay."

"What about you? I'm not sleeping alone."

God, but he adored this woman. Jamie was more resilient than any person he'd met. "Trust me. You won't be."

She smiled then began sorting the food. Max went to work lighting the wood stove. He liked having Jamie around. She brought life to these old walls. It was what he'd been missing in his life these past eleven years.

A few minutes later, a cabinet door banged shut, and Jamie

stepped into the living room. "All finished."

The fire was heating the place nicely. He tossed in one more log and stood. "Great. Let me show you to the bedroom." Halfway down the hall, he grabbed some fresh towels from the linen closet. "Thought you might like to shower. If there's anything you need, just holler."

"Thank you. I'm not sure how long I'll stay up. I'm exhausted."

The emotional toll would have felled even the strongest person. "Me, too. While you shower, I've got some calls to make. I also want to check on my gear. Take your time." It would be better if she didn't hear the conversation.

Once he showed Jamie the bathroom, Max slipped back into the living room. While he didn't expect trouble, he wanted to be prepared in case Hank called. They'd only have a few minutes to get out. That also meant they'd have to leave by the back route, which would take longer.

The flight would require cash, and the men he could hit up for the money at a moment's notice was limited. Trent, Dan, Thad, and Cade were his only choices, and Cade was in Hawaii on his honeymoon.

Max called Trent first. Before he had a chance to say hello, Trent responded. "You in trouble?"

"Not yet, but my sixth sense is acting up."

"Mine would be, too, if I thought terrorists were after my girlfriend."

He liked the idea of having Jamie in his life. Whether she was willing to be in his would soon be tested. "You learn anything else after we left?"

"Just finishing up now. Chuck Forbes said he and his men will be scouring the area for any suspicious behavior."

The added manpower should speed up the capture. Max leaned against the counter, keeping his eye on the hallway. "Need a favor."

"Shoot."

That was one of the reasons he liked Trent. The man got straight to the point. "Need some cash."

Trent whistled. "How soon do you need it?" Trent would give a man in need the shirt off his back.

"As soon as I can get it. I'm thinking two grand should get us pretty far if we need to get out of here."

"I should be able to drum up that much. Have you gotten burner phones yet?"

At the ease with which his request could be met, Max blew out a breath. "Weather permitting, I'll head back down to Hank's tomorrow."

"How is the old guy?"

When Trent had come up last summer, the three of them had gone fishing for the day. "Still feisty."

"You'll have to dump your car, too, you know."

Shit. He'd just bought the SUV. "I was hoping I wouldn't have to do that." Actually, he didn't want to admit he'd need to.

"If these men can trace credit cards, they can find a car. As soon as I hang up, I'll ask Dan and Thad to round up the cash."

Max was touched by his friends' generosity. "I'll pay you guys back. I just don't want to withdraw anything from my account."

"No problem."

They discussed how to handle the exchange, and concluded the best way would be for Trent to leave the money with Hank. Max didn't need to have his friend followed to their doorstep. No telling what these men would do once they found out Jamie had flown the coop.

"I appreciate this more than you can know."

"You'd do the same for me," Trent said. "I'll work on getting what you need on my end."

"Thanks." When Max disconnected the call, he felt a bit more settled having taken care of that issue.

Now it was time to go into survival mode. First, he wanted to create a bug-out bag and make sure the cabin was booby trapped for the night.

The wind had already started to howl, rattling the windows. Damn. They didn't need the snow. On the other hand, it would make it more difficult for an intruder to come and go unnoticed. It was hard to cover tracks. He wouldn't be surprised if in a couple of days this terrorist cell sent a scout to check out his place. His name was in the public record as owner. Hiding in the technological age was getting harder and harder.

The shower turned off, and the image of Jamie wet and naked flashed in his mind. He wanted to snuggle with her, kiss every inch of her delicious body, and then make slow, gentle love with her. But she said she was exhausted, and he agreed, she needed her rest.

Max gathered some bottled water, canned soup, and a few power bars she'd purchased to put in his emergency stash. Tomorrow, if they made it to Hank's, he'd grab some dried meals.

Max strode to the closet where he kept his gear. Fishing poles, batteries, flashlights, sleeping bags, stoves, and anything else he'd need to survive was there—including his weapons. Not knowing how long they could stay there, he gathered what he thought they'd need, and took the gear into the living room. He was carefully packing the items in a duffel bag when Jamie came out, looking clean and quite refreshed.

She was dressed in gray sweats and sneakers, but she couldn't have looked more adorable if she tried. He immediately squashed his longing. Her hair was wet and barely combed. He now regretted having tossed Marie's hairdryer.

"What are you doing?" she asked. He didn't like the hitch in her voice.

"Being practical. I like to be ready to leave at a moment's notice, even if that possibility is slim."

She walked over to the pile of gear on the floor and sank down in front of him. Her blue eyes were wide with worry. "You think they'll find us?"

Shit. He hadn't meant to upset her again. "They may try, but they won't succeed. I trust every person who knows we're here."

"People aren't always trustworthy."

It was time to find out what really happened to Jamie to make her so skittish. He knew the basics, and that she'd been burned badly. If he understood her better, he'd be able to anticipate how she'd react under difference circumstances. "How about hopping up on the couch, and I'll get us a glass of wine?"

Her eyes shone. "I'll fall asleep."

"Then I'll carry you to bed. Red or white?" He stood.

"White. You really are prepared aren't you?"

"You have no idea."

From the cabinet, he located a nice Chardonnay and poured them a glass. He could have sat across from Jamie in the leather chair, but he wanted to be close to her, to be able to hold her if she needed comfort.

Max held out the glass. "You said people can fool you. Want to tell me about it? You might be thinking I'm trying to pry, but I need to learn what could set you off, what makes you afraid." That was the truth.

She returned her gaze to him. "You mean will I freak if I see someone with a gun?"

Jamie was smart. "In part."

She closed her eyes for a moment and inhaled. "Okay. I'll tell you if you think it'll help. My friends all know the story anyway."

"Thank you. It means a lot that you trust me."

That brought out a smile. "If there's one thing I'm certain of, it's that I trust you."

Her words meant the world to him. "Thank you." He tapped his glass to hers, and they both shared a moment.

A slight blush crept up her face, and she inhaled deeply.

"Benny and I had been dating for about three years when his mom's deteriorating condition took a turn for the worse."

"Amber told me his mother had ALS."

"Yes. I really can't say if that was the trigger for him changing, or if it was when he asked to marry me and I said no, but the fact was, he went crazy."

Max hadn't heard about the proposal. "If you'd been together for so long, why did you say no?" He held up a hand. "You don't have to answer that." He'd said he wanted information to help him judge her reaction to certain stressors. Knowing why she broke up wasn't needed, but he wanted to learn everything about her. Learn who'd hurt her and why.

"It's fine. Benny and I got along really well for a long time. We both loved to watch old movies, and we both were in the medical field. He was interested in my patients and how I tried to make a person's last few weeks on earth more comfortable."

"Sounds like you and he were a good fit."

"We were for a while. I think I was attracted to him because he was so nice. My life growing up had basically sucked, and when I moved to Rock Hard, Benny was there to pick up the pieces." A lovely smile crossed her face, but then her cheer disappeared. "I once had a dog named Beau. When he died, I didn't know what to do, so I called Benny. He loved animals, too, and handled everything. That was before we started dating. When he came over and was so caring, I knew he was the one for me." She looked off to the side. "Or so I thought."

Max set down his glass then removed hers from her fingers. "Come here." He slipped her onto his lap and held her tight. Max kissed her forehead. She looked up at him with a small smile on her face. "Then his mom became incapacitated?" he asked.

"That actually occurred a few years later. Benny began to change slowly. I didn't see it right away. When the deaths at the hospital occurred, I was really shaken. I started to examine my life and I realized I wanted a man with focus, purpose, ambition. Benny had none of those traits anymore. He started to look to me more and more to make the decisions."

"Like which movie to watch or where to go to dinner?"

"Yes!"

He chuckled at her enthusiasm. "When did you know it was time to call it quits?" Jamie fascinated him. Most women would have blamed the man, but she seemed to have a good handle on what she wanted. He also wanted to never make any of those mistakes with her.

"I'm not really sure. I kept hesitating because Benny had more empathy than any person I'd ever met. In the end that one positive trait was his downfall."

"What do you mean?"

"Benny had so much sympathy for the terminally sick people that he decided to put the patients out of their misery. He thought that would cut short my suffering."

"So he killed them." Cade had told him that part of the story.

"Yes, but I never suspected he'd go that far." Her voice drifted. It was almost like she was reliving that terrible moment.

Max hugged her. "It's not your fault, you know."

She planted a palm on his chest, and her touch seeped deep into him. "Zoey helped me see that, but it's still hard."

"You're a strong woman, Jamie Henderson."

"I try to be."

She looked up at him, and when she smiled, Max knew then and there, he'd fallen for her. Hard.

Chapter Twenty

Now that her story was out, Jamie was glad he'd asked her to explain those terrible days. She was tired of tap dancing around the issue. She wanted Max to know her and understand everything she'd experienced. With all she and Max had been through since the wedding, she felt comfortable blurting out her pain to him. She appreciated that he never judged her.

The strange part was when she recounted Benny's good points, Max seemed to fit the bill, too. He had a good heart. No one else had taken the time to visit Agent Vic Hart in the hospital, no one else had insisted on driving her to and from work every day, and no one she'd ever met would have put his life on the line for her. His compassion had been above and beyond the call of duty. That must mean he really cared.

His amber eyes half closed. "We've had a hard day. What do you say we get some sleep?"

His lips descended, and the ache in her heart disappeared as she banished all thoughts of her past. Suddenly, she was wide awake. She wanted this man. Right here. Right now.

When he teased open her lips, she let him in willingly. As their tongues dipped and probed, she slid her hands under his shirt. The moment her fingers touched his hot skin, her body exploded with need. The suddenness of her desire stunned her, but she couldn't halt what was happening, even if she wanted to. Jamie didn't want to think about men chasing her or friends dying. It was just the two of them here. Safe. Exciting. Wonderful.

Max's breaths increased, and he pulled back. "Jamie. I want to make love with you, but if you're too tired I'll—."

"No. I want that, too." This was what she'd dreamed of. To be with a man who knew what he wanted.

Max stood, scooped her up in his arms, and kissed her hard. Even though he never took his gaze off her face, he managed to get them to the bedroom without bumping into a wall. He set her on the bed, knelt down in front of her, and slipped off her socks. Benny never undressed her.

Stop thinking about stupid Benny. I'm with Max now.

"How about leaning back and letting me take care of you?" he said in the gentlest of tones.

"Last time, you let me strip you."

He cocked a brow. "That was last time. Besides, you were too slow."

"Slow is good." She ran her gaze over his body and she couldn't wait to touch what was underneath those form-fitting clothes.

He flashed her a smile. "I'll think about it."

Letting a man take charge was novel for her. Given all that had happened, Jamie wasn't sure she was ready to give up total control yet. "Oh, come on. Fair is fair."

He chuckled. "You warm enough?"

She didn't miss that he hadn't commented on her request. "Yes." He'd heated her body completely.

With one tug, he pulled down her sweats. "Nice undies."

The phone call from Trent the last time had interrupted him before he could see them. Max placed a knee on the bed and lifted her sweatshirt over her head. The shine in his eyes and the twist of his lips emboldened her.

Jamie lifted her chin. "I want to see you naked, too."

"Fine, but if you want to help, better hop to it."

"I'll be quick." *Or maybe not.*

Since Max was kneeling on the bed, undoing his jeans would be the best way to start. She slipped the button through the hole easily, but lowering the zipper proved more difficult since his cock was putting pressure on the metal. When she managed to open his jeans, her breath caught at his size. She'd been a bit stunned the last time, too, but she didn't remember his bulge being so large.

"Can you take off your boots?" she asked.

"Yes, ma'am." Max stood, toed the heel, and discarded first his right shoe, then his left. He slipped off his socks. He stepped back, daring her to get up. "Have at me."

Even though he'd seen her naked breasts, she was still a little self-conscious. All she wore now were her panties. Hmm. Should she go fast or slow? He said she was too slow last time. *Fast it is, then.*

"You going to just stand there and stare, honey? Or should I help? I'm not a patient man when I know what I want." The hint of humor unlocked her inhibitions.

Heart beating against her ribs, Jamie wedged her thumbs under the denim waistband. She was so out of her league. Max was pure male. Aggressive, focused, powerful. And to think he wanted her. Wow.

With a hard tug, she lowered the material a few inches. Getting them over his well-defined ass took a bit of work. In order to drag the material to his ankles, she was forced to drop to her knees. "Can you lift your leg?"

Jamie glanced at his hidden erection. Since she was already on her knees, she was tempted to pull down his briefs and suck on his cock.

"Don't even think about it." She swore the words sounded like a growl.

"You going to stop me?" She glanced up and smiled. His returned frown made her laugh.

"Perhaps."

With a cheeky grin, he stepped out of one side of his jeans, then the other. All that was left was his shirt and briefs. Jamie stood and couldn't help but stare at the corded muscles in his legs. Her fingers ached to touch his well-defined body.

"Take off the shirt next."

"Yes, sir."

She ripped off his pullover and tossed it on the floor. His body was amazing. She leaned her face against his muscled chest and inhaled. He smelled of the mint soap he kept in the bathroom.

"You can take off my briefs now," he said with a smug expression.

The man did like to take control. Jamie pulled on the elastic waistband and eased his briefs downward. "Holy shit. You're huge."

Max smiled. "Better to love you, honey."

"Can I suck on him now?"

He laughed. "There will be time for that later." He lifted her up, gently placed her on the bed, and then stepped back. After retrieving his wallet from the back pocket of his jeans, he extracted a condom. "Hope these are still good."

"They might be bad?" Part of her was happy he didn't sleep with every woman, but she wanted to be safe.

"I'm sure they're fine, but it's been a while."

"For me, too."

"We're about to change that." Max tossed the foil packet on the bed next to them then crawled on top of her. "You make me happy."

His words lit her up. Max leaned over and nipped her bottom lip between his teeth. His grip was gentle but assertive, and his touch caused delicious shivers to travel down her body. Jamie reached up and ran her hands over his back. Muscles covered muscles. He was better than her wildest imagination.

"I have to taste you," he said.

He slid lower, and when he swirled his tongue around her nipple, her pussy clenched. The intensity of the thrill was oh, so welcome. She lifted her arms and threaded her fingers through his thick hair, gripping the strands hard.

"More." She wanted to feel everything he was willing to give her. She needed to know she had survived.

Max sucked on her other nipple, and a strong ache bulldozed straight down her body. His fingers clasped her waist. As he dragged his chin down her belly, his rough stubble ignited her skin in its wake.

Latent desire sprang to life. "Hurry." Jamie didn't care if he knew she'd been thinking of this moment ever since she'd had a taste of his lips.

"I want to make this memorable for you." He looked up at her with dreamy eyes, the color now closer to light-brown than gold.

"It's already burned in my mind." To be one with Max would close the door to her past forever.

He placed his palm over her panties and fingered the material, letting out a guttural moan. He then laid his cheek on her belly and inhaled. "You smell so sweet. You drive me crazy."

No man had ever talked to her like that, his words enticing her. Jamie slid the soles of her feet toward her body and pressed her hips upward, wanting him to possess her.

Quicker than she could blink, he pulled down her panties and threw them on the floor. She wanted him to impale her now, to feel all of him. As much as she'd wanted to suck on his cock before, her need to have him inside her overpowered her. "Take me."

Her arousal perfumed the air. She was wetter and more ready than she'd ever been in her life, and she had Max to thank for that.

He reached for the condom, tore the foil first, and then rolled the rubber down his length. "I want to take my time, but I need you too much."

"Yes," she whispered.

Max spread her legs, and when he swiped his tongue across her slit, the rush nearly took her breath away. Her inner walls contracted. Dear God, but this was more than she ever imagined.

He pressed a finger to her clit, and her hips seemed to fly off the bed. She grabbed his shoulders and dug her fingers into his skin. "I'm so close. Please."

Jamie barely recognized her own strangled voice. When had she become so easy? Max was surely to blame.

He moaned and crawled up her body. "I'm about to burst too, honey. God help me, but I'll try to take it easy."

His lips took hers, the kiss transporting her someplace she'd never been, and his exploration made her yearn for more. Her breath caught as their tongues dueled and parried. It was as if only the two of them existed for that moment in time.

Max nudged open her legs with his knees, gently pressing his cock against her opening. From his increased breathing, he was fighting for control.

He broke the kiss and sucked in a loud breath. "I want you, Jamie Henderson."

"I want you, too."

With one long, slow thrust, he slid into her, stretching her wide. Her pulse soared. She tried to relax, but he was so damned big. Needing to take charge for a bit, she pulled down his head and kissed him with every ounce of pent-up passion she possessed. He filled her mouth and body at the same time, making her a prisoner to her own desires. As if he'd flipped a switch, lust, and need slammed into her.

Her senses on overload, she lifted her hips to meet each one of his thrusts. Blood pounded in her head as she spiraled out of control. Jamie squeezed her eyes shut, wanting to think of nothing but what Max was doing to her body. Electric tremors raced across her skin, setting every cell on fire.

"Oh, honey." Max's strangled groan tossed her over the ledge of total ecstasy.

Stars burst behind her lids, and, as her climax consumed her, joy blasted her. He kissed her again, dragging his lips across her chin, finally landing on a tender part of her throat. Max pumped three more times, then held her tight as his cock felt as if it had doubled in size. She couldn't help but clamp down on him.

He buried his head in her neck and let out a feral cry. His hot cum filled the condom, and nearly seared her. They were one. Together.

Hearts beating fast, she absorbed his passion. Time stood still. Max held her as if she were some precious gift he never wanted to let go.

Finally, he eased out of her. "What you do to me. Be right back." He ducked out of the room and returned a moment later with a warm cloth to clean her.

"Thank you." She wasn't sure she would have had the energy to drag the cloth between her legs.

"I need to get something." He disappeared again. This time, he was gone for a few minutes. Doors banged open and shut. Max returned dressed in flannel bottoms and a T-shirt, looking macho and cute all at the same time. Jamie was riding high until she saw the gun in his hand. Her joy evaporated.

"Max?" Her heart skipped a beat.

Chapter Twenty-One

From the anxiety in Jamie's voice, Max had screwed up again. He shouldn't have waltzed in here with a weapon in his hand. What had he been thinking?

He placed the gun in the bedside table drawer. "It's a precaution in the remote chance someone comes knocking."

"I don't like weapons. That's all."

"I wish it didn't have to be this way, hon. I know Benny shot you." He'd seen the scar on her arm. It wasn't large, but it must have hurt like a bitch. "But I'm not him."

Her face softened. "I'm not scared of you. God no. I'm afraid of the terrorists. I know what they'll do to a person who gets in their way." She wrapped her arms around her body, and he'd bet it wasn't because she was cold.

He sat on the edge of the bed and drew her to his chest. "If it makes you feel any better, I put sleigh bells on the door handle. If they manage to get through the lock when they open the door, it will make a lot of noise." He smoothed the hair from her face. Jamie was so sweet.

"That was smart of you to think of that."

He leaned back and lifted her chin. "That's me. Mr. Smart."

Max actually got a slight smile out of her. Holding her tight, he crawled in next to her. How this tiny woman had gotten under his skin so fast, he didn't know. For years, he'd pushed every woman away, never letting anyone close to his heart for fear of losing her, convinced the devastation would kill him the next time. Jamie made him realize that being alone was no way to live. She was this sensitive spitfire of a woman that made him love life. He still couldn't believe she was here—with him.

He reached behind him and turned off the light.

"Can you leave the hallway light on or something?" Her plea was like knives slicing his body. Damn. Here, he'd prided himself on knowing what would scare her.

"I have a better idea." He turned the light back on, slipped out of bed, and carried the table lamp as far as the cord would reach. "How's that?" Shadows covered most of the ceiling.

"Perfect."

One hurdle jumped. Max crawled back into bed again. Already the winds had picked up, causing the tree branches to slap against the windows. He wouldn't be surprised to find a foot of snow when they woke up tomorrow. If the wind subsided, he had a plan to do something fun—an activity that would also help keep them safe. He bet Jamie would appreciate the diversion. Hell, so would he.

He kissed her good night as if he'd done it a million times. The best part was that she kissed him back. While they were in the eye of the storm, he'd enjoy it. "Roll over and let me hold you."

"That sounds wonderful." She smiled, and he lost another piece of his heart.

Jamie woke up with a start and sat up. She grabbed hold of the warm blanket, drew it up to her neck, and looked around. She spotted the illuminated lamp glowing in the corner, but the bed was empty. She placed her hand on the spot where Max had slept. It was still warm.

The rich aroma of coffee entered her nose, and she smiled. He was up. She yawned and stretched, not wanting to admit what was real and what wasn't. Yesterday had been a blur of emotions. What started out as depression, morphed into fear, and then bloomed into amazing desire. It was surreal. How was it possible to have experienced two tragedies and an ultimate high in such a short period of time?

She had yet to wrap her mind around the wonders of making love with Max Gruden, but the tenderness in her body attested to the fact they had made love, completely, totally, wonderfully.

The blanket slipped down to her waist, and the cool air chilled her. She was naked and needed to dress. Stepping onto the cold floor, she shivered, and moved over to her suitcases she'd left open on the far side of the room. She crouched down and pawed through her possessions for something warm to wear. Max implied they could be forced to leave at a moment's notice, so she hadn't wanted to put her clothes in the dresser or closet.

She quickly dressed, then pulled back the curtains to look outside. Her breath caught at the beauty. Pristine snow covered the ground and made the boughs of the branches hang low. Maybe she could convince him to let her go outside—assuming he believed it was safe.

Thinking Max might need help with breakfast, she hurried out to the kitchen. He was at the counter, cracking eggs into a bowl. Two cups of steaming coffee sat on the counter. The scene was idyllic. This was what life should be like all the time.

When he spotted her, his grin came out wide, teasing her body into wake up mode. While he was more handsome than a man deserved to be, she didn't like the puffiness under his eyes. That implied he hadn't slept well.

"Good morning," he said with what seemed like forced cheer. "You sleep good?"

He couldn't tell? Benny always said once she was asleep, she didn't move. "Yes. I didn't snore, did I?"

He laughed. "No. Come on over and help me."

She'd spent so much time by herself that she'd forgotten what it was like to do something with a man. "What would you like me to do?"

He had said she was supposed to do all the cooking. When she stepped close, he pulled her to his chest, and kissed her. That woke her up.

"Can you handle making bacon?" he asked.

At least he hadn't suggested she try her hand at a cheese omelet. "Totally." She nodded to the hot drinks. "Which one is mine?"

"The red cup."

The first sip took the chill out of her bones. "Delicious."

In companionable silence, they worked together. He put bread in the toaster then poured the scrambled eggs in the frying pan, while she placed the bacon in a second skillet.

"Are you up for a little adventure today?" he asked with a glint in his eye.

Her pulse soared with excitement. "You're letting me out?"

He laughed. "Only with me."

"I wouldn't want to go by myself." He must know that.

"After breakfast, we need to head back down to the store. I'm afraid I wasn't thinking straight yesterday. We'll need to get burner phones." His jaw tightened as if he expected her to complain.

"Do I have to smash the one I have? Or can I turn it off?"

"Turning it off won't work, nor will smashing the screen like they do in the movies. We'd have to remove the battery, and that takes a special tool that I don't have. I've been told wrapping it in aluminum foil will do the trick."

"Is that the same for my computer? Will it prevent the terrorists from tracing my location if I wrap it?"

"That I don't know, but just in case, I'll ask Hank to hold

onto it for a while. He's got a metal gun safe that should keep prying eyes away."

That was good news. "If I have to choose between giving up my laptop and staying alive, I'll donate my computer to the greater good."

"Let's hope it doesn't come to that. My car won't be as easy to disguise. I'm going to have to see if I can get Hank to swap vehicles with me. Last time I looked, he drove a real slow camper."

Poor Max. "Do you think those men saw you drive me to work?"

"Most likely. I'm guessing they followed us to your house, or asked around, because they believed you have something that belonged to them."

Goose bumps pebbled her arms. She understood that Max wasn't saying that to scare her, but was trying to make sure she understood what was at stake. "Only I didn't."

"They don't know that, nor do they believe it. They're determined buggers, I'll grant them that."

"Changing vehicles makes sense if we have to be on the run."

He smiled. "Way to look on the bright side."

Max scraped the eggs from the pan and placed them on a dish, while she put the sizzling bacon on a plate.

"This looks fantastic," Jamie said as she shuffled over to the small table.

Max held out the seat for her. "I think you've now experienced the entire repertoire of my cooking skills."

She doubted that. "Guess I better try these eggs, then." The first bite had her mouth watering. "Fantastic. And you said you couldn't cook."

He grinned, and stuffed in a mouthful of eggs. When they finished eating, Jamie insisted on cleaning up.

"I'll gather what we need," he said.

Just as she finished drying the last dish, Max returned with some gear. "Go put on your jacket and boots, while I install the chains on the tires."

Jamie was actually excited to go outside. The sun was shining, and the day appeared calm. It was perfect weather to be outdoors. She drew on her coat, hat, scarf, and gloves. As she rushed back to the living room, Max was coming in through the front door.

"Are we going to the store just to get phones?" She slipped her computer into her purse. Thankfully, she had online backup so she could recover her files if things went south. She wondered if he had something else in mind besides visiting Hank's.

"There might be more." Max slipped the sleigh bells from the door handle and placed them on the counter.

She liked their alarm system. The bad guys couldn't cut power to the house, so they'd never lose light. Sometimes old-fashioned devices worked best.

The drive to the store was magical. The road and landscape was pristine. Because she didn't spot any other tire tracks, it gave her confidence she'd be safe for a while.

"I love how the snow is clean and is piled high on the branches. It's breathtaking."

"It is."

When they arrived at the small store, a car was parked in the lot.

"Shit." Max drove on by instead of stopping.

Jamie's nerves nearly burned. "You think that's one of them?" Damn. Here she'd believed they hadn't been discovered.

"I have no idea. Let me call Hank. If he doesn't know, I'll have Trent run the plates, though I'm not sure how a name will help us. It's not like a person registers a car under the name, John Doe, terrorist extraordinaire."

She liked his sense of humor. He dialed Hank. "It's me. I know you can't talk, but I spotted a brown Toyota Camry in the lot. Do you know who it belongs to? We'll be right there." Max's shoulders lowered. He clicked off the phone, stuffed it in his pocket, and then executed a three-point turn. "The car belongs to Hilary Stanhogler, Hank's sister."

Jamie's blood pressure dropped a good twenty points. "Thank goodness."

As he parked, a woman was leaving the store with an armful of groceries. Max jumped out, and opened Jamie's side.

He moved toward the woman. "Hilary!"

The lady stopped. Then recognition dawned and her eyes widened. "Well, I'll be damned. If it isn't our Rock Hard hero. Hank said you were back in town. Let me set these down and give you a hug." She placed the items on the hood of her truck, came over, and gave him a bear hug. They chatted a bit, and once more Max introduced Jamie by her fake name.

When Jamie shook the woman's hand, it was clear from her skin's roughness that Hilary had no problem with hard work. "Nice to meet you."

"Stop on by sometime. Both of you." Hilary faced Max. "You know Carl would love to see you again."

"We aren't staying long, but the next time we're back in town, we will."

"I'll hold you to it."

Once Hilary's engine fired up, Max hustled Jamie inside the store.

Hank rushed over. "You had a visitor this morning."

Max was holding her hand, and the tension through his fingers nearly crushed hers.

"Who?"

"Trent. Left a package for you. Said he couldn't stay because he had to get back. Let me find it for you." Max let go of her hand. Hank went over to the counter and withdrew an envelope from inside the cash drawer. "He also said you might want to give me that fine ride of yours for my beat-to-shit camper."

Max laughed. "Leave it to Trent to pave the way for me."

"Boy looks out for you."

"That he does." Max glanced around. "Need two burner phones and a place to keep a computer."

He nodded to Jamie. She extracted her prized possession and placed it on the counter.

"Let me get those phones." Hank returned a minute later. "These here are ready to go. As for the computer, got a gun safe in the back. I don't think any of those fancy Wi-Fi waves can reach through steel. If you want to leave your phones, I can store them, too."

Max smiled. "That would be great." They placed the aluminum-wrapped items on the counter.

"I see you're one step ahead of me." Hank fished a hand in his pocket. "Here are the keys to Edith. She's already gassed up. Even set out clean bedding for you all." He winked.

Heat rushed up her face as Max exchanged keys. "She parked out back?"

"You bet."

Max withdrew cash from the envelope and placed several bills on the counter. "This will help fill up my truck. We'll be at the cabin until trouble arrives. I'll give you a call with my new number."

Max picked up some packaged food, paid, and escorted her out the back. It took him a minute fiddling with the key to get the door to the camper open. Once he did, she checked out their new ride. The VW Vanagon was old, but it looked functional. Just as they were driving out, Hank was pulling Max's car around back.

They both honked and waved. So far, so good.

Max glanced over at her with raised brows. "What do you say to a snowmobile ride?"

Excitement was immediately dampened by caution. "Is that wise? I thought you wanted us to stay around the cabin."

Max pulled onto the road that led to his place. "Relax. We'll both go stir crazy sitting in the house. I figure we can check out the perimeter. With the fresh snow, we'll be able to see if there are any tracks."

She swallowed her concern. "Of the human kind, I'm guessing."

He winced. "Yes. I'm not expecting any, though. By the way, have you ever shot a rifle?"

She hadn't seen that question coming. "Me? Never? I told you I didn't like weapons."

"I know, honey, but I think you should learn."

Well, damn.

Chapter Twenty-Two

"Hold on tight," Max said as he started the snowmobile. He only owned one snowmobile helmet, so he opted to use motorcycle helmets, each of which had a built-in microphone. If Jamie needed to tell him to slow down, she could.

She wrapped her arms around his waist and pressed her chest against his back. The sensation of closeness seemed to alter something inside him. Everything had changed once he made love with her. He'd expected Jamie to be tentative, conservative, and a bit naïve. Boy, had he been wrong. Jamie had more passion that anyone he'd ever been with. She was uninhibited, and her level of trust had been the ultimate stimulation. A woman like Jamie could alter a man's thinking—permanently.

He just had to make sure not to forget why they were there. Jamie's life was at stake, and he needed to protect her. They'd been lucky Hank hadn't sounded the alarm last night, though if he had, Max would have been ready. He'd trained himself to be a light sleeper.

He couldn't wait to show Jamie around the property. However, because she'd never been on a snowmobile before, he needed to take it slow. That worked for him, because part of his mission was to check for footprints. The second part was to teach her how to shoot a rifle. He didn't expect them to be a situation that required her to defend herself, but on the off-chance they did, he wanted her to be prepared.

Max started the ride off easy since there were many trees close to his house. Once he drove past the property line, there was a big field where they could have some fun. It was also a good spot to shoot a rifle, as no one lived behind him.

"How are you doing?" he asked as he decelerated.

"Good. This is fun." She tightened her grip around his waist.

Once she confirmed she was enjoying the adventure, Max revved the engine and raced down a hill. Jamie let out a little squeal, but she didn't sound scared. When Max didn't spot any evidence that anyone had been there today, exhilaration shot through him. He circled the property once before bringing her to the area where they could practice.

He pulled to a stop. "Lesson time."

"Do we have to?" While her words sounded like a complaint, there was a lot of happiness in her tone, too.

"Only if you want to stay alive, missy." He tried for as much pep as he could muster.

She lightly punched his back. "Way to bring me back to reality."

He laughed. "Hop off." Once she dismounted, he did the same. With his Glock secure in his shoulder holster, he grabbed the rifle case, along with some targets.

He kept his hand on her back as they trudged over to a spot he often used for practice. Placing the empty tin can on a stump about thirty feet away, he had her stand behind a lone tree.

"Let me show you how to load the shotgun, how to cock it, and how to aim. We'll start with how to load one shell." With care, he demonstrated how to port load the shell by placing it in the chamber. "I won't run the action forward because I want you to do it. The key here is to remember to keep the metal end facing you."

She bit her bottom lip and looked adorable. "Okay, but

move behind me so I don't accidentally shoot you."

He chuckled, but followed her request. Jamie managed to load the rifle on the first try.

"Perfect. In a moment, I'll show you how to use the magazine to load multiple shots. Stand behind the tree like so, and use the edge to keep the gun steady. The tree will protect you in case there is a shootout." She winced, but he didn't know of a way to sugarcoat it.

"I guess I should learn, though I'm betting we'll be in a car or by a building if we're attacked."

"That would be my guess." He was happy she was willing to give this a go, despite not wanting anything to do with guns. He handed her earplugs. Rifle shots were loud. Max enjoyed standing behind her. He wrapped his arms around her outstretched ones. "In a standoff, the key is to keep shooting. Doesn't really matter if you hit anything."

"Really?"

"Yes." He'd be the one to do the damage. He was trained. Jamie was not. Civilians might never live down a kill.

"Okay."

Once he adjusted her stance, he bent down to help her aim for the can. He didn't expect her to hit it, but having something to shoot at was helpful. "Now pull the trigger when you're ready."

Wanting Jamie to fully experience her first trigger pull, Max stepped back. She shot, but the can remained unharmed. She lowered the weapon and turned around. "Aw. I want to go again."

He grinned. The competitive Jamie had come to play.

✧ ✧ ✧

By the time they returned to the cabin, Jamie's hands were frozen and her ears were ringing from the report. It didn't matter she'd worn ear protection. The rifle had been freaking loud. Learning to shoot had been frustrating, but with Max's help, she'd actually hit the can once. Knowing this exercise could save her life someday helped with having to handle a weapon.

Max put the snowmobile back in the shed, and then escorted her inside. "That was fun," he said. "Hope you had a good time."

"I did. I loved riding around. The landscape here is fantastic." The town of Rock Hard had been mostly cleared for the buildings. She wished they'd left more trees.

Max washed his hands. "I'm starving. What are we having?"

She laughed. "You're putting me in charge?"

"You said you wanted to help."

"You got me there." The normalcy of her day had done wonders for her attitude. While on the back of the snowmobile, she'd pretended she was on vacation and not in hiding.

Max headed toward the bedroom. Since Jamie had put the groceries away, she was able to find the bread and sandwich meat. "Ham and cheese sandwiches with tomato soup good?" She had to shout so he could hear her down the hall.

Max returned to the living room a few seconds later. "Perfect. I'll stoke the fire."

This cabin living was growing on her, though she knew not to get too comfortable. They were a phone call away from total danger. Max had asked her to pack one of her two suitcases with enough clothes to get along for a few days. He said they'd each keep a bag in their new ride. That way if Hank called, she could grab a few essential items and go.

"Don't forget to call Hank with your number. We want him to be able to contact us."

He chuckled. "Already did that when I brought around the snowmobile." He shoved more logs in the stove and closed the metal door.

The man was good. Now that she had a phone, she should

call Sasha to see how her friend was holding up. Jamie also wanted to find out about the funeral arrangements for Yolanda. She wasn't sure Max would let her attend, but she wanted to find out when it was. In all honesty, Jamie didn't think it would be wise to go either. While she doubted the terrorists would attack her in a church full of people, they could follow her afterwards. Stupid men. If they would just tell her what they wanted, she could assure them she didn't have it.

Max moved behind her and wrapped his arms around her waist. He squeezed, and then let go. "You did great today." His words were colored with surprise.

She twisted to face him, making sure not to dislodge his welcomed embrace. "Did you think I'd freak or something?"

He shrugged. "It's all part of the learning process of me understanding you. I don't think any of us know exactly how we'll react in a given situation until it happens. Triggers can occur at any time. While I've witnessed a dozen or more blazes since my house burned and haven't *freaked*, as you would say, the next one might send me over the edge."

She lowered her gaze as his words sunk in. "I hope that won't happen to me. It was probably good for me to see what it would be like to handle a gun. If someone shoots at me, I want to know I won't freeze." Max grinned at her comment. "What's up with the smile?"

"I think you're a remarkable woman. Resilient, trusting, and loving."

"I am, aren't I?"

When Max lowered his arms, Jamie waved the butter. "You want to spread this on the bread?"

"Can do."

Max had asked her to learn how to shoot, claiming he wanted to learn more about how she'd react when the gun went off. She, too, wanted to discover everything about him. This pressure cooker they were in could cause unexpected reactions. She hoped she didn't fold. "Can I ask you something?"

Max removed a frying pan from the cabinet and placed it on the stove. "Sure."

"You asked why I became a hospice nurse. I'd like to ask you the same thing."

"I never studied medicine, honey, at least not in the same way you did," he said with a straight face.

"Funny man." Of all the men she'd met, she never thought Max Gruden would be the one with a sense of humor. "You told me why you went into law enforcement, but I'd like to learn why you left."

"You mean why did I become obsessed with finding the man who set fire to my house that killed my wife and young son?"

Ouch. His pain sliced through her at the nerve she'd hit. "Sorry. It's okay if you don't want to talk about it."

He blew out a long breath. "No. You should know where I'm coming from. It's part of who I am. If there was one thing I learned from these last eleven years, it was that obsessions are bad. They can take over your life and put everyone else at a lower priority."

She busied herself with finding the can opener for the soup. "I so get that. I feel terrible I haven't spent enough time with my friends." She twisted around and leaned against the counter. "Benny's betrayal forced me to change who I was. I thought after those men chased me at the clinic, I'd figured out how to take back some control. Now I'm not so sure."

"It takes time. Trust me. I know." Once he finished preparing the bread, he grabbed the packages of meat and cheese and opened them. "As for shutting out your friends, it's easy to be blind to what's important in your life, especially when you want something badly enough."

Max must be talking about himself. Before she met him, the only thing she'd ever wanted badly enough, was to help others. "Want to tell me about your quest for retribution?"

He gripped the knife and pressed his lips together. He probably was deciding if he wanted to spill the beans.

"I was on a task force to bring down this drug cartel headed by Santori Anderson—a very bad man. We'd received some intel about a warehouse full of drugs, and when the six of us went in, all but one of the dealers scattered."

"Santori Anderson?"

"You got it. He spotted me, took aim, and shot." Max tapped his leg. "Shattered my femur." She hissed. "I was able to get off a round before I almost passed out. That one bullet hit him in the side of his head, and ended up blinding him in his eye."

She refused to feel sorry for the dealer. "I thought Amber said he got away."

"He did. Long story short, while he was recovering in hiding, he hired a man by the name of Warren Dominguez to torch my house to pay me back for ruining his life."

"Anderson was a drug dealer and he shot you first. What did he expect the cops to do? Shake his hand?"

He graced her with a small smile. "Apparently, his sense of right and wrong wasn't as strong as ours." He placed the buttered bread of each sandwich face down on the skillet.

She didn't ask about his child dying or the torment he went through when he learned of his family's death. She honestly couldn't imagine something that intolerable. Even what she'd recently gone through paled compared to the pain he must have experienced. It was why she trusted him with her emotions. "Why leave the force? Why not look for the man yourself?"

"I didn't leave right away. After a two-year search, we captured Santori Anderson, but he wouldn't reveal the name of the arsonist. I stayed for another year, spending countless hours tracking down clues, and eventually the case went cold. But I couldn't let it go. I figured the only way to find the bastard was to learn about his other fires. Arsonists usually have a certain signature."

"So you studied fires in order to find this man?" That was

smart. Proactive. Control-taking. She could learn something from him. Hell, perhaps that was why he wanted her to know how to load and shoot a gun. She had to admit, shooting the rifle had empowered her.

"Yes, but even then I wasn't all that successful. I wanted to know more. I needed to think like an arsonist. That was when I went back to school and studied fire science. I could only go part time, though. Took me years to get my degree." He topped the heating bread with cheese and ham. "In the end, I spent a fourth of my life tracking down this man. I would find clues to his location and pass the information onto Dan. Even though I wasn't a cop anymore, I went on a lot of the investigations. Eventually, things fell our way, and we got him."

"That must have been an incredible relief."

"It was, but when it all over, I had a big void in my life." Max placed the top on the sandwich, lifted the bread with a spatula, and flipped it over. "I'm slowly returning to life, and I have you to thank."

"Really?" Jamie turned her back to him as heat raced up her face. She managed to remove the can top, then poured the soup into the saucepan.

She carried to pot over to the stove and turned on the burner. Max slid the sandwiches onto a plate. Once he dumped the pan in the sink, he returned to the stove and changed the setting of her pot from medium to low.

He clasped her shoulders. "I don't know why you're surprised. Don't you feel more alive since we've met?"

She looked up at him. "More alive? Try just alive. Before the fire and the break-in, I was dead inside, going to and from work, helping others. I liked what I did, but there was no real joy in my life."

Max slid his hands down her arms to her waist, walked her backward to the counter, and lifted her on top. They were eye-to-eye. "And now?"

Chapter Twenty-Three

Before Jamie had the chance to tell Max what a difference he'd made in her life, he stepped between her legs and kissed her. Now that all the rage and fear had been exposed—and they seemed to be dealing with it together—they could start fresh. His fingers slid under her shirt, and he brushed his thumbs across her nipples. Damn bra.

Max broke the kiss. "I promised myself that I would stay away from you so I could make sure you were always safe, but I have no control when I'm around you. I want you naked. Then I'm going to fuck you hard and often."

Maybe it was from the release of tension, but she giggled. Actually giggled. That was something she hadn't done in years. His words gave her strength.

"Okay, but only if I can suck on your cock first." She wouldn't compare having made love with Max to anyone else, but suffice it to say she'd only given a blow job a few times. You-know-who didn't like them. Being able to lick and suck on Max would be such a high. This time she hoped she didn't get sidetracked.

Instead of him responding to her comment, he yanked her shirt over her head. "Nice."

She had packed some of her nicer bras and panties, and was glad she'd worn a pretty set this morning. Not wanting him to change his mind, she opened the waistband on his jeans and tore down the zipper. Damn. He'd worn briefs again. Oh, well.

"How about we both take off our shoes," she suggested. That would make the disrobing process move faster.

He tugged off her footwear, before removing his own boots, and kicked them aside. Jamie tried to lift his shirt over his head, just as he was unzipping her jeans. It became almost comical.

"Let me slip off the counter," she said.

Max set her down as if she weighed nothing. "It'll go faster if I do this myself." In one quick move, his shirt disappeared. His pants and briefs were next. "I need you too badly."

If Jamie hadn't been so mesmerized, she would have finished taking off her jeans, too. Only after Max reached behind her and unhooked her bra did she realize she'd been staring. She wet her lips in anticipation of what was to come.

He tossed her bra on the counter. "Condoms. Damn. Remind me to get more next time we're at Hank's."

"How embarrassing. He'll know what we're doing."

Max laughed and fished another one from the pocket of his jeans. He tossed it on the counter. "I think Hank already assumes we are doing just that." Max lowered his gaze and leaned closer. "You said you wanted to do something first?" He dragged a thumb over her nipple, and her thoughts scattered.

"Yes."

Jamie bent over, and when she cupped his heavy sac, he groaned like she'd hoped he would. *Yes.* The man wasn't immune at all. Being short suddenly had an advantage. She studied his length trying to decide how to proceed.

"You've got ten seconds or I'm taking over."

She looked up at him. The seriousness in his expression compelled her to lower her head and draw his upright cock into her mouth. She sucked hard. Max combed his fingers through her hair and pressed on her scalp. Dragging her mouth down his length, she twirled her tongue around his hard shaft.

"Fuck, but that feels so good." Max's free hand cupped her breast and twisted the nipple between his fingers, sending delightful pulses down the sides of her body. The man could turn her inside out with a touch.

She rolled his balls while she grabbed his cock with her other hand. Between drawing him in and running her tongue along his pulsating vein, her movements turned more frantic. Suddenly, Max drew her upright and pulled her close. His lips descended on hers like a starving man. When his dick pressed against her open jeans, her pussy dampened, and a deep yearning bubbled inside her. She needed him. Wanted him. Desired him, but she didn't have the strength to break the kiss. Their tongues explored, tasted, and probed with desperation. She clamped her fingers onto his corded shoulders and drew him near, wanting to melt right into him.

Max pulled back, his eyelids half closed. He fumbled with the foil package. As soon as he extracted the rubber from its case, he peeled it down over his cock. Why couldn't she remember to ask if she could do the honors? It was Max's fault for distracting her.

He tugged off her jeans taking her panties with it, and then lifted her onto the counter. Drawing open her legs, he bent over. His fingers dug into her thighs as he swiped his rough tongue across her slit. His lick caused spasms of electricity to ignite her already burning body. Her breath caught and her mind swirled. This was where she needed to be.

"I love how you taste." Max dipped his tongue into her opening and rubbed her clit with the pad of his thumb. She nearly lifted off the counter.

She grabbed his hair and yanked hard, unsure whether she could control herself for much longer. "I need you."

Max straightened, slid her to the floor, and turned her around. He grabbed her hips, and with a quick pull, Jamie's body was parallel to the ground, her arms outstretched.

"I want to savor every part of you." He placed his cock at her wet entrance and plucked her nipples. "What you do to me, girl."

He pinched the tips again, sending ripples of electric pulses straight between her thighs. Then he impaled her.

"Dear God in heaven." Her cry came out strangled. Without thinking, she clamped down hard on his cock.

"Jamie. Don't. I can't hold off much longer."

She couldn't either. She pressed her hips back against him, and Max drove into her hard and fast, setting her body on fire. She didn't need an expert to tell her the cause of the blaze. It was all Max Gruden.

Jamie dropped her head and let him transport her to heaven. Between him lavishing his attention on her nipples and turning on every nerve ending in her body, Jamie let herself go. She floated and soared, blocking out her fears. She was in a different world. With her eyes shut, pinpricks of light burst in her vision.

"I'm close, honey. Hold on."

She wanted to go over the edge with him. Grabbing onto the counter with all her might, she arched her back and gave into her desires. Passion, pleasure, and lust filled her. When he slipped a hand between her legs and pressed on her clit, her tiny button lit her up. Her climax swooped in and took over her mind.

Max pressed his chest against her back and wiggled her little pearl again. Each time he shifted his weight, his muscles rippled, causing more fireworks to go off inside her. Max grunted a second before his cock expanded and stretched her wide. He detonated his hot cum into the condom.

"Jamie, Jamie." He lowered his lips onto her neck and nibbled. For the next few minutes, as he held her tight, her world shrunk. She was at peace.

Max finally slipped his cock out and stepped over to the sink. Water ran behind her. "Let's clean you up."

Her legs were like rubber, and she had to lean against the

counter for support. "We forgot to eat."

"I don't know about you, but I just had my feast."

Jamie laughed. Where had he been her whole life?

By the time they dressed, reheated the grilled ham and cheese sandwiches, and ate, it was late afternoon. "I need to call Sasha. I'm worried about her." Jamie pulled out her burner phone. "Shit."

Max stilled. "What is it?"

"I don't have her home number." She snapped her fingers. "No wait, I do. Sasha wrote it down for me on a scrap of paper in case I needed a ride home from the bar the other night. It may still be in my purse." Jamie rushed to the bedroom and brought her bag back to the kitchen table. She stuck her hand in the morass, but failed to find it. "Stupid mess."

Frustrated, she dumped everything out onto the tabletop and separated the contents. In the middle of the pile was the piece of paper she was looking for. "Here it is."

Max picked up a yellow movie toy. "What is this?"

"You don't recognize this little fellow?"

"'Fraid not."

"It's a rubber minion from the movie Despicable Me. I found it in my coat pocket right after I treated Katie Danvers. I figured she slipped it in there after I told her mom that part of Katie's problem might be that she put too much unclean stuff in her mouth. She's six and the cutest thing. I put it in my purse, so that when she came back for her next treatment, I could return it to her."

Max's brows pinched. "Do you always wear your coat when you treat your patients?"

Jamie's mind spun. "No. Never. The free clinic has good heat. Maybe I'd forgotten to take if off, though that had never happened before."

"But you remember taking it out of your coat pocket and putting this in your purse?"

What was she missing? "I do, but at the time, I didn't think about how it got there. The only child I'd treated that day was Katie, so I assumed she must have given it to me."

Max tugged on it and it separated. "It's not a toy. It's a flash drive."

Her heart sank as her mind spun. A flash drive? Oh, shit. "You don't think Jonathan—I mean Vic—slipped it in my pocket, do you?" She recreated the last time she'd seen him. "Oh, my God."

Max placed a hand on her shoulder. "What is it?"

"The day of the robbery, I'd brought food for both Vic and Larry. Only Larry hadn't shown up yet. I was bending over to put the bags on the ground, when a gust of wind pushed me forward. As I tried to regain my balance, Vic reached up to steady me. I remember thinking how strong his grip was."

"Could he have slipped this in your pocket then?"

She couldn't be certain. "It's possible."

"The only way the terrorists would know you had this was if they saw Vic put it there."

She replayed that moment. "Right before the gust of wind made me stubble, Vic looked off to the side. He'd just told me a rather funny knock-knock joke, but his smile completely disappeared for a moment. Do you think he saw someone he suspected was a terrorist? Is that why he gave it to me? Shit. He had to have known they'd come after me."

"Not necessarily, honey. If you didn't feel him place the drive in your pocket, he might have thought the observer only saw him help steady you."

"I hope so."

"We need to take a look at what's on here," he said.

"Do you have one here? My computer's at Hanks." Her

heart was pounding harder than ten jack hammers.

"No, but I know where we can use one. Get dressed. There's an Internet café a few towns over. We'll be safe there."

She liked the word "safe," but there was an undercurrent of anxiety that threatened to push her panic button. Jamie shoved back her chair and dashed into the bedroom to bundle up. Getting out twice in one day was a real treat, but only if it was for fun.

Max was waiting for her when she stepped back into the main room.

"Ready?" he asked.

He seemed to ask that a lot. "As much as I can be."

Max hugged her. "I know it's tough, but there's no way they can know Hank and I have switched vehicles."

"What if they come after Hank and force the answer out of him?" Putting anyone in danger would cause her endless guilt.

"He's tougher than he looks."

"Easy for you to say. You won't be the one facing those terrible men. They have guns. Remember they shot and killed Yolanda."

He waved the drive. "Maybe there's nothing on this."

"You don't believe that."

He locked up and led her to the camper. "Doesn't matter what I believe. We both need to relax. Acting nervous at the café will only make people talk. We're visitors. People will notice us more."

She'd been to small towns like that before. He said the café was only a few towns over, but in Montana that could be miles. "How far away is this Internet café?" Jamie hopped up in and secured her seatbelt.

"Twenty minutes maybe. Kind of depends on whether the roads have been cleared or not." On the way down to Hank's store, Max kept quiet. From the way his cheeks were moving, he was thinking. "I'm betting Vic planned on retrieving the flash drive from you the next day, with you none the wiser."

She blew out a breath. Max always was able to see the glass half full. His background in law enforcement gave him a good perspective. "I hope that's true."

For the next few minutes, she let her mind wander over to the other events that had recently occurred to see if in light of this new evidence, she might figure something else out.

Jamie sat up and twisted toward Max. "Remember, I mentioned that I gave Becky a present in front of Banner's Bar?"

He glanced at her. "What about it?"

"It was a small pin. The box might have been two inches by one inch at the most. I slipped it out of my coat pocket and handed it to her. While we were standing outside the bar door, another friend came toward us, and Becky slipped it in her pocket. Could the man in the baseball cap have seen me pass something to her? Did he think it might have been the flash drive? Is that why he followed her?"

Max's lips lifted slightly. "I think you should be a cop. You have good instincts. We may never know, but it is logical."

"I can do logical sometimes, but I'm more comfortable with the emotional half of my brain."

Max reached out and rubbed her leg. "I like that there are two sides to you."

Max had such a wonderful calming effect on her. He always could bring her thinking in line with reality. After all she'd been through, Jamie should be a complete mess, but she wasn't. If she'd been alone when she found her house broken into or learned of Yolanda's death, Jamie might have had a nervous breakdown.

Max glanced over at her. "Did you call your friend, Sasha?"

"Crap. Finding the flash drive distracted me."

"I understand."

"I'll call her later. I don't think I could keep from telling her something." Jamie picked up the flash drive. "If this is from Vic

Hart, what do you suppose is on it?"

Max's fingers tightened on the wheel. "Something damned important."

"He might have found out the location of the terrorist cell and maybe even their identities."

"Wouldn't that be nice, but I kind of doubt it. If he did have that kind of information, he would have called it in. Putting information on an electronic device is risky."

"I never saw him with a phone, and he certainly didn't have a computer, unless he kept it in his backpack."

"Undercover isn't always a twenty-four hour a day job. I'm betting Vic slept in a warm bed most nights and drove a nice car, compliments of the US Government. He could have risen very early in the morning, put on his makeup, and parked close to town. He then could have limped over to his usual spot near the clinic with no one the wiser."

"He didn't limp." Which meant he might not even have shrapnel in his leg. "Why do you suppose he picked the clinic area?"

"That, my dear, can only be answered by Vic."

She exhaled, picturing the tube down his throat and the saline drip into his arm. "I hope he's awake."

"I could call Dan from my burner phone, but I think the less contact the better. Truthfully, Vic's condition doesn't affect us right now. Agent Forbes and his men will make sure Vic stays safe."

She remembered Max telling Dan to call him if something came up. "Dan will need your new number, too."

Max chuckled. "You seem to forget that I was a cop. I already contacted him as well as Trent."

"I hope they can keep a secret."

"Don't worry."

It took them about twenty-five minutes to reach the cute town of Winding River. Along the way one of her favorite songs came on the radio, and she turned up the volume. Pushing aside all of her worries, she hummed the refrain.

"You a big Toby Brunnell fan?"

"Yes." She sighed. "There's something about country western songs that speak to me."

"His song, Montana Fire, is one of my favorites."

She looked over at him. "Mine, too!" Max smiled, those dimpled cheeks sending her mind in a different direction.

He shook his head. "It's kind of sad, really. The hero in the song seems so in love with his fantasy woman, but she doesn't have a clue."

Jamie leaned back her head. "Yeah, but she figures it out in the end. It has a happy ending."

Max laughed. "You are a romantic."

"Very true." They entered the town—all four blocks of it. Few people were parked in the street and none were walking around. "It looks deserted."

"It's early still. I bet around dinner time and afterwards, the place will be bustling. Or at least as bustling as a town of two thousand can be." Max cut the engine and jogged over to her side.

Jamie slipped her purse over her shoulder and let him help her down. The snow had piled up on the sidewalk, so she had to walk carefully to avoid slipping. Once inside the café, Jamie relaxed. Comfy sofas and mismatched chairs were scattered in the front half of the café. A long table with four computers hugged the right wall. Fortunately, none of the stools were taken. This must be their lucky day.

"Want coffee and a snack?" he asked.

A food counter was located in back. Tea tins lined the wall, but it was the aroma of coffee beans and chocolate that piqued her interest. "Sure." They went up to the glass counter, where there was everything from cookies to pies to tea sandwiches.

The cashier came over. "What can I get you two?"

While Jamie was a bit nervous to eat, the food looked too good to pass up. "I'll have the fudge brownie and a black coffee."

"Same for me," Max said.

Max paid—again. Jamie wanted to address his need to take care of her, but she wasn't in a position to do much since they had to pay in cash, and she was a credit card girl.

"I'll bring it over when it's ready," the server said.

Max escorted Jamie to the computer that was the farthest from the window. They tapped the mouse and the computer sprang to life. "Go ahead and plug it in," he said.

Jamie's stomach twisted. "If there is some juicy info, what are we going to do with it?"

"I have Agent Forbes's card, but let's take a look first."

Jamie loaded the drive and waited. There were two files. She clicked the first one, and it sprang open. Max leaned closer and scanned the contents. "Fuck me."

Chapter Twenty-Four

The document on the flash drive contained a list of names. Next to each one was an item and an amount. Only these weren't the type of things one would buy in a grocery store.

She ran her finger across the screen and started reading quietly. "Rich Phillips—duct tape: twelve rolls. Justin Andrews—hydrogen peroxide: four gallons." The list went on and on. "What do you think this means?"

Max leaned close and whispered. "It looks like ingredients used to make a bomb. Or rather, a lot of bombs."

Her stomach twisted. "Holy shit."

"We've got to get this to the Feds, ASAP. Open the second file. Then we'll make a copy." His words came out clipped.

She didn't want to ask what he thought might happen to the flash drive, but having a backup made sense. Jamie clicked on the second icon. Neither said a word for a minute. The information made less sense than the first list. "What would row 27, seat 3 mean?"

"It looks like theater seat numbers."

"You think a theater could be their intended target?" Jamie's throat nearly closed.

Max shrugged a shoulder. "Or a football stadium, or any large venue that has numbered seats. Is there any more information? A date would be extremely helpful."

She scrolled down. "There's nothing more. Just this one page."

"Shit."

"Wait a minute. Look." Jamie pointed to the bottom right hand portion of the screen. "This could be a date: 5/3."

"It's possible. No year, though. I'll go out on a limb and say it's this year, assuming it is a date."

"What do you think CF is?" The initials were centered at the bottom.

Max leaned back in his seat. "Given the location on the page, it could be the initials of the person who sent this." He shifted his gaze toward the window, his fingers tapping out a beat.

Jamie read the list again, trying to think of all the places that had a large number of seats. "The university has a football stadium." The idea that a large population could be killed sent chills up her spine.

"I can list a few places, too. Think of all the movies theaters in town and school gyms, not to mention our indoor soccer stadium."

She was more scared now than before. "Now what?"

The waitress came over with their coffee and dessert. "Here you go."

Jamie looked up at her and smiled. "Thank you."

"You're welcome, hon."

If anyone came in and asked questions about either of them, Jamie didn't want the woman to remember that Jamie had been the nervous lady with the blonde hair. Absently, she fingered her light-colored strands. "You know I've always wanted to be a redhead."

Max's brows rose. "You'd look great as one, though I like you just the way you are."

He had a knack of boosting her confidence just when she needed it. "Thank you."

"You're thinking you want to be a little less identifiable. Is that it?"

He caught on fast. "Yes. It's bad enough being short and skinny. I'm rather hard to miss, but if I dyed my hair and changed my makeup—or rather wore makeup—the bad men might look right past me."

"Smart."

She'd deal with the transformation shortly. Right now the chocolate was calling her name. Jamie bit into her brownie. "Mmm. This is really good." Perhaps it was so tasty, in part, because some of the mystery had been solved. "If I were a terrorist, and I knew I'd lost this flash drive, I'd be freaking out."

"Which was exactly what they did. I'm hoping they become bolder and make a mistake." Max shoved back his chair. "I need to make a call."

"To Agent Forbes?" Jamie kept her voice low.

"Not to him, yet."

She thought he'd said he wanted to pass this off to the Feds as soon as possible. Knowing Max, he'd want to check to see that Forbes could be trusted. Max moved over to the front of the café where no one could hear him, kept his back to the customers, and scanned the street. A cold streak raced up her spine. Did Max suspect someone might have followed them? Was it his cop instinct kicking in, or was it his habit to check everything?

The bell above the door jangled and Jamie's senses shot to high alert. A twenty-something year old man with a shaved head and a neck full of tattoos strode in. Far be it from her to judge a man by his appearance, but given how taut her nerves were of late, she couldn't help but wonder if he was a terrorist and their location had been discovered.

Her pulse quickened and her mouth turned dry, until she saw that he didn't even look her way. That didn't mean he wouldn't spot her once he placed his order. Jamie shot a glance at Max to see what he thought they should do. Damn. He was still talking on the phone.

A second later, Max walked over to her, but he didn't seem to have noticed the newcomer. Max stepped next to her, picked up his coffee and brownie, and motioned they sit at a vacant table.

Jamie followed him. "Did you see the man who just walked in?" she whispered, then nodded in the man's direction.

"Yes."

"Could he be a *person of interest*?" Why wasn't Max rushing her out of the café or questioning the guy? Guess Max couldn't just stroll up and ask if this man wanted revenge for a wrong our government had perpetuated against some unknown group of people.

"Stay calm. If he is with *them*, leaving now will only confirm that we have what he wants. I can see our van from here. No one is inside searching it. We're good."

Max's back was to the front, so how could he know that? Jamie didn't say a word. She trusted he knew what he was doing. "So, now what?"

"We need to print a copy then get back to Marie."

She looked at him with skepticism. "I'm no computer expert, but once we make a copy, shouldn't we delete the file, or write over it?"

Max's shoulders slumped. "We can't. It's illegal to tamper with a Federal investigation."

"Damn."

The bell above the door rang again, and Jamie twisted back around. The man left with a drink and a to-go bag. The big question was whether he was rushing to his team members to tell them who he'd found, or was he an innocent bystander who'd come in for a snack?

"I'm not cut out to do this." She wrapped her arms around her chest.

"No one is, honey. Come on, let's do what we need to do and get out of here."

Jamie stepped over the computer again, plugged in the drive, and printed the information. She quickly ejected the drive and handed it to Max. She wanted no part of it.

Max waited at the printer. He grabbed the paper, folded it, and stuffed it in his pocket. "How about we take the coffee and food back to the camper where we can figure out our next move?"

She liked that idea of not being so exposed. "Good."

Once they were in the van, Max turned on the heater. She faced him. "Have you decided if you're going to call Agent Forbes?" she asked.

Max twisted in his seat. "Before we turn over any sensitive information to the FBI, I want to make sure Forbes is who he said he was. I asked Dan to check. Once he gives me the thumbs up, I will."

"You didn't believe him when he said he was with the FBI? He had a badge."

"You keep asking me if I trust Hank, or if I trust Dan and Trent."

"Yes."

"I trust them a lot because I've known them a long time. I don't know Chuck Forbes from Adam. For all I know, he could have bought the identification on line."

The ramification made her sick. "You think?"

"Probably not, but I'm cautious. Even if he's legit, I'm not going to discuss anything over the phone. It might be a burn phone, but I can't be positive it can't be traced. So that we don't waste precious time, I asked Trent to meet us at Hank's. I'll give him the flash drive, and if agent Forbes checks out, Trent can hand deliver the information to him."

Max had really thought this through. "I like the part about handing it over. I'm not sure I'm ready to go back to Rock Hard though." She immediately stuffed half of the brownie in her mouth, chewed, and groaned at the wonderful sweetness. "It's too bad we can't videotape you handing off the drive to Trent, and put it up on YouTube. That way these crazy guys will leave us alone."

Max chuckled. "If you posted something like that, Trent would be the one in danger."

"Strike that idea, then."

Max reached out and placed a hand over hers. "Speaking of handing over the evidence, when Trent arrives at Hank's store, I want you safely out of the way."

Jamie held up her other palm. "You won't catch me out in the open."

"We should head back." Max started the engine.

He pulled onto the street and was on the two-lane highway in no time. Being in the camper lessened their chances of being spotted. Jamie relaxed as much as was possible given what was about to occur.

"When do you think Trent will get to Marie?" She was curious how long they'd have to wait around for him.

"He was hopping in his car as we spoke."

"Did Trent say how Jon—I mean—Vic is?"

Max shook his head. "I think he's leaving your friend's welfare up to the FBI. They have a lot to lose if anything happens to him."

"Good."

When they arrived at Hank's, there wasn't anyone in the lot, which made her feel better. In fact, the lights were once more off in the store.

"Hank must be eating dinner," Max said. He pulled out his phone.

"You don't need to disturb him just to hand off the disk, do you?"

He stroked her cheek. "You are a very considerate person,

but didn't you say you wanted some hair dye? Besides, Trent won't get here for another hour or more."

She cocked a brow. "You're right. You think the store will have what I want?"

"It might not be some fancy salon brand or one that has highlights and shit, but you'd be surprised what he carries."

"Sounds good."

A few minutes after Max dialed his friend, the lights clicked on in the store. Just as Max stepped from the car, his cell rang. He pulled open her door. "Hey, Trent. Yeah, we just pulled up. We'll be here." Max ended the call and helped her out. "That was Trent checking in. Go on inside. I want to look around."

Jamie knew better than to ask what he was looking for. She knew he wanted to check to see if those creeps had tracked them down. She couldn't be certain someone in the café hadn't sounded the alarm.

She stepped inside and liked that the bell above the door rang. Hank emerged from the back. "Where's Max?"

"Looking for bad guys."

Hank nodded and returned to the back room.

Before Max came back, Jamie decided to look for her dye. Halfway through her search, the front door opened, and she jumped at the sound of the bell. It had to be Max or a customer Max didn't feel was a threat.

"There you are," Max said, his nose and cheeks a bit red from the cold.

Her heart skipped a beat when he rounded the corner. "I'm presuming it's safe out there?"

"So far."

Way to keep me calm. She picked up a box of hair dye she thought would work. "When do you think these terrorists will know I don't have the drive anymore?"

"You mean when will it be safe to go home and walk the streets without looking over your shoulder?"

He'd nailed it. "Yes."

"Hard to say. How would they know you don't have the information they want? Trent's not going to take out an ad in the newspaper."

"Damn." Jamie held up the box of dye. "What do you think of this one? Color good?" She needed to focus on something other than the terror that was building in her chest again.

Max moved closer. Instead of focusing on what she had in her hand, his gaze remained on her face. "I like it."

She lowered her find. "You didn't even look." *Men.*

"Don't have to. I'll like whatever makes you feel good." As if to prove his point, he wrapped his arms around her waist, drew her near, and kissed her.

The contact started out soft, but then Max broke the seal. Instead of diving back in, he hovered his lips over hers, their breaths becoming one. His hand roamed down her jacket and over her ass, sending lust straight through her.

He squeezed one butt cheek. "You have too many clothes on."

Max pressed his hips forward and his hard cock was evident even through his jeans. "Are you kidding? You want to have sex in the store where anyone can come in? You know Trent will be here soon." Not to mention Hank was rummaging around the back for something.

"Not for a while. We have time. Besides, I locked the front door."

Holy shit. "Are you crazy?" Or was this the release they both needed?

Max didn't wait for her to respond. He unzipped her jacket, and then continued to undo her jeans.

"Max," she whispered. "What about Hank?"

Max extracted a condom from his wallet, shucked off his boots, and stepped out of his jeans. "Don't worry about him. He'll hear us making noise and know what we're doing. He knows better than to interfere."

Heat raced up her face. Jamie never thought she was that sheltered, but apparently she was. She'd never done anything close to this in her life. Some kind of moral code should be telling her to stop him, but her body wanted this worse than anything. Whether it was because of the stress or the possibility that their lives could end any minute, Jamie had never felt more alive. "What if Trent drives faster than we expected?"

"Hank will stall him."

Once more, Max seemed to have thought of everything. If he believed it was safe, then she'd go along. She, too, kicked off her shoes, and dragged down her jeans, leaving only her undies—and her jacket and top. Getting totally naked was a step she needed to think about. With his gaze glued to her face, Max back-pedaled her to the end of the aisle and leaned her against a small post.

He slid his hands up her back. "I want you real bad, honey. When I'm around you, I can't stop."

She loved his sentiment. "Ditto."

His lips descended once more. This time, they devoured each other as his fingers unhooked her bra. The second her breasts were freed, he dragged his palms to her front and flicked her nipples. His touch caused a chain reaction of lust to slam into her hard. She reached around his back, cupped his ass, and squeezed.

Footsteps neared, then stopped. "Oh, sorry." It was Hank. Damn.

As soon as she heard the back door close, Jamie blanked her mind to everything but the amazing sensations coursing through her. Their tongues dipped and swirled, sending sparks of need all over her body.

Max broke away. His golden brown eyes were dreamy and full of desire as his fingers slid to her panties. "Need you to open wide for me. I'm going to impale you. Then you'll be mine."

She'd be his? Or was he just saying that? *Stop thinking.* It didn't matter. His macho talk turned her on. "Okay."

That was a dumb thing to say, but no other words came to mind.

He yanked off her undies so quickly, acting as if he couldn't wait another moment. He then stepped out his briefs. Quicker than she could count to ten, his big dick was sheathed. Damn.

"I want you, honey."

Max lowered his head and dragged his palm down her belly. With a slowness meant to drive her crazy, he slipped a finger between her pussy lips.

Max smiled. "I see someone's excited." Her inner folds had become slick with need.

Before she could respond, he slanted his lips across hers. The moment another finger joined the first, she moaned, unable to keep quiet. When he drove both fingers into her pussy, she rose on her toes in search of more.

He leaned back then dropped to one knee. "Keep your legs open wide and don't move. Say nothing."

His command changed something inside her. Heat raced up her body, and he hadn't even licked her yet. Because she was now hot, Jamie slipped off her jacket and tossed it on the ground. Her fingers then found his scalp. She loved running her hands through his thick hair.

His tongue replaced his fingers and she almost climaxed right there. When he moved his mouth to her clit, she bit down on her lip to keep from coming. "Hurry."

Max flicked her tiny nub back and forth. With each swipe, he drove her closer to the edge of her climax. As amazing as this was, she needed his cock more. Jamie pressed her fingers against his head.

He abandoned his sexual assault and stood. "Need you." His voice was harder than gravel, and sexier than ever. Max lifted her up. "Wrap your legs around me and get ready for a ride neither of us will ever forget."

Her body melted at his words. She did as he asked. He placed her back against the pole for support and she clasped his strong shoulders. Digging her feet into his thighs, she lifted her hips, and Max pressed his big shaft against her opening.

He kissed her with tenderness then clasped her waist. In one smooth move, he thrust his dick upward, impaling her fully. The sensation defied description. Her walls clamped down on his cock and Max hissed. Jamie gurgled something unintelligent as his dick throbbed and pulsed inside her.

A few seconds elapsed before she was able to draw in a full breath. Staying fully sheathed inside her, he lifted off her shirt and bra with one hand while firmly supporting her butt. Max leaned over, and sucked hard on her nipple, electric sparks bursting to life. She thought she'd take off right then.

"Please, Max." Jamie rarely begged, but she prayed his need was as great as hers.

Max lifted his chin and took her mouth prisoner. He partly withdrew his cock then pistoned into her again. More sparks flew. Jamie squeezed her thighs tight and joined in the thrusting. Nothing mattered but each other. They kissed, rubbed, and fucked hard and furiously, until he drove into her so far she skyrocketed out of control.

"I'm coming," she yelled. The moment her screaming words registered, Jamie snapped her mouth shut, but failed to stop her orgasm from claiming her.

Max held her tight and pounded into her hard. He buried his face against her neck, and grunted as his hot cum exploded. Her eyes shut, she let him take her to a peaceful place where no sounds entered her brain. She'd been transported to heaven.

Only when he lifted her off his cock, did she remember where they were. Heat rushed up her face and she looked around. Thankfully, the store was as empty as when they'd arrived.

Max grinned as if he could read every expression on her face. "Be right back." He pulled off the condom then slipped on his briefs with one hand. When he jogged down the aisle, she couldn't believe he was in plain view of the outside world.

While she waited for him to return, she put on her bra and slipped into her shirt. Had she really made love in the aisle of a store?

Apparently.

Max returned quickly with a towel and wiped her clean. Seconds later they were fully dressed. Other than Hank, no one would ever know what a marvelously mind-altering experience had occurred in aisle three. In those few minutes, domestic terrorists had ceased to exist. For that, she'd be eternally grateful to Max.

He retrieved a few dollars out of his pocket and handed her the money. "Why don't you pay for your hair dye while I wait for Trent by the door?" He lifted her chin. "While I believe it's safe, can you stay inside? Please?"

He acted like she was in the habit of disobeying him. "I said I would." Besides, it was cold outside.

✧ ✧ ✧

Max needed to have his head examined. What had he been thinking having sex when he was expecting Trent to arrive any minute? Thank God, Jamie seemed to enjoy their incredible encounter. If their escapade took the edge off this bad situation, then it was worth it.

He kept reminding himself he needed to keep away from her until this mess was over, but every time a situation presented itself, he'd tossed caution to the wind.

Right before they'd made love, he'd placed his gun on a shelf at the end of the aisle in case he'd needed it. He never would have put Jamie in real danger. It was just his heart that might break when this was all over.

Christ. They'd never spoken of a possible future. He couldn't even remember if she said she liked him. The fact she trusted him, however, boded well for them.

Max never thought he'd even consider having a permanent relationship again, but with Jamie it seemed right.

Headlights pierced the darkness, cutting off his musings, and a car turned off the main road. It was hard to miss the red Jeep with the rack on top. It was Trent's vehicle. Max relaxed a bit.

He jammed his hand in his pocket, grabbed the flash drive, and stepped outside. This stupid looking toy had caused so much harm. He'd be glad when the FBI had it. Let them deal with these crazies.

I don't really believe that.

Max wanted to be part of the capture. Needed to bring down these men, if only to see the defeat in their eyes. They'd caused enough destruction.

Trent pulled in, parked next to Edith, and jumped out. "Where's Jamie?" He jogged up to Max.

"Inside. I want to keep her safe." Max handed him the drive. "Take care of this. Enough people have died."

"What's on it?"

When Max had called Trent, he didn't want to say anything over the phone. Max detailed the list of names and the needed supplies, along with a list of seat numbers. "The items look like materials to make a bomb. It's possible the seat number refers to where to place the charges." He pulled out the printed copies and handed them to Trent.

Trent stuffed the flash drive in his pocket and studied both sheets. "Christ. You have any idea what they're targeting?"

"No. I can think of a lot of places with seat locations, though." Max slipped the sheets from Trent's fingers. "Look at this. See down here? This looks like a possible date. And this could be a signature of the head man."

Trent's brows rose. "CF? Did that match any of the names on the list?" Max didn't like the tentative tone to his friend's voice.

"No, though we can't be positive it is a signature. You have someone in mind?" There were a lot of shady people in Rock Hard. Trent would know more of them than Max would.

Trent waved a dismissive hand. "No, though it's ironic that Chuck Forbes has the initials CF."

Max stilled. "You think our trusty FBI man is a double agent?"

"No. Dan asked the mayor to check if Forbes was on the up and up. The mayor called in a few favors. The FBI vouched for their agent. To be sure, one of the crime scene techs sent in a photo of the guy. Feds confirmed Chuck was their man. A high source said he's one of their best agents."

"Good. If he's that smart, he'll be able to make sense of this." Max folded the two sheets of paper and stuffed them back in his pocket.

"I'm thinking CF could either be another man's name or the initials of the target."

Max never liked to make assumptions. "I agree, but which one?"

"Let's hope Forbes can tell us." Trent pressed a palm to Max's shoulder. "Times a wastin'. Need to get this back to Rock Hard. Let's hope the Feds can do their magic."

Trent headed back to his Jeep. Max wanted to get inside and tell Jamie the transfer was complete. Just as he reached the door, a shuffle sounded behind him, followed by the sound of bone meeting flesh. Max drew his weapon and spun around. Trent was on the ground, out cold, his face bloodied. Adrenaline surged through Max.

"Trent!" Max shouted, panic ripping through him.

Keeping his eyes on the two men racing away, Max charged toward his friend. Fuck. Max didn't spot a getaway car, not could he hear a motor turning over. They must have hidden their car. The man in the rear stopped, turned back around, and fired at Max.

Oh, shit.

Chapter Twenty-Five

The front pane of the storefront shattered.

Jamie!

Max was torn. He wanted to check on her. He needed to help Trent, but he also couldn't let these bastards get away. Jamie had promised him she'd hide if anything happened. When he left her, she was on the west side of the store. Hank would see to it that she stayed safe.

Feet pounded on the road. His police training kicked into gear.

"Stop!" Max called after them, knowing his command wouldn't be obeyed.

Another shot fired. Max crouched down, aimed at the men who'd just tried to kill him, and pulled the trigger. The man stumbled, grunted, and fell.

One down, one to go.

Max rose, and when he returned to Trent, his friend had come to. He lifted up on his elbows, shaking his head, if he was trying to figure out what happened. Blood stained his neck, and his cheek was bright red.

Max leaned over him, his heart pounding. "You okay?"

"Yes. Go," Trent said, pain lacing his voice. He dragged a hand over his neck. When he checked the damage, his palm was covered in blood. Fuck. "The man. He got the drive."

"Damn."

Trent would live, and as much as Max wanted to stay and help his friend, many lives were at stake. Max needed to stop the thief. The man pounded his way down the road. How far he planned to run was anyone's guess, but no matter what, Max wouldn't let him get away.

If the terrorist reached his vehicle and was able to drive off, Max would never catch him. Once the terrorist cell learned Max had killed one of their own, they'd want retribution. He couldn't let that happen. He'd give his life before he let anyone near Jamie.

Dodging and weaving to lessen the chance of getting shot, Max chased after the man. The guy slowed, turned, and lifted his weapon. He fired. A second later a deep pain seared Max's thigh. *No!* He stumbled, but managed to stay upright.

Don't stop. Keep going.

Warm blood soaked his pants, both in the front and back of his thigh, but the adrenaline kept much of the pain at bay. The man took off again—and vanished just as quickly. Max kept going, keeping low.

Where the hell was he? Between the quarter moon and the lights from Hank's store, Max could detect shadows, but not much else. Nothing moved, not even the leaves. It was as if he'd stepped into a movie theater and someone had punched pause.

Then snow crunched. The man was on the move again. Max changed directions, heading toward the sound. Shit. He'd so focused on locating the man that Max almost tripped over the person he'd shot.

To make sure the criminal on the ground wouldn't come to and starting firing, Max took a knee and felt for the man's pulse. *Dead.* Jesus. Max had hoped to get some information out of him—like the name of the target. Now that wouldn't happen.

Max stayed on his knee to conserve his energy, his hand over his wound. He scanned the area in front of him. People didn't disappear. The terrorist must be hiding. Waiting.

But where?

He needed to figure out his next move. Max's leg burned, and it became harder to ignore the throbbing pain.

Before he'd come up with a concrete plan, an engine roared to life, jacking Max's senses into overdrive. The sound came from about a hundred feet away. Max jumped up, and charged toward him, trying to force the sharp ache out of his mind. With each step his limp became more severe, and he tripped. His knees smashed to the ground. The snow cushioned part of the fall.

Get. Up.

For Jamie, he had to stop him.

Seconds later, the getaway vehicle bounced over the uneven ground toward the pavement. This was it. Max's last chance. "I want you, motherfucker."

He rose to his feet. Putting his weight on his good leg, he kept his arm steady, inhaled, and pulled the trigger. Glass shattered. He shot again. And again. Until he had one bullet remaining.

The horn sounded, and the car slowed. It was as if the movie had started up again, only this time in slow motion. The car veered to the left, hit the slippery slope, and skidded down the embankment, heading straight toward a tree. The impact sounded more like a thud than a crash.

Steam sizzled out of the engine, and relief helped spur Max on. This vehicle wasn't going anywhere, but Max had to make sure the driver wasn't either.

Moving as fast as his body would let him, he made his way to the vehicle, his hand on his bloodied thigh. Keeping his weapon aimed at the where the driver's head should be, Max yanked open the door and swallowed a groan as pain rushed up his body.

Stay awake.

The driver's head was on the wheel, the airbag deflated. Max's aim had hit its mark. The man had two bullets in his body—one at his shoulder and the other a few inches closer to center. The man groaned. Good. Max needed him alive.

Spotting a weapon on the passenger seat, Max quickly pulled the driver from the car, biting back the pain.

"Watch it. I'm shot, you fucker."

"Too bad." Max worked hard to sound gruff. He didn't need this ass to know he'd been shot, too.

Keeping his gun aimed at the possible terrorist, Max pushed him toward the store. When they reached the parking lot, Trent was gone. Max let go of his prisoner, and the man dropped to his knees. The shooter's upper back was covered in blood. As much as Max wanted to beat the location of the intended target out of the man, he needed to call for help more.

For the man. For himself.

"Hank!" Max shouted using what little energy he had left. With the front door shattered, Hank should be able to hear him.

His friend rushed outside, gun in hand. "Holy shit, man. What happened to you?"

"Don't worry about me. Call Sheriff Duncan. Got one man dead 'bout a hundred feet down the road."

Max waved his gun and faced the man. "You're under arrest for assaulting an officer, stealing government property, and for the attempted murder of … me." It didn't matter the flash drive came from the terrorists in the first place.

"Fuck you."

Max looked over at Hank. "Jamie okay?" His vision suddenly blurred, and his mind fogged.

"She's safe, but I imagine is scared to death." Hank stepped toward Max. "You need to get inside. I'll call the sheriff and wait for him."

"No. I can—"

Before he could finish his sentence, Max's knees buckled,

and he crashed to the graveled lot. His vision turned black.

✧ ✧ ✧

At the sound of gunshots, Jamie had frozen. Before she could move to see if Max was okay, the glass on the front door came crashing down. Scared out of her mind, she'd dropped to her knees between the aisles and covered her head. Chills had raced up her body, and her heart banged against her ribs.

After what seemed like ten more shots, silence filled the air, her mind jumping to every bad conclusion. She knew that if anything happened to Max, she'd crack. The man had claimed her heart—totally, completely. When she'd fallen in love with him, she couldn't say. All she knew was that she had.

Footsteps sounded a minute later, and Trent had staggered in. Hank raced up to him, grabbed a hold of the injured man and warned her to stay still. Not understanding what was happening outside, she followed his instruction. It was only when she'd heard Max call for Hank that she began to breathe again.

Because she hadn't been sure if it was safe to leave her spot, she'd remained huddled near the loaves of bread and waited. Hank ran past her, a gun in his hand.

When she heard Max tell Hank to call the sheriff, she shot to her feet. Miraculously, she had the strength to make it to the end of the aisle and peek out. Oh, my God. Max was on the ground and Hank was standing over him, a phone against his ear.

Trent appeared at the end of the aisle and looked over at her. His neck was caked in blood, but he didn't seem to be bleeding. His eye was swollen shut and his lip cut, but he was alert.

"Do you know what happened?" From where he stood, he would have been able to see the exchange outside.

"No, but we better get the first aid kit. It's on the counter." Glass crunched. Trent was going out to help.

Happy to be useful, she rushed toward the back of the store.

She hoped they'd called 911, though she had no idea where the nearest hospital or fire station might be.

With bandages in hand, she ran outside. Cold air blasted her, but she couldn't worry about freezing to death right now.

Trent drew his weapon and aimed at the other man on the ground.

"I'll get something to secure this fucker," Hank said. He rushed back inside.

Jamie's gaze shot to Max. Oh, no. His thigh was spurting blood. The bullet must have nicked an artery. Her pulse pounded. If she couldn't stop the bleeding soon, he'd die.

Don't fall apart on him now.

She was trained for this. Then why were her fingers trembling?

Jamie dropped down next to him. The rough gravel bit into her knees. "Max?" He didn't respond. She pinched his shoulder, trying to rouse him. He was going into volume shock. "Max?"

He groaned. Damn. Grabbing a handful of gauze pads, she opened the packages then placed them on top as well as underneath his thigh. The through and through was on the outer edge of his leg. She applied pressure and prayed.

Hank returned and quickly used tie wraps to secure the downed man.

"Watch it, fucker." He glanced at her. "I'm shot, too. Hey chickie. When you're done with him, come help me."

She didn't answer. "Hank did you call for an ambulance. Max really needs help."

"Called for two. Sheriff should be here any minute to take this scum off our hands."

The captive let out a series of expletives, but it was nothing she hadn't heard before.

"How close is the nearest hospital?" Max was losing blood fast.

"Less than ten minutes away."

Jamie nodded. She lifted the pad on Max's thigh, but she didn't seem able to slow the flow.

"Jamie?" Max opened his eyes and tried to smile, but his lips wavered.

"I'm here. You're going to be okay. Help is on the way."

He lifted up on his elbows and grunted. "I'm good."

"You are not good." Stubborn man. "You're bleeding badly."

With a herculean effort, Max sat up. He glanced down at her hand holding the pad on his upper thigh. He swatted her arm away and lifted the bloody bandage. "Hmm. Just a scratch." He looked up at Hank, barely able to lift his eyelids. "Where's the sheriff?"

"He's coming."

"Hold this and apply pressure," she said to Max. With her free hand she grabbed the roll of tape, and wound it around his leg.

Max looked at Jamie. "Where's your coat? You'll… get c…cold." It was as if Max was having a hard time finding the right words. This wasn't good.

"I'm fine."

Flashing lights and a sudden siren made her jump. A Sheriff's vehicle pulled to a stop in the lot, and a tall, thin man eased out of the driver's side while a second man exited the passenger side.

They both trotted over. Trent explained who the criminal was, but Max interrupted. "Need to… frisk him for the stolen property," Max's words came out slurred.

"I didn't steal nothing."

The sheriff searched the man, but came up empty handed.

"Then his partner has it," Trent said.

The man still didn't respond. More sirens sounded in the background. Thank God the ambulance was here.

A minute later, two ambulances skidded into the lot. Paramedics jumped out, pulled out a stretcher, and rushed over. Jamie relayed what had happened, despite Max complaining the whole way.

She stood back and let the emergency team do their job. She then joined Hank. "I want to follow Max to the hospital."

Hank withdrew the keys to Max's SUV. "His car will get you there faster. Go north on the main road here. As soon as you cross US 2, take a right on Sunnyview road. Can't miss it."

"You need the keys to Edith." She ran up to ambulance. "Max. We need Hank's keys."

Max pressed his lips together, dug into his pocket, and handed them to one of EMTs who gave them to her. "We need to take him, ma'am."

Her heart ached. Max was strong. He would make it.

Once the second ambulance loaded the prisoner, the deputy hopped in back. Max's ambulance drove off, followed by the second one.

Jamie strode up to Max's friend. "Trent you need someone to look at your injuries."

"I'm good."

What was up with all this macho shit? "Don't be silly."

"Hey, Sheriff. We need to find that drive," Trent said.

They headed down the road in the direction of the headlights that were illuminating part of the forest.

"Trent needs medical help, too," she told Hank. "I'm not leaving without him."

"He'll be back soon."

Jamie rushed inside to grab her coat and purse then waited by the broken door until they returned.

The sheriff stepped over to his car, and Trent walked up to her. "I'm going to follow you to the hospital in Kalispell. I want to be there for Max," he said.

Trent was in no shape to be behind the wheel. "How about I drive? I want the company." That wasn't entirely true, but Trent seemed as pigheaded as Max.

"Give me a sec, then."

She bet he wouldn't have given in so easily if he'd been able to see out of both eyes. He stepped next to his Jeep, squatted down in front, and ran his fingers under the front bumper. He moved to the back, and repeated the check.

"Fuckers." He stood, dropped something on the ground, and smashed it with the heel of his boot. Trent returned to her. "Those assholes must have been watching me. They put a tracking device on my car. That was how come I didn't see them follow me."

She placed a hand on his arm. "It's not your fault."

"Like hell it isn't."

It was too late now to be doling out blame. "There's nothing you can do. Come on. We need to get to the hospital."

Her stomach wouldn't stop churning. If these two found them, how many more would learn of their location? The men's superiors would surely expect a call saying the drive had been secured. Damn. When was this going to end?

Chapter Twenty-Six

It took Jamie twenty minutes to get to the hospital. After Trent showed the ward clerk his badge, the woman called someone to check on Max's status. Sympathy filled her face. "He's being prepped for surgery now."

Jamie hoped they could repair the damaged artery in time.

A nurse came up to Trent and placed a hand on his arm. "Sir, how about I take a look at that neck and lip?" She ran her gaze around his face.

"I'm good."

Men. "Trent. Please," Jamie pleaded. "That cut on your neck could get infected, as could your lip. As long as we're waiting, you might as well let her tend to you."

He let out an exasperated sigh. "Fine." He slipped his hand in his pocket and faced Jamie. "When Agent Forbes gets here, give him this. Tell him about the other man who's at the hospital."

She took the flash drive disguised as a yellow toy and deposited it in her pocket. She couldn't wait to turn it over to the authorities. She wasn't so naïve to think she'd suddenly be out of danger. Far from it. With one of their men dead, and another injured, the terrorist cell might come after her with renewed vengeance.

"I'm coming with you." She decided it might not be safe

being in the waiting room herself.

He nodded. "You're right. Guess my brains got scrambled."

The nurse escorted Trent inside, and Jamie followed. She took the seat in the corner of the exam room. Now that Max was in good hands, and Trent was being taken care of, exhaustion finally claimed her. Her nerves had been taut the entire drive up.

Jamie closed her eyes and couldn't help but relive the shots over and over again. Each time a gun had fired, her pulse skyrocketed. Poor Max. She still couldn't believe he'd put himself in that kind of danger. What had he been thinking running after two armed men? It didn't matter that he had a weapon, too. What if he'd been killed?

She opened her eyes to stop the nightmare. Max had been a real hero. In truth, if he hadn't stopped those men, the FBI might not have learned some of the names of the terrorists until it was too late.

On the drive up here, Trent had relayed what he remembered. Max was about to go into the store when a man came out of nowhere, drew a knife blade across Trent's throat, and then smashed his elbow into his face. Trent said it had happened so fast, he didn't have time to react. He was lucky he hadn't been hurt worse.

Jaime checked the time. "When did you call Agent Forbes?"

"Over an hour and a half ago."

He'd be here shortly. "Maybe I should wait for him in the other room."

Trent's jaw hardened. "No." He turned to the nurse. "You almost done?"

The nurse had placed a few stitches above his brow and was now tending to his lip.

"Just about," the nurse said.

Max still had the paper copy of what was on the file. Until the agent could find a computer, he'd have to be satisfied with her memory, which at the moment was having a hard time staying focused.

"All finished." The nurse stepped back.

Trent got up from the exam table. "Thanks."

After he filled out some paperwork, they returned to the waiting room. Even though Trent was a cop, Jamie scanned the waiting room. There were only three other people waiting. One was a mother and her young son, and the other was an older man who appeared asleep. None were males in their twenties or thirties, but she wouldn't discount these three as being associated with terrorists. At this point, she might question her own mother.

Trent stretched out his legs and winced, as if more than just his head had received a pummeling. "So you and Max are tight?" he asked.

Jamie hadn't expected that question. She wasn't even sure what she should say. Trent might be a good friend, but she wasn't about to tell him that she was falling in love with Max. She hadn't even told Max! "I like him."

He cocked a brow. "Just *like*? I know my buddy must be crazy about you."

That caught her interest. Or was he trying to distract her? "Why do you say that? Did he tell you something?" A vein throbbed next to her eye. The stress was getting to her.

"Didn't have to. Every year, since the beginning of time, Max and I always go to the Monster Truck Rally at the County Fairgrounds. This year, he asked you instead."

Her heart raced. She had no idea that the event was so special to him. "You could come with us."

Trent laughed, then immediately sobered. He placed a hand over his lip. "Shouldn't do that."

"Sorry." Something Trent said rang a bell. "Is the rally always at the County Fairgrounds?"

"Yes."

She'd never been. "Is it stadium seating there?" When she'd gone to one of the Monster Truck events in California, it had been held at a large football stadium.

He twisted toward her. "Yes. What are you getting at?"

"CF could stand for County Fairgrounds."

His eyes widened. "Oh, fuck. Max showed me the initials, but I thought it was a signature. There was a date at the bottom of the paper. The rally is May 3rd. That must be it."

Excitement coursed through her. "We need to tell Forbes."

He slightly shook his head. "Max never told me you had the ability to use mental telepathy. After the stunt *they* pulled bugging my car, I'm not trusting my phone. They probably listened in when Max told me he had the drive."

"Right. I wasn't thinking. So what happens now?" She'd left her burn phone in Hank's van. Damn.

"That's up to Forbes." Trent sat up, and looked toward the door then back again, acting as if it wasn't safe to be talking about this. "So tell me about yourself," he said.

While they waited for Forbes, Jamie gave Trent a sanitized version of her life. Before she finished, Forbes arrived. But he wasn't alone. With him were three men dressed in suits. She would have thought they'd have tried to blend in. Both she and Trent jumped up.

Forbes approached. "How's Max?" He sounded concerned.

"In surgery."

The agent raised his brows. "Perhaps you both would like to get some fresh air."

Trent nodded. Jamie pulled on her coat and followed the agent outside. She understood it wouldn't be wise to hand off the flash drive in plain sight.

Once they were away from the entrance, she handed him the information.

"Do you know what's on it?" Agent Forbes asked. "Max didn't say."

Jamie detailed the list, the items, the seat numbers, and her guess what it all meant.

Forbes whistled. "This is huge. I'll get on this right away. Knowing some of the identities should make it easier to find them and take them down."

Max would be so disappointed not to have a hand in the final showdown. "I'll let Max know."

Forbes nodded. "I'm going to station one of my men outside his room."

He didn't have to tell her why. There were more terrorists than the two Max had stopped. "Thank you. What about the man Max injured?" She assumed Trent had told him about him.

"My men are checking on him now. Once he's stable, we'll be speaking with him."

There wasn't much else to say. "Thank you."

Trent turned to her. "Will you be okay by yourself?"

She assumed that meant he would be leaving. "I'm good. The FBI has my back."

"I know Max well. Whatever you do, don't let him out of here until the doctor releases him."

She didn't like how serious he'd become. "You think Max would try to leave?" As soon as she said the words, she realized her mistake. "Never mind. He's more stubborn than you are."

He chuckled. "Take good care of him. He needs you." Trent hugged her goodbye. He turned to Agent Forbes. "Can I trouble you for a ride back to Marie?"

"Sure. I'll have one of my agents stay with Ms. Henderson."

"I appreciate it."

Jamie rushed back inside to warmth. The agent was standing close to the entrance, his back against the wall.

Close to an hour later, a doctor came through the door. "Ms. Henderson?"

She jumped up. "Yes?"

His face remained inscrutable, but she didn't expect anything different. "Your friend, Max, is in recovery now. We had to repair an artery, but everything looks good. Nothing vital was hit."

"Thank God. When can I see him?"

"He'll be moved to the surgical wing in about an hour. The nurse will let you know when you can see him."

Two hours later, Jamie was told she could visit Max. The agent with her nodded, but he didn't move. Apparently, he'd be keeping watch at this end. When she reached Max's room, another agent who'd come with Forbes was standing guard. He pushed open the door and she entered.

Jamie pulled up a chair and picked up Max's hand. It was cold.

He opened his eyes. "Hey."

His face was pale, but otherwise, he looked good. Right now, she'd take anything other than dead. "How are you feeling?"

"Groggy." He glanced down at his wound. "Am I going to live?" He smiled.

"Yes, but you'll have to rest for a couple of days." She wanted to kiss every inch of his body, but she didn't want him to get excited and move about.

"Not going to happen. I need to speak with Forbes."

The anesthesia must be messing with his head. "I already gave him the drive."

"He showed up already?"

Jamie squeezed his hand. "You were in surgery for hours. Trent went back with Forbes." She still didn't think Trent should be driving, though his eye looked less swollen when he left.

"What did Forbes say? Did he know what CF meant?"

"We didn't ask him. Trent and I think we figured it out. Mr. FBI Man was very impressed with all that you'd done."

"You figured it out?"

He didn't seem to care about the accolade. She reminded him that the Monster Truck Rally was being held at the Country

Fairgrounds on May 3rd. "CF could stand for County Fairgrounds. The date matches, too."

"I'll be damned. The stadium will be packed. If they'd succeeded, close to a thousand people could have died."

It would have been a huge tragedy. "Forbes said that with the list of names, he and his men should be able to locate the terrorist cell quickly."

"I need to go." Max unhooked the IV from the port in his arm and sat up. He looked around. "Where are my clothes?"

The man must be delusional. "You aren't going anywhere, buster."

"Yes, I am. Honey. Listen. I don't care if the FBI said they were taking over my case. It's still my case. I want to see this through to the end."

She could let him get out of bed and attempt to find his clothes that weren't there, but all the movement might reopen his wound. "Not only won't I give you the keys to the car, or drive you anywhere, there's an FBI agent guarding the door that won't let you out of here. As much as I like it when you go all heroic on me, I need you to get better." Jamie hooked up the IV again.

"Well, damn."

✧ ✧ ✧

Max was about to climb the walls. Three days was too long to lie in a hospital bed. As far as he was concerned, his injury looked pretty much healed. He might limp a bit, but now he had matching wounds. Once from the bullet eleven years ago, now this one on the other leg.

Stupid doctor acted like he needed Max able to run a marathon before signing the release papers. If Max had been able to explain the real reason for wanting to get out of there, he bet the doctor would have sent him on his way. Too bad Max couldn't blurt out that he had to help the FBI take down a bunch of terrorists.

It wasn't all bad, though. He got be with Jamie. Wonderful Jaime. She'd been incredibly patient and caring, if not rather stubborn. He'd been quite capable of getting out of bed by himself to go to the bathroom, but she'd insisted on wrapping an arm around his waist to make sure he didn't fall.

As much as he liked having her around, he could see it was taking a toll on her, too. Agent Forbes had requested a female agent from a local field office to stay with Jamie at a nearby hotel each night. One afternoon, when Jamie was with him, the agent had purchased clothes for her. Max liked how her eyes had lit up when she saw them.

After a bit of arguing, he convinced Jamie to ask to borrow the agent's phone. It would be secure. Max didn't want to be kept in the dark any longer. Actually, he wanted to know if when he got out, whether he could help with taking down the cell.

Max called Dan, but when he asked him about the progress, his former boss acted rather strange. "I haven't heard. You know the FBI. They keep a tight lid on things."

"I thought Forbes was going to keep you in the loop. Let you help."

"He did."

Max knew Dan well. "What aren't you telling me?" Max had enough of this shit. He was ready to knock the agent outside over the head and leave.

"Forbes is on the other line. I gotta take this. Talk to you soon." He then had the balls to hang up.

Jamie looked at him with eagerness. "So? What did Dan say?"

Poor Jamie. All Max wanted to do was wash away her pain. She was forced into seclusion until these men were brought to justice. "He didn't know anything, but I don't believe him."

She slumped back in her seat. A knock sounded on the door

and they both turned. The agent never knocked, nor did the nurses. Trent walked in, looking almost as good as new. A nice change to the last time Max had seen his friend on the ground.

"What's up, dude?" Trent said with a smile.

"Nice of you to stop by. You look like shit, by the way." Max had to say something.

Trent's smile didn't diminish. He pulled up a second chair. "I have some good news."

Max waited for him to spill it, but he kept looking between the two of them. "What is it? Tell us."

Chapter Twenty-Seven

"For starters, you both are being heralded as heroes." Trent brushed his knuckles across his chest. "I, also, was given kudos for my role in taking down the terrorist cell."

Jamie sat there stunned for a minute. "Taking them down? They've been arrested?"

"They have. After an intricately planned operation, the FBI, in conjunction with the fabulous RHPD, captured all those responsible for the attempt to bomb the Monster Truck Rally."

"Oh, thank God." She sagged in relief. The rally was scheduled for this weekend, and she feared the FBI wouldn't be able to stop them in time.

Trent nodded. "It will continue as scheduled."

Jamie glanced over at Max. She expected to see frustration written all over his face. Instead, he was smiling. She didn't get it. "I thought you'd be upset that you didn't get to charge in on your white stead and shoot everyone one of the bastards."

He and Trent burst out laughing. "That would have been nice, but I'm good, knowing you'll be safe."

"Safe. I'd forgotten what that word meant."

"Max," Trent said, "guess who the kingpin was."

Max wasn't always the most patient man when it came to guessing games. His furrowed brows implied that now wasn't the time either. "Who?"

"Ed Hanson."

The name didn't sound familiar. "Who's that?" she asked.

Max answered. "The man who owned the burned warehouse. That's quite interesting."

Her wheels spun. "Do you think Vic suspected him and that was why he planted himself in front of the abandoned building each day?"

"That makes sense," Trent said.

The room door opened, and Max's doctor strode in, clipboard in hand. Half a dozen nurses had already been in to day to check on Max. The fact that several repeated the same tests, Jamie suspected they just wanted to take another look at their hot charge.

The doctor set down his clipboard, and checked Max's wound. "Excellent. You're healing nicely. You ready to go home, Mr. Gruden?"

"Hell, ya."

"Take it easy for a few days. I'll send up a wheelchair then you can be on your way."

"Thank you."

Because Max's damaged jeans were been beyond repair, Jamie had asked the female FBI agent to purchase him a new pair.

Trent slapped his thighs. "I'll leave you two lovebirds. I need to get back to Rock Hard. Wanted to be the one to share the good news."

Max swung his legs over the side of the bed. "Appreciate it."

Max got dressed, looking almost like his old self.

As soon as the nurse arrived to take Max down, Jamie hustled out to get the car. She wanted to be waiting by the entrance when he came out. Being outside without worry was exhilarating, but she couldn't help but glance around a few times to check for more black vans.

When she drove up to the entrance, Max was already waiting. He pulled open the driver's side door. "I'll drive."

The man was crazy. "I'm good."

"Jamie."

They only needed to go back to Marie. He'd be good for that long. She slid across the bench seat.

He closed the door and put the car in gear. "I know you'll probably ask that we head back to Rock Hard so you can go to work tomorrow, but how about we take a few days at the cabin and just enjoy each other. Would you like that?"

Would she ever. "Now that is the best idea you've ever had."

✧ ✧ ✧

Jamie wouldn't let him do anything the first two days, and it drove him crazy. Even when Max had to go outside to get more wood for the stove, she'd fussed. Max had enough.

"Jamie. Please come here." She was in the kitchen making dinner.

She rushed up to him. "Is something wrong?"

"As a matter of fact, yes." Her gaze shot straight to his leg. He exaggerated his limp and sat on the couch. "Can you look at my leg?"

"Of course." She dropped down next to him.

At least she didn't insist on helping him off with his boots. Once he divested himself of those, he slid off his jeans. He had a raging hard-on, and if he didn't get some relief soon, he was going to burst. He couldn't take being around her any longer. He had to make love with her.

"I have a serious problem."

She burst out laughing. "So I can see."

"How about you coming into the bedroom and help me relieve this ache?"

"Only if you let me ride you."

They discussed that if he was on top, it might put too much pressure on his leg. He disagreed, but she was the medical professional. "Deal."

They both stood. To prove he was good as new, he faced her, and lifted her over his shoulder in a fireman's hold.

"Max! Put me down. You'll hurt yourself."

She didn't weigh enough to do any damage. "Won't happen. You're mine, and I'm going to prove it to you."

She giggled. He entered his bedroom and set her down. Just looking at her made his blood run hot. "I want you naked."

"Yes, sir." Her fingers shot to the buttons on her blouse.

He swatted them away. "I meant, I'm going to get you naked. Just stand there." Max was ready. He wanted to tear her clothes from her body, but then he'd miss savoring every inch of her. After opening the front, he slipped the material off her shoulders. Jamie was delicate, sweet, and divine. "What a shame that bra has to come off, but if I don't feast on your tits, I might die."

"You're silly."

He grinned. "We'll see if what I do feels silly to you." Max unhooked the back and lowered the straps an inch at a time. It was like Christmas all over again. "So pretty."

Jaime drew in a large breath as he lowered his head and licked one nipple then the other. He alternated between them until her tiny nubs were wet and taut. As much as he wanted to tease her mercilessly, he needed to taste the rest of her. Max lifted her up and placed her on the bed. First came her shoes, and then her pants.

Max straddled her and tossed off his shirt. He needed to remove her panties, so he could drive her crazy.

"You promised." Jamie scooted back on her elbows. "You said you'd lie down and let me get on top, remember?"

"I'm not going to hurt my leg. I've been walking fine."

"Max Gruden." Her attempt at a stern face had him smiling.

"Fine. What the lady wants, the lady shall get. At least temporarily."

She huffed. Max did as he'd promised. Stretching out his legs, he rolled on his back and rested his head on his bent arms. "I am now yours. Have at me."

When she giggled, he completely lost his heart. Again.

✧ ✧ ✧

Jamie placed her palm on his flat abs and lightly brushed her hand up and down his faint treasure trail. She loved the peaks and valleys of his hard muscles, along with the way his hair tickled her hand. The three times they'd made love, they'd been too desperate to really explore what each other had to offer. This time, she wanted to touch and lick his delicious body until he burst—well, until he almost burst.

Once up on her knees, she leaned over and dragged her tongue from his belly button downward. As she neared his erect cock, she diverted the path to the side.

"You missed."

He was grasping the sheets as if he wanted to touch her. Too bad. She was in control right now. "Lift up your hips."

He obeyed, and she dragged down his briefs and tossed them behind her. Her pulse sputtered at his size. She placed her mouth within a hair's breath of his skin and blew across his entire length.

"You're asking for it, honey."

Not wanting him to take over because she was teasing him too much, she flicked the tip of her tongue along the throbbing vein to give him some satisfaction.

"Suck. On. Him." Max's plea came out garbled.

He didn't sound all that upset, but from set of his firmed lips, he was working hard to hold it together.

"Now look who's easy." He was all man, so full of steely

resolve. She inhaled deeply, loving the way he smelled—fresh and minty.

Jamie lifted his cock and placed the mushroom-shaped head in her mouth. Max groaned the moment her lips touched his skin. He always drove her crazy with his tongue, and she wanted to repay him.

She eased downward. His fingers plowed through her hair. The deeper she went, the tighter his hold. With her other hand she pumped her fist at the same time she swirled her tongue around his length.

"Deeper."

Jamie wanted to please him. She tried to take in more of him, but she gagged and had to withdraw. Not one to give up, she inhaled and tried again. This time, she was able to go farther.

In a flash, she was flat on her back. "Two can play at torturing each other."

"Your leg!"

"It's fine. I'm on my stomach. No pressure."

She supposed since he'd been walking without much of a limp that he could support himself. Still, she wanted to ride him.

Max spread her legs wide and slid between them. Excitement slickened her. She thought he'd lick her pussy, but instead he tongued her inner thighs, going over and over the same spot until the tension grew so high, she dug her nails into his skin.

"Higher." It had come out as a command, but Max wasn't the type to follow her request unless he wanted to.

"Soon."

He wedged his shoulders between her thighs and opened her pussy lips with his thumbs. He inhaled deeply. "Love your honeyed scent. I can't get enough."

His head dipped, and when he nibbled on the hood of her clit, sparks of need jumped up her body. Pleasure threatened to tip her over the edge. No way, she'd come first, but God it was hard not to.

"Kiss me." She had to draw him away from licking her clit, or she'd go off like a ten-megaton bomb.

Using his elbows, Max looked like a lion on the prowl as he crawled over her. When his lips were lined up with hers, he cupped her cheeks and nipped her bottom lip. That didn't count as a real kiss, but it twisted her insides and heated her to the core nonetheless. The man could do things to her body that should be illegal.

Jamie opened her mouth in invitation and he finally obliged. The moment their tongues touched, they both groaned. She clasped his shoulders then dragged her hands down his back, loving how his corded muscles flexed and rolled with every movement. Max was powerful, demanding, and oh, so sexy.

Once they broke from the kiss, she dragged air into her lungs. Max slid lower and licked her taut nipple. Shimmers of delight rippled over her body, and she arched her back for more, desiring a bit of pain to feel alive. Max obliged by nabbing the engorged tip between his teeth and tugging with the right amount of pressure. Heaven. But with heaven, came that ever-nearing orgasm.

"Yes!" *Don't come. Not yet.*

He slid his hand down her body and pressed a finger into her wet opening. Oh, my God. She let out a gurgled response. Her pussy walls were slightly swollen, making his touch a powerful aphrodisiac.

When he curled his finger and hit her sweet spot, Jamie lost it. Her climax slammed into her so hard, she bucked and gasped for breath. Her fingers dug into his scalp and she let out a cry as waves of ecstasy slammed into her. Her vision turned dark. When she was with Max, she was weak, unable to keep her emotions from overflowing.

Max rolled off her. She didn't dare open her eyes, not wanting to see any disappointment on his face. The drawer slid open and foil ripped. She tore open her eyes, and when Max met her gaze, he grinned.

"I can't help myself. I have to have you."

Jamie sat up and held out her hand. "My turn."

Indecision crossed her face. "Be quick."

"Very quick. Please get on your back." He had promised.

Max grinned and assumed the position. She hadn't been sure he would let her take the lead. Using her teeth, she finally got the damned foil package opened. She placed the condom on tip on his cock and eased it forward. She took her time, wanting to keep the sides even. This was harder than it looked.

When he was properly sheathed, she sat back on her haunches. "Done."

"Ride me, lady. Ride me as hard as you want."

Those words were music to her ears. Before she obeyed, she kissed him with all the pent up passion in her body. Max was everything she wanted. She pretended tomorrow didn't exist. Their breaths mingled and she knew their hearts did, too.

She was on her knees in a flash, straddling him, her legs wide. His cock was pressing hard on her slit, causing the anticipation to grow. He raised his hips as if he were begging her to begin. Jamie couldn't wait any longer. She lifted up, grabbed hold of his meaty shaft, and aimed her pussy over him. This was so exciting. She'd never ridden a man before. Having this much control was heady.

The tip of his cock touched her opening and her juices flowed around him. Knowing she couldn't take all of him in one shot, she eased down. His girth stretched her so wide, she had to gulp in more air.

Planting her hands on his chest, she rose up again only to lower once more. This time, she clamped down on his cock. Max's eyes widened. *Aha!* The problem with too much teasing was that he might explode before she was ready.

She planned to take her time, but he had the nerve to tweak both of her nipples at the same time, twirling, and pressing on them hard. The ache grew and grew until a bolt of electricity shot down to her clit and ignited her.

"Ah, ah, ah." Jamie didn't want to come. Not yet. She had to hold on.

He let go of her swollen crests and rubbed them, soothing her raging libido. No words were needed. His touch was all she required.

When she lifted once more, Max grabbed her hips, held her still, and drove up into her. No one could withstand that kind of torture. She let out a scream as her orgasm swept in and dragged her into the lustful world of ecstasy.

Max's eyes closed and his mouth opened. His dick swelled and throbbed, and then heat shot out like a cannonball. Her heartbeat flooded her ears, blocking out all noise. He held her tight for what seemed like forever then gently lifted her off to the side.

Like a limp doll, she lay there, unable to think. The mattress dipped and feet sounded on the floor. She wanted to look at his retreating ass, but she didn't have the strength. Max returned with a warm towel and cleaned her up.

Damn. She should have been the one to get up.

Faint evening light flooded the room, and all she wanted to do was sleep, but she had to finish making dinner.

She could get used to this life. Given how fast Max had mended, she suspected they'd be leaving tomorrow, getting back to their old lives of work, work, work. The big question was where did she fit in his life?

Chapter Twenty-Eight

"Wake up, sleepy head."

Max's deep voice entered her brain, but it took a few seconds to register. Jamie opened her eyes to find a smiling Max next to the bed—fully clothed.

She sat up. "What time is it?"

"Ten in the morning."

"Oh, shit."

She never slept in, but after they made love and eaten, they'd spent hours talking about their work. They didn't get to bed until after midnight, where they made love again. She couldn't get enough of him.

He chuckled. "We need to eat then hit the road." They had decided to head back today since the Monster Truck Rally was tonight, and Max didn't want to miss it. Neither did she.

"What did Dan say when you called?" Max had called to find out more about the security at the event.

"The FBI promised to have a ton of their men just in case someone had slipped through the cracks."

"I'm glad." Now she could enjoy herself.

Jamie dressed and insisted on making breakfast while Max rested. After they ate, it was time to finish packing and load up the SUV. Leaving was bittersweet. She loved this cabin. She could have done without the tension and the shooting, but she had learned a lot about Max, and herself as well. The healing process was never fun, but having Max by her side had made the journey life affirming.

She snapped closed her suitcase and took it into the living room. They'd already picked up their cases from Hank, and collected her laptop and their phones. It was time to say goodbye to Marie, Montana.

She glanced around one final time, refusing to think about whether she'd ever see this place again. Jamie wouldn't assume Max wanted her permanently in his life. If she thought he did, and then he didn't ask her, she might never survive.

"You all set?" he asked.

"Yes." She picked up her suitcase to take to the car.

Max huffed. "I can carry it, you know."

"Humor me. I promise once we arrive in Rock Hard, I'll let you go all macho on me again."

He laughed. After they packed up the perishables, they were soon on their way. Max drove, despite her offer to be the chauffeur. When they passed Hank's store, Jamie waved even though he wouldn't see her. She liked the storeowner. She could see why Max was so fond of him.

Had they not said their goodbyes yesterday when they'd picked up her laptop and phones, they would have stopped.

This time when Max pulled onto the main road that would take them to Rock Hard, she tried to tell herself that she didn't need to check the side mirror. She doubted she'd succeed. They might be safe from these terrorists, but Jamie would never be so naïve to believe there wasn't evil lurking somewhere.

As they neared Rock Hard, Max glanced over at her. "What do you say we stop by the hospital and check on Vic? Dan said the FBI would soon be transporting him back to DC for therapy."

"I'd like that."

Mixed emotions filled her. Vic had been her friend, and for

that she wanted to make sure he was on the mend. However, he never should have entrusted her with something as valuable as a flash drive. Depending on his condition, she might even give him a stern talking to.

Less than two hours later, Max pulled into the LACE parking lot. To her surprise, the anxiety didn't assault her like it usually did. Jamie wanted to believe that she'd truly moved on.

After she checked Vic was in the same room, they headed to the sixth floor. A man in a suit was stationed outside the door. Max showed his badge and explained who they were. Apparently Agent Forbes had already mentioned they might stop by.

Jamie knocked and entered. Vic was sitting up in bed, but had his eyes closed. He still had the saline drip, and except for his bandages and the bruises around his eyes, he almost looked good.

"Jonathan?" Jamie didn't know which name to use, but she wasn't ready to speak his real name out loud yet. There was another man wearing a suit in the corner. It didn't matter that he might be another agent, she wanted to be careful.

Vic cracked open his eyes and studied her. "Jamie?" His voice actually sounded stronger, like he was no longer trying to appear frail.

When Vic reached out his arm, she moved closer and clasped his hand in hers. Tears burned the back of her lids. She should be pissed that he'd put her life in danger, but she understood hundreds could have been injured if he hadn't.

"That's me." She smiled, but the corners of her lips wobbled.

He glanced behind her and lifted his chin. "Is that Max?"

"How did you know?" The man on the bed looked so different from the homeless man that she had a hard time believing it really was Jonathan, or rather Vic.

"Chuck described him." He squeezed her hand, then let go. He elevated the bed. "You know the worst part of this?" He waved a hand over his burns.

The list would be too long to enumerate. "What?"

"That I put you in danger."

Her heart nearly cracked. Max stepped next to her and wrapped a possessive arm around her waist. The agent in the corner straightened as if there might be a confrontation.

"Why did you do it?" Max's voice sounded like ground glass.

Vic wet his lips and faced her. "Chuck told me you found the flash drive. I never meant for them to come after you. I swear I was going to retrieve it as soon as I could, but a few men had other ideas."

"What happened exactly?" The events of the tragedy never made sense to her.

Vic blew out a breath. "I was sitting on the steps like always, when you showed up. Your visit was the highlight of my day. Earlier that morning, I'd seen two men who I believed were members of the cell exchange something—something I wanted to check out. I got up from my stoop, slowly made my way over to them, swaying and staggering as if I'd have too much to drink. As soon as the two men parted, I accidentally bumped into the man with the interesting item. Given I'm a highly trained pickpocket, seconds later I had said item in my hand. It felt like a toy, but I soon discovered it was a flash drive."

"Didn't the man suspect something when you bumped into him?"

"Apparently not at first. He was too busy being horrified that a filthy human had come that close to him. He walked away, and I went back to the steps. I had to figure out a way to get the information back to my team. I didn't have any idea what was on the drive, but I figured it was important from the way they were looking around. A few minutes later, you appeared—and so did the two men. I realized I might have been made."

That made sense. "That was why you stopped smiling after telling me that knock-knock joke."

"I guess. I don't know what I looked like, but those men did distract me."

"When you slipped something into my pocket, they must have figured you'd given me what you'd stolen from them."

"That's what I would have thought if I were them."

Max pulled her close. "If you're good at sleight of hand, how did the men know you'd put it in Jamie's coat pocket?"

"I don't think they knew for sure. That was why they came after me—to check. As soon as I spotted them striding toward me, I hightailed it out of there. I had to stay alive long enough to get the flash drive back from Jamie and warn her of the danger. I thought I had succeeded, but they found me. After that was a blur until I woke up here."

Max leaned forward. "Do you remember the fire?"

Vic shook his head. "No."

Jamie's sympathy soared. Vic hadn't meant her any harm. Things had just gotten out of control. "I'm sorry."

He lifted a shoulder. "We're taught that being made is the risk we take. I'm the one who's sorry that you were caught in the middle."

She glanced up at Max. "It had its positive side effects."

Vic grinned, the sparkle back in his eye. He shifted his gaze to the man in the corner, then back at her. "Knock, knock."

Her throat clogged. This man might have put her in danger, but he was still the kind hero on the stoop. "Who's there?"

"Iva."

"Iva who?"

"Iva sore hand from knocking!"

She grinned. "That was so bad. I think your brain got addled."

"Could be." His tone came out wistful.

She cleared her throat. "Max said you were going back to DC? When?"

"As soon as Chuck can set up a transport. I'll be treated for my burns, not to mention having many hours of debriefing." He squeezed her hand. "I won't forget you, Jamie."

She'd never forget him either. "What about Charlotte? Does she exist? Or was that part of your cover?" Her words were tinged with a bit too much unintentional anger. She regretted her tone the moment the words spilled out.

"Oh, she's very much alive." His pain was evident.

"You really don't speak?"

He shook his head. "It's kind of mutual. She never approved of my life's work. I get that. When she was growing up, the FBI was my life. I pushed her away. Once she left home, I stayed away from her because I feared retaliation by those I'd pissed off."

Max's fingers tightened on her waist. He'd suffered that kind of retribution. It was a pain few could survive, and none could forget.

"I wish you luck," she said. Closing a chapter was hard, but she did hope the best for him.

"You, too, Miss Jamie."

The nickname choked her up. If she didn't think she'd bump into his shoulder burn, she'd have given him a hug. "If you ever make your way to Montana again, please stop by."

"Will do."

Fearing she'd break down, she turned on her heels. It was dumb to be so sentimental. The two of them hadn't spoken more than a few hundred words to each other in the short time they'd known each other. The man had lied to her, put her life in danger, and yet there had been a connection she couldn't let go of.

Once in the hall, she leaned against the wall and drew in more air.

"You okay, honey?"

Max always seemed to want to make her life easier. "Yes. Thank you for coming with me."

"I wouldn't have let you come alone." He tapped her nose. "I have an idea."

"What's that?"

"Why don't we pick up your car? That might make you feel better." Max's voice came out soft, almost like he could tell the experience with Vic had been difficult.

"That would be great." Or would it be? Her car meant her freedom, which also meant there wouldn't be a need to be with Max all day. At least the rally started in a few hours, so they'd be together for the evening.

On the drive to the shop, Max kept quiet. He was probably trying to decide how to handle the next phase of their relationship. After tonight, would he walk away, only calling on occasion to see how she was doing? Would he stop over for a quickie because he had to focus on his job? Or would he ask her to be part of his life?

Stop it.

Their time together might have been short, but they'd shared an unbelievable experience. She'd seen the real Max Gruden, and by God, she would do whatever she needed to do to keep him.

When they arrived at Richardson's Automotive, Grayson was on the lot. Once inside, the mechanic dropped the keys in her palm along with the bill. Her heart nearly stopped at the amount. She'd pay as her car was the last link to her dad. She wasn't quite ready to give up his memory.

"I'll follow you back to your house," Max said.

She'd told him she wanted to check on the condition of her place. "Thank you."

As she entered her drive, her gaze shot to the living room window. *Yes.* It had been repaired. Max pulled in beside her. He opened her door, and helped her out.

"Looks good so far," she said. She walked over to his SUV to gather her luggage.

"How about we get your stuff later? Let's check inside first."

He probably figured if the place was in the same condition as when they'd left it, she'd want to stay at his place another night. That worked for her.

Max slipped the car keys from her hands, led her up to the front, and opened the door. She must have been spacing out or something.

The second she walked in, her pulse raced. "It's perfect. How is that possible?" While the items on the credenza weren't in the same order as how she'd had it, everything was picked up. What was missing was probably beyond repair.

"Dan can be a miracle worker." Max placed a hand on her back. "Let's check out the rest of the house."

She didn't know why he seemed to be in such a hurry, but that worked for her. Jamie was anxious to see what the rest of the place looked like, too. The office looked fine. When she eased open the bedroom door, she couldn't believe it.

"Someone even made the bed."

All of her clothes were put away, too. Jamie needed to do something nice for Dan Hartwick, or whoever had cleaned up.

"Does it feel like home?" Max stepped behind her and wrapped his arms around her waist.

She glanced up at him. "It never really felt like home." She twisted in his arms. "I like your house better."

"You do? I thought it was too sterile."

"It is, but a woman's touch could do a lot to change that." *Hint, hint.*

He grinned. "I'd like that. What you do say, you come on over and give me some pointers? My place is closer to the Fairgrounds anyway."

Closer by only three miles, but she'd do anything to be with him. "Works for me."

"You might want to bring a change of clothes, in case you want to spend the night."

Oh, yeah. Did Jaime have plans for him or what?

Chapter Twenty-Nine

Max drove them to his house, saying he'd be happy to drop her back home tomorrow. He carried the leftover food from the cabin as well as her overnight bag. Because they'd been gone for a while, the inside of his home was rather chilly. Even with a jacket, Jamie was cold. She rubbed her arms.

"I'll light the fire. Before you know it, the room will be toasty. How about making us some coffee to help warm us up?"

"Sure." Jamie liked how at ease they were around each other.

While Max lit the fire, Jamie brewed the coffee. When she carried out both mugs, the flames were shooting up the flume. He smiled and lifted his mug from her fingers.

"Nice fire," she said stepping closer to absorb the warmth.

"Well, I am the fire marshal. I love all types of fires. They fascinate me, but if I never see another house or building burn again, I'll be happy."

"I could sit and look at the flames for hours." There was something romantic about a blaze.

"Enough, my little pyromaniac. Come sit with me. I have something I want to discuss with you."

His tone wasn't tinged with despair, so it must not be too bad. She sat on the sofa next to him. "I'm listening."

"I thought it was time to talk about us."

Her heart nearly jumped out of her body. "Us?"

"Us." He dragged a hand over his chin. "I never planned to fall in love again. Hell, I worked hard to steel my heart against getting close to anyone. I had this fear that if I loved someone and then lost her, I'd never recover. But with you, I'm willing to take the chance. You make me so happy, Jamie Henderson. Happier than, perhaps, I deserve, but I'm determined to do what it takes to keep you in my life."

She couldn't believe her ears. "You love me?"

Max cupped her face. "Yes, I love you. You couldn't tell? You have a resiliency about life that I admire, and you have a way at looking at things that's so incredible. I figure if you can put up with an old coot like me, I'd like to see where we can take this relationship."

Tears fell. "I love you, too," she sobbed. It sounded anticlimactic after his proclamation, but it was no less true. "I never thought I'd ever trust another man. To be honest, I'm not even sure I've ever known real love—until I met you."

In a flash, she was on his lap with his arms wrapped around her. He kissed the top of her head. "You make me so happy, honey."

She twisted around and looked up at him. "You, too."

Jamie had a whole speech practically memorized about how he needed to give love a chance, and how good they were together, but his words were so much more poetic.

Max hugged her. "You really mean it? You love me?"

She'd never heard any doubt come out of Max's mouth before, but this had to be a big step for him, too. "Yes. With my whole heart and soul."

He grinned. "Then I say we celebrate in a way that will be mutually exciting."

She couldn't agree more. *Go for it. Tell him.* For years, she'd wanted this. "I want to live life to the fullest. Do something crazy like experiment in bed." She whispered the last three words. Benny never wanted to do anything unusual.

Max had the audacity to lean back his head and laugh. "Are you shitting me? Care to elaborate?"

Maybe she'd gone too far. "Nothing too out there, but I've always fantasized about being tied up."

"Oh, yeah? I never thought you'd be such a wild child, but I like it."

She pursed her lips. "I'm not a child. I'm a grown woman."

"All five-foot-one of you."

"Five-feet-two," she corrected.

He held up a palm. "Woman. Excuse me. You are far more woman than anyone I've been with."

She detected a hint of exaggeration on his part, but she let it pass. "Good."

Max jumped up. "Wait here."

She knew better than to ask what he had planned. Down the hall, drawers opened and closed. He returned waiving a handful of neckties. "Huh? You think this will work for you?"

"I've never seen you wear a tie." She hadn't known he'd owned one.

"I can be classy when the need arises." Max pulled her to a stand. "I want this to be the best lovemaking experience of our lives. We've pledged our love. Now it's time to show it."

Her heart thudded. Max couldn't be more perfect.

✧ ✧ ✧

Max was excited. Jamie was his. All his. He needed to go slow in order to bring her the best climax she'd ever experienced. He'd been too hasty before. Now it was about showing Jamie Henderson how much he loved and cherished her.

Max stood, clasped her hand and walked her over to the fireplace. "How about closing your eyes?"

Her breath hitched. "Okay, but can I touch you?"

He'd never be able to last if she did. "No. And no talking either, unless it's to ask me a question or tell me what an amazing job I'm doing turning you on."

Her eyes popped open. "How about if I want to ask you to take off your clothes? Does that count? That's a question."

He cocked a brow, hoping she'd understand that he was in charge. "No."

She lifted her chin. "Fine, but next time I get to decide what we do."

He laughed. "I'd like to see you try. Now shush. Relax and enjoy."

Max wanted to create the most sensual experience for her, to show her how amazing it could be between them. She wore the prettiest white blouse that hugged her curves. It made his mouth water just contemplating what was underneath. She must have wanted him to work to get her naked because the top had a good ten buttons. That was okay. Max could be the most patient man alive when he wanted something badly enough.

He passed the first button through the hole and eased open the lapel. Instead of moving on to the next one, he kissed her smooth skin then dipped his head lower and lower as he undid each button. She moaned and he had to hold in his own groan. He didn't want her to know how much she affected him.

Her fingers were moving as if they itched to touch him. She better not even think about helping undress either one of them. This was all his operation.

He eased open the next two buttons, exposing the tops of her delicate breasts. Damn, but Max had to work hard not to think about her precious nipples, and how she would respond to each and every lick. Why did he have to promise himself to go slow?

"Let's get you out of those boots." They were the slip on kind, so divesting her of them would be easy.

He held her elbow while she lifted her leg and yanked them

off one by one. She was being such a good girl to keep her eyes closed. Jamie trusted him. Even though her shirt wasn't completely open, he turned his attention to her jeans. With a flick of a snap, and a quick unzip, her waistband lay wide. Then he took off her jeans.

"You warm enough?" he asked.

"Yes."

She drew in her bottom lip. Thank God she wasn't looking at him, or she'd have seen him struggle with control. He had to adjust himself every few seconds to keep from throwing her on the sofa and making passionate love to her right then and there. But this wasn't about his needs. It was about Jamie's.

Desiring more skin-to-skin contact, he undid the last two buttons on her shirt and dragged the silky material down over her bare arms. His breath caught at the white lace bra, which was simple in style, but highly effective in driving him crazy.

"I see you like to please a man."

She smiled. "I don't like to please *a* man." Had she waited another second before continuing, he would have asked her to explain. "I want to please *my* man."

That brought out a grin on his face. "Then, thank you."

He placed her blouse on the back of the sofa. With her back to the fire, the light was haloing her blonde hair. She truly was an angel.

Jamie reached out and waved her arms, but as he returned, Max was able to step out of the way. "What did we decide about you touching me?"

She pouted, but it was clearly for effect. "That's not fair."

"Do you trust me to bring you to the highest cliff in the world before we dive into total glory together?"

"Yes." She giggled. "You are a poet."

"I doubt that. You inspire me."

"Aw."

He stepped close. "Let me take off this frilly lingerie." He unhooked the back and lowered the bra straps, revealing her delicious breasts one at a time. His cock turned to steel the moment the material cleared her pebbled tits. "So perfect." She opened her lips, but he was able to stay her comment with a finger. "Remember. Shh."

"Grr."

He silently chuckled. Jamie was going to be a fabulous challenge. "Place your hands on your head, honey."

Her lips formed a "W," as if she wanted to ask him why, but then she refrained.

What had he done to deserve such an incredible woman?

Jamie looked hot in her tiny panties. So as not to feel a burn on her back, he twisted her around to face the fire. Max dropped to his knees in front of her and pulled down her undies.

"I'm naked." As soon as the words came out, Jamie clamped a hand over her mouth.

He silently laughed, pleased she seemed to be enjoying herself. Max couldn't wait any longer. He had to taste her. He leaned over and dragged his tongue through her wet folds. When he opened her pussy lips, Jamie bent her knees, and her tiny mewling sound almost broke him. How was he going to last?

"I'm glad." He stood. "Let me get some cushions for you." He grabbed two and placed them on the floor. He then gently guided her down and had her get on her back.

His cock was throbbing something fierce.

She's all mine.

✧ ✧ ✧

Jamie was bursting at the seams. Not opening her eyes had made Max's touch set every cell on fire. The whisper of his jeans sliding down his thighs added to the anticipation.

"Keep your eyes closed now."

She did—mostly. Jamie lifted her chin, and through her

lashes, watched him undress. Max was amazing. He'd lost so much and had even been shot twice, yet he still had a zest for life. She couldn't love him more.

"Ja-mie." His deep, throaty voice caused pinpricks of delight to skitter across her skin.

"Fine." She shut her eyes tight this time.

When soft material encircled her wrists, she nearly squealed. This was a dream come true.

With care, Max wrapped her hands together and tied a knot. "That okay?"

She loved how concerned he was about her comfort. "Yes."

He lifted her hands above her head, and then fiddled with something. A moment later, when she tugged, she had little leeway to move. She stretched out her fingers and hit hard wood. Ah, it was the chair. Her man was clever.

Even though she was near the fire, her nipples hardened at the thought of being at his total mercy.

"I want your pussy real bad, but I have too much to lick and touch and kiss first."

"I'm ready."

"Sure you're warm enough?" Max placed his palms over her breasts.

"I am now."

With her pussy vibrating, Max crawled on top of her, but she barely felt the pressure of his body. His hard chest replaced his warm hands. Jamie yanked on her restraint, needing to touch him. She couldn't move. Damn.

His lips gently touched hers. He remained still as if he were memorizing the moment. Jamie opened her mouth and drew him in. Their tongues touched and she melted. She wanted to wrap her arms around his back and feel the muscles ripple so bad, but when she'd couldn't, it made her want him more. She was helpless, vulnerable, and very much was enjoying this wanton need building inside her.

Jamie groaned and lifted her hips. She wanted his cock. Max broke the kiss and slid lower. When his lips latched onto one nipple and his palm caressed the other breast, she thought she was going to blow. Her climax was building, and she wasn't sure she could stop it from taking over. This was about them. About their love. She had to wait.

His warm tongue swirled around the other nipple, causing streaks of delight to shimmy down her belly. When he drew the tip between his teeth and tugged, she gasped for breath.

"Please, Max. I need you."

"Easy, honey. A little longer. I want to love each one again." He switched to the other side and tugged until her juices flowed hard.

"I can't. Please."

He must have finally believed she was on the edge. Instead of giving her his cock, Max moved lower and licked her clean. She yelled out his name. "Untie me. Now."

If she didn't touch him, she would go insane. With one quick tug, she was free, able to lower her arms. She dug her nails into his back then ran them over his muscular shoulders, loving the sensuous hardness of his smooth skin.

"I want you." His words came out on a gurgle.

She opened her eyes to watch Max don a condom. If she hadn't been so out of control, she would have begged to let her suck on him first.

"You want to ride me again?" Max asked. He kissed her quick, and then nibbled on her ear. Pinpricks of lust soared through her.

She hoped it was because he'd enjoyed it yesterday and not because his leg hurt. "Yes!"

He laughed. "Better hurry. Offer only last five more seconds."

Jaime rolled onto the floor. "Get on the cushions."

Max stretched out, looking like a god. He quickly dragged

her on top of his chest.

Jamie pushed up onto her knees, and grabbed his thick cock.

"Easy there. He's about to detonate."

Needing Max to last a little longer, Jamie positioned herself over him. Torturing him would be fun, but she was too needy. Bending her knees, she sank down on him.

"Ah, ah, ah. It grew."

Max grinned. "You got that right."

Jamie lifted up a bit, and slid back down, her slick walls welcoming him. Now it was time to tease and tempt him. She leaned over and lifted his head so that his mouth was pressed against her breast. He captured a swollen nipple between his teeth and nipped one tit, then the other. New sensations sparked a need deep inside her. Without thinking, she clamped down hard on his cock.

"You've gone too far, honey." Max grabbed her hips and thrust all the way into her. Her eyes watered at his massive size. "Jamie, oh, Jamie."

Max closed his eyes and plowed into her again. Over and over, his hard cock pounded against her back wall. Her body heated and her heart rejoiced.

"I love you, Max Gruden."

After that, nothing but pure bliss entered her mind. Max dipped his thumb between her legs and pressed on her clit. That was it. She burst into flames like a blazing inferno. Nothing could douse the fire in her body.

"I'm coming, honey."

Just as he spoke the words, he gripped her hips hard, drove up, and held on tight. Her orgasm claimed her as his hot cum filled the condom. Jamie squeezed her eyes tight, and let the wonder of it all transport her to another universe.

When her climax ebbed, she collapsed onto his chest, and rested her head on his shoulder. His hands roamed over her back and butt as his kisses hit everywhere he could reach.

The fire crackled and the last log fell. "If I could stay here all night I would," she said.

Max rolled her off him. At the moment, Jamie was willing to give up going to the rally, but from what Trent said, Max had looked forward it all year. In a flash, he returned with a damp towel.

"What do you say we shower and head on over to the Fairgrounds? Afterwards, I'd like to take you to the Steerhouse for dinner."

Not only was Jamie taken aback that he hadn't asked her to Italiano's, but Steerhouse had to be the most expensive restaurant in town. "I'd love that. Is there some reason why we aren't going to your usual haunt?"

Jamie sat up with her back to the fire and crossed her legs. Max knelt next to her and lifted her hands. "I thought we'd celebrate."

"Celebrate the capture of those terrible people?"

"That and I was hoping we could toast to our new beginning."

That sounded wonderful. "New beginning?" Why did she have to repeat everything he said?

"I'd love for you to move in with me."

Her heart skipped a beat. "Yes. I'd really like that."

He gave her his patented smile and she wanted to pull him down onto the cushions and do him all over again.

Chapter Thirty

The Monster Truck Rally had been a ton of fun. Jamie had spotted a few of the FBI agents who she'd met either at the Kalispell hospital or at LACE, only this time, they were dressed in jeans and boots. Smart. From what she could tell, no one seemed to notice them. She bet few even suspected there'd been a threat.

After the rally, she and Max had a wonderful dinner at the Steerhouse, where they discussed her move. She couldn't have been more excited about this new path. As much as she wanted to spend a few days shopping with him to pick out artwork for his walls, they both had jobs to go back to. Next weekend, they would take the time to choose which pieces of furniture of hers she wanted to keep and which things she wanted to donate.

The days seemed to fly by. Getting back to work had been hard, but working with patients again was rewarding at the same time. Dr. McDermott had announced they were closing the clinic early on Wednesday so that the staff could attend Yolanda's funeral. Jamie was pleased the service hadn't already occurred. Apparently, Yolanda's family was coming in from all over the country.

Jamie promised she'd say a few words, but when she faced the crowd, ready to put into words how much Yolanda had meant to her, it had been a lot harder than she had ever imagined. Had Max not been there nodding his encouragement, she would have broken down for sure.

The next day, it was close to six when Sasha found her in the clinic hallway. "I'm ready for my first happy hour with your friends."

Sasha's bowling league had ended, and she wasn't planning on signing up in the near future. Jamie guessed than many of the nurses had been rethinking their priorities.

"Great. Let me grab my purse and coat."

Once Jamie returned, they said their goodbyes to the rest of the staff and headed out. They'd both parked in the lot next to where the warehouse used to be. While someone had torn down the burned remains, there wasn't any evidence yet of new construction. With Ed Hanson in jail, she wondered what would happen to the property. It would be nice if the city built a park there.

Once they reached town, Jamie spotted a space in front of Banner's. She drove on by, letting Sasha take it. Jamie parked a block away and hurried to meet her friends. Thankfully, the snow had melted. She could only hope the last of winter was now history.

Sasha was waiting for her by the door. "Let's do this," Jamie said, pulling back the handle.

As soon as she stepped inside, it was as if her troubles disappeared. Jamie forgot about work and focused on her wonderful friends. Once they reached the table, Amber jumped up from her seat and hugged her. Between the cabin and moving, they hadn't seen each other except briefly at the funeral. Jamie then embraced Zoey, Becky, and Melissa. Apparently, Lydia was still at work.

Jamie introduced Sasha. As they finished shaking hands, Abby came over for their drink orders. Jamie looked to each girl. "How about we get a pitcher of Sangria. I'm buying."

That caused a stir. Melissa leaned on her elbows. "Are we

celebrating something?"

"Maybe."

That started the chatter. Jamie couldn't exactly say she'd been the target of terrorists, but Dan, Trent, and Max suggested she say the warehouse arsonist came after Max, and he feared they'd come after Jamie, too. That was why they had to go into hiding. "Okay, here's what happened."

Becky's eyes remained wide throughout her tale. "You mean you spent a whole week in a cabin with Max?"

"I did."

She placed a hand over her chest. "He is so dreamy. I wish I could find someone like him."

As was their usual refrain, everyone assured her that her time would come.

Becky glanced to the ceiling. "For two days, I had Trent Lawson checking up on me, asking about my stalker. He's gorgeous, and nice."

"If you like the good looking, strong, capable kind of man. He's okay," Jamie said.

They all laughed.

She didn't feel comfortable talking any more about her experience as she feared she might let something slip. "I will let you in on a secret. Max told me he loved me and asked me to move in with him."

Amber, Zoey, and Sasha knew of the change in her life, but Jamie hadn't had a chance to tell Becky or Melissa, who squealed and clapped.

"Ladies." Abby set down the pitcher of Sangria, along with the glasses.

Jamie poured.

Zoey lifted her glass first, and they all followed. "To love!"

"To love," they said in unison.

Zoey set down her glass. "I want to hear all about Amber's honeymoon, but first I need to tell you all something. I'm afraid some of you might not be too happy."

They all turned toward Zoey. Even though Jamie had confided in her about Max, Zoey hadn't told Jamie anything.

Amber stilled. "What is it?"

"Yesterday, Thad and Pete surprised me with tickets to New York City."

Jamie couldn't have been happier for her friend. "That's fantastic. Why wouldn't we be happy?"

"Because the men convinced me to elope instead of getting married in Rock Hard as I'd planned."

The crescendo of noise made Jamie's ears hurt. Amber, Melissa, Becky, and even Sasha asked questions all at once.

Zoey held up her hand like a school teacher. "I know you all wanted to be in the wedding, but for many reasons, we thought it would be more romantic to get married by a justice of the peace at Rockefeller Center. Thad really wants to go to a Broadway play."

Jamie's heart melted. "That's so romantic, but won't that bother you not to have the wedding gown and all that stuff?" She didn't want that, but Zoey had always talked about the perfect wedding.

She smiled. "I had that with Amber's wedding." Zoey glanced at her friend with much love.

"Me, too," Jamie said. "I wouldn't like all the attention thrown my way."

"Never say never," Zoey said.

And so began a lengthy discussion of the pros and cons of weddings.

Six months later

Max escorted Jamie into Cade, Stone, and Amber's backyard where they were having a huge Labor Day party. It seemed as if every member of RHPD and the fire department was there. As soon as she and Max arrived, Amber and Zoey came over and gave her a hug.

"So glad you two could make it," Amber said.

Jamie blushed. They were an hour late. "We were a bit delayed."

"Uh-huh." Amber glanced between them. "Come into the TV room. There's someone there to see you." Amber grinned.

"Who?"

"It wouldn't be a surprise if I told you, now would it?"

Jamie had no idea what the surprise might be. She looked at Max, but he just shrugged. They both followed Amber into the den where Cade was chatting with a man whose back was to her. Amber slipped next to her husband and motioned that Jamie was behind them.

The stranger turned around. When he smiled, Jamie's heart jumped. His white teeth and fit body made him look so different. Surprisingly, the burn on his jawline didn't detract from his good looks.

"Jon—I mean Vic?" She studied him. He seemed taller, but perhaps it was because he was always seated when she walked by. He had to be close to six feet.

He stepped over to her. "The one and only." He gave her a light hug then held his hand out to Max.

Max shook it briefly, and then placed a possessive hand around her waist. "What are you doing back in Rock Hard?"

Jamie detected a slight abruptness to his voice. She couldn't blame him for not warming up to Vic after what happened, even though Max had seemed to understand why Vic had pawned off the drive to Jamie.

"I've left the FBI."

"Why?" She never expected him to tell her that.

"Many reasons. In part, it's hard to fit in with the way I look."

He was being silly. Did he think because he had a scar on his jaw that he looked bad? "You look fine. Scars on men are sexy. Women will be flocking to you, wanting to know your story."

"I wish, but thank you for the confidence boost. It was time to move on. I did what I wanted to do—uncover those terrorists. The best part is that Charlotte and I have reconnected. It's all good."

Joy filled her. "I'm so happy for you."

Max's fingers relaxed from around her waist. "You planning on getting a job at RHPD?"

Vic shook his head. "No. I'm opening my own Investigation firm in Rock Hard, called Hart's Investigations."

She smiled. "That's fantastic. How long have you been back in town?"

"I returned yesterday. Have you seen Larry since the fire?"

She shook her head. "No."

"I'll try to track him down. I liked the guy."

"Me, too. I hope he's okay, but I wouldn't be surprised if he's somewhere in Florida."

"I hope you're right." Vic shoved his hands in his pocket. "Since I'll be staying, I'll be looking for a house. If you hear of anything, let me know."

"I might know of a place." She mentioned she was renting her house, but the tenants had only signed a six-month lease. "It's small, but it's in good shape. We'll have to talk."

"Sounds promising." He touched her arm. "I won't keep you, but I'm thrilled to see you and Max together.

Cade glanced down at his wife with total love. "Is it time?"

"Now that the new lovebirds have arrived it is."

Jamie was confused. "What are you talking about?"

"Come back outside. We have an announcement to make." Amber smiled, but Jamie couldn't get a read on her.

Jamie and Max followed them out with Vic right behind them. Country music was playing over the speakers, and Stone was at the grill cooking. He looked up, grinned, and turned down the volume.

Cade shouted for everyone to listen up. Thirty seconds later the crowd finally quieted.

Amber stepped next to Cade. Stone lifted the burgers off the grill, placed them on a plate, and strode over to them. Cade and Stone bordered Amber.

"I'd like to make an announcement everyone," Amber said. "We want our friends to be the first to know that we are expecting a child."

The hoots and hollers drowned out any chance of Amber continuing. Finally, they calmed. "We're due next March, so let's all celebrate!"

The music sprang up and Max turned to her. "I think it's time we talked about kids."

Jamie reached out to steady herself on his arm. They'd fallen head over heels in love in the last half-year or so, and she'd never been happier, but she'd never had the courage to push Max into wanting to start a family. For her, having children would be a dream come true.

"Okay."

He glanced to the sky and rolled his eyes as if he was the dumbest man alive. "I guess I should have done things in order." Max got down on his knee and held out a ring. It was as if the sea had parted. The music muted and the crowd gathered. "Will you, Jamie Henderson, marry me?"

Tears clogged her throat. She couldn't even say the word, yes. All she could do was nod. Max stood and slipped the ring on her finger. It was a beautiful diamond, with two smaller diamonds on each side of the main one. "It's incredible."

Max gathered her in his arms. "Not half as incredible as you."

She sniffled, and he produced a white handkerchief from his pocket. "I figured you'd need this."

Jamie swatted his arm. "Funny, funny."

"So how many?"

Her mind wasn't thinking straight. "How many what?"

"Kids, silly."

"One girl and one boy. For starters."

He laughed. "That works for me. I guess I'll have to keep in shape so I can walk my daughter down the aisle."

Jamie probably shouldn't have kidded him about the age difference. "You better."

A long line of their friends congratulated them. Their song came on.

Max held out his hand. "I know how much you love the song, Montana Fire, so I asked Cade to play it. Let's dance."

Jamie stepped into his arms and placed her face against his chest. "I love you, Max Gruden."

He tilted up her face. "I love you more."

They probably would spend the next fifty years competing. Oh, what a fantastic fifty years it was going to be.

The End

About the Author

I love to read, write, dream, and connect with people. A book with a happily ever after is a must, as is having characters I can relate to. My men are always wonderful, dynamic, smart, strong, and the best lovers in the world.

I love hearing from readers, too!!

You can contact me at:
velladayauthor@gmail.com

Visit my website at:
www.velladay.com

Check me out on facebook, too at:
www.facebook.com/vella.day.90

Follow me on twitter at:
www.twitter.com/velladay4

I also write as Melody Snow Monroe:
www.melodymonroe.com

Want to know more? Sign up for my newsletter:
http://eepurl.com/I0OX5

OTHER BOOKS BY THE AUTHOR

PACK WARS

NOTE: These THREE novellas (50K each) were previously released as single titles.

GENRE: Paranormal Werewolf Romance, Paranormal Erotica, Paranormal Menage (MFM)

TRAINING THEIR MATE (BOOK 1)

She failed to stop him. Now he's coming after her.

Liz Wharton has one goal—to kill the man who raped her mother. Had she known Harvey Couch was a werewolf, she never would have tried to take him on by herself.

Determined to put an end to the pest bent on revenge, Harvey sends his goons after her. When two wolves attack her, Liz is sure she's hallucinating. Good thing Trax Field is there to stop them.

Trax and Dante Field, members of the Pack, have devoted their lives to stopping bad shifters like Harvey Couch. Saving Liz would have been just an ordinary day, but when Trax finds her huddled in an alley, bruised and shaken, he's convinced she's his mate.

To keep her safe, Trax and Dante hold her captive in their loft apartment. When they aren't searching for Couch, Trax and his brother spend the night training their future mate in the art of bondage and sensual pleasures. How will they be able to convert her into embracing not only their lifestyle but also their animalistic side?

CLAIMING THEIR MATE (BOOK 2)

She saw the killer. Now he wants her dead.

Realtor Chelsea Wilson enters a vacant home she wants to show and comes face-to-face with a dead man—and a killer. Freaked out, she runs, but the killer nabs her.

Ricardo Mendez, a werewolf who runs a drug operation, doesn't need a witness to the murder. He viciously attacks her, but the dead man's brother, werewolf Kurt Wendlick and his Pack partner, Drake Stanton stop the final assault.

When Kurt and Drake save Chelsea, they're certain she's their mate and will do anything to keep her safe. Her loving ways puts Kurt in a tailspin. He wants to claim her, but first he needs to avenge his brother's murder.

What can Chelsea do to help the tormented man? Will the three ever explore the world of BSDM together?

RESCUING THEIR VIRGIN MATE (BOOK 3)

She's sold into slavery. Now she's on the run.

All Elena Sanchez wanted was to get on the plane to Costa Rica and visit her parents. When the authorities tell her they need to search her, she finds herself drugged and caged by a sadistic bastard who plans to sell her virginity to the highest bidder.

Two Pack members, Clay Demmers and Dirk Tilton, learn that Elena, Harvey Couch's former secretary, is a victim of a human trafficking scheme. They go undercover and bid for her. As soon as they see her, they realize she's their mate. More determined than ever to save her, they buy her, but at what cost?

Elena doesn't know who to trust. They inform her they're werewolves, but is that any better than being sold into slavery to humans? With care, Clay and Dirk teach her how to embrace her submissive ways. The problem is this good Catholic girl likes it. Will the guilt from her upbringing prevent her from having the best ménage relationship possible or can she find a way to have both?

PUBLISHER'S NOTE: This adult contemporary romance contains explicit sexual content, graphic language, and situations that some readers may find objectionable (double penetration, ménage, violence). Not intended for those under the age of 18.

THE BURIED TRILOGY
BY TIA MASON

Check out this boxed set by Tia Mason.

NOTE: These books have been published previously under their separate titles.

GENRE: Romance, Mystery, Thriller, Suspense, Serial killer

BURIED ALIVE (BOOK 1)

When loner homicide detective, Hunter Markum, finds the skeletons of four women in a mass grave just outside Tampa, Florida, he's distraught as hell. It leaves a bitter taste in his mouth, as it's a harsh reminder of his own sister's unsolved murder.

For the first time in his career, the usually detached Hunter feels a more personal connection to this case, and agrees to team up with Dr. Kerry Herlihy, a forensic anthropologist, in the hopes she can decipher the buried bones. Her compassion for these cold case victims draws her to him.

Kerry too finds Hunter's strong family attachment appealing, as her family abandoned her as a child, but she tamps down her desires. The case must come first.

Against their will, the attraction ignites, and their quest to find the killer soon reveals the identities of the victims and the chilling fact that each woman had been abused. When Kerry's work throws her directly in the killer's path, Hunter realizes how much she's come to mean to him. In a race against the clock, Hunter must apprehend the murderer if he hopes to save the woman he loves once she's buried alive.

BURIED SECRETS (BOOK 2)

When rookie Tampa Police Officer, Jenna Holliday, goes undercover at a local occult store to investigate a rash of grave robberies, she never expects to become the victim of a black magic death spell.

Dr. Sam Bonita, a forensic anthropologist, in search of answers regarding a headless body, visits the store where Jenna works and is enchanted by her.

Believing Sam holds the key to her case, Jenna tries to get close to him. When his house is burned to the ground, with both of them inside, she's unsure if her cover has been blown or if Sam is the object of some deranged killer.

Only after a series of murders, and a few death threats, do Jenna and Sam suspect a serial killer is on the loose and after both of them.

BURIED DEEP (BOOK 3)

When forensic anthropologist, Dr. Lara Romano, first examines the exhumed skeletons of two Native American men buried in Tampa, she has no idea she's caught the eye of a serial killer who's intent on dipping her in plaster and covering her in hot wax to complete a twisted ode to his Seminole mother.

Isolated by her profound hearing loss she suffered as a child, Lara jumps at the chance to work in the field and prove she's as competent as any hearing scientist. Not even the easy-on-the-eyes cop bucking to work with her will distract her from her goal.

Missing Persons detective, Jake Kinsey, needs a high profile case to land him a job in Homicide. Though he suspects the attractive rookie scientist may hinder his success, he believes the cadavers in Lara's investigation are linked to his current case—eight missing men, all Native Americans, believed to be dead.

What Jake and Lara don't realize is that the missing bodies have been left in plain sight as part of a tableau constructed by the madman who plans to use Lara and Jake for his final scene.

MONTANA PROMISES

GENRE: Medical Romance, Contemporary Western Romance, Erotica ménage romance, (MFM)

PROMISES OF MERCY (BOOK 1)

Killing is wrong. The reason doesn't matter.

When oncology nurse, Amber Delacroix, learns her reckless brother has been in a paralyzing motorcycle accident, sorrow fills her soul. He's murdered a few days later, and now she's utterly devastated. Adding to life's cruelty, the cowboy cop assigned to her brother's case brings her in for questioning.

Stone Benson, the paramedic who brought Amber's brother into the hospital, stays by her side throughout the tragedy. He treats her with kindness and compassion—something she hasn't experienced much in her life. Amber yearns for more than his comforting words, and they embark on a tremulous journey. Just when she feels that their relationship is at a turning point, he reveals that he likes to share his women with his good friend and roommate, Cade. That turns out to be a huge problem, because Cade is the cop who believes she's guilty of killing her brother.

As chance would have it, another murder occurs when both Cade and Amber are in the same location. Realizing she's not the mercy killer, Cade offers a heartfelt apology—one that includes dinner and a sharing of souls. When things heat up between them, she succumbs to his passionate ways. The big question that plagues her now is where does Stone fit in?

Stone knows exactly where Amber needs to be. Right between him and his best friend, Cade. He'll do whatever is necessary to convince her that she has finally met two men she can trust and build a life with.

Too bad the killer has other ideas. When he goes after Amber, what will the men need to do to save her in time to pursue a loving ménage relationship?

PUBLISHER'S NOTE: This adult contemporary romance contains explicit sexual content, graphic language, and situations that some readers may find objectionable (double penetration, ménage, violence). Not intended for those under the age of 18.

CAVEAT: But if you love medical erotica with a contemporary western setting, this book is for you.

FOUNDATION FOR THREE (BOOK 2)

You aren't free to love until you realize you can't make someone love you back.

As builder Pete Banks is finishing a remodel for psychologist Zoey Donovan, she arrives home dazed, injured, and distraught. As he calms her down, she draws him in with her halting story of how Thad Dalton, a local cop and Pete's roommate, saved her life. When Pete learns Thad was shot, he's torn between staying with a woman in need and being there for his roommate.

Zoey never intended to blurt out to a man she's never met how she almost died, but Pete's understanding nature alters something inside her. Usually, she's the one trying to figure out her clients' needs, not the other way around. While Pete Banks is one of kind, she can't tear her mind from Thad, the man who risked his life for her.

Detective Thad Dalton was never so scared in his life when a madman grabs Zoey in the hospital corridor and threatens to kill her if his demands aren't met. Thad ends up taking a bullet to save her but would do it again if it means having her in his life.

When Zoey, Thad, and Pete attend Thad's parents' anniversary party sparks fly. She realizes she wants a more personal connection to these two men. While Thad's on board, Pete doesn't think he's worthy. His self-loathing forces him to retreat and casts doubt on their future together.

Zoey and Thad are justifiably both mad and hurt. It's going to take a miracle to patch this threesome back together for their happily ever after.

PUBLISHER'S NOTE: This adult contemporary romance contains explicit sexual content, graphic language, and situations that some readers may find objectionable (double penetration, ménage, violence). Not intended for those under the age of 18.

MONTANA FIRE (BOOK 3)

No good deed goes unpunished.

Free clinic nurse, Jamie Henderson, has been slogging through life in cement-filled boots for the past six months. It's been damned hard to get past her recent betrayal, but she's determined to try.

Her attempt is derailed, however, when danger chases her. While she manages to escape, the near attack shakes her to the core. Now more than ever, she needs to take back control of her life.

Arson investigator, Max Gruden, is called to a blaze at an abandoned warehouse only to learn a man was found clinging to life inside. After the victim is rushed to the hospital, Jamie, a woman who has intrigued Max for a while, tries to cross the police barrier, searching for answers about her friend who was caught in the fire.

What starts out as a simple friendship between Max and Jamie quickly turns into a blaze of passion. When she finds herself a target in a terrorist plot, Max is enraged and promises to do everything in his power to keep her safe.

PUBLISHER'S NOTE: This adult contemporary romance contains explicit sexual content and graphic language. Not intended for those under the age of 18.

Made in the USA
Middletown, DE
28 October 2018